Recent college graduate, Ethan Moore, flies to San Francisco for a job interview with an advertising firm. That evening, he goes to a gay club where meets a gorgeous man who seduces him, but leaves his hotel room in the morning with only a note. A few weeks later, Ethan begins his new job and discovers that the man he slept with is his boss, Chance Harlow. He's fallen for the playboy, but wants to keep their relationship strictly professional. His efforts fail miserably as Ethan keeps succumbing to Chance's advances.

Ethan is selected to accompany Chance to Bali for a huge account. He will be spending ten days at a luxurious resort with the man he's fallen in love with. Chance has made his intentions known, and he won't pressure him, but if Ethan doesn't want him, there are plenty of men who will. Ethan struggles with this until one evening they are in the hot tub with two hot swingers who want to play. He flees after watching Chance make out with one of the men. Will Ethan finally give in to the playboy, or did his actions lose him the man he loves?

TAKING A CHANCE

Emjay Haze

Published by
NineStar Press
PO Box 91792
Albuquerque, New Mexico, 87199
www.ninestarpress.com

Warning: This book contains sexually explicit content, which is only suitable for mature readers.

Print ISBN #978-1-947139-22-0
Cover by Natasha Snow
Edited by Elizabeth Coldwell

Chapter One

ETHAN

A loud knock on his bedroom door startled Ethan. Expecting his mom or brother, he glanced up from his laptop. "Come in," he shouted, looking past the scattered drawings on his bed and back at the screen, opened to a job website. He'd applied to advertising companies all over the country but hadn't received any responses to his resume, so he kept searching online.

"Hey, buddy. Is this where you've been hiding?" His best friend poked his head in and opened the door fully before stepping inside. Realizing it was company, Ethan quickly gathered his drawings into a neat pile and sat up.

"Mark." Ethan shut the screen. "What are you doing here?"

He shrugged. "It's kind of boring being back home. Thought I'd see what you're up to."

"Gee, thanks." Ethan chuckled, not taking offense at all.

"You know what I mean."

Ethan put the laptop down and lay back on his bed, his hands folded behind his head. He did. He'd been bored too. Ethan couldn't wait to get out of this place, and he'd only been back for a few weeks.

"Have you started looking for a job yet?" They both had graduated from the University of Iowa in the spring. Ethan's degree was in advertising and marketing with a minor in graphic design. He'd always been a doodler.

Mark shook his head. "I'm working with my dad again this summer. I was accepted into grad school in the fall." Mark was the business major, and his dad was prepping him to take over the family business.

"Oh, right." Ethan felt like a loser. All their other friends seemed to have everything already figured out. Maybe *he* should go to graduate school. "I've applied everywhere but haven't heard from anyone yet."

"Where?" Mark asked, interested. He took a seat next to Ethan on his bed.

"Boston and New York, mostly."

"Those are big places, and far away." Mark never shared Ethan's aversion to their hometown. But then again, he wasn't gay.

Ethan stood up and walked over to his door, peering out to make sure they were alone, and then he closed it and sat on the bed again. "I can't wait to get out of here. I'm going crazy already."

Mark looked at him and shrugged. "It's not that bad." They lived in a small town west of Omaha, just over the border into Iowa. Ratchet Falls, population 6200. Who the hell names a town that?

Ethan sat on the edge of his bed. "Are you kidding? There's not even a gay bar here."

Mark laughed. "You wouldn't go even if there was one."

True. Ethan was only sort of out. He'd been so afraid of anyone finding out in high school that he even had a girlfriend, if you could call her that; they never even kissed. She was cool though when she figured it out, and they became friends. She called herself his beard, but he never liked the sound of that. When Ethan went away to college, he met a few guys, but he didn't like the weird feeling he got the next day after a hookup and had to face the guy on campus. That was never not awkward—for Ethan, at least.

"Maybe I would if you went with me?" They'd had this conversation many times. The closest gay club was thirty minutes away, in the city. It was far enough no one would recognize him, but he didn't have anyone to go with, and he was too chicken to go alone.

"I love you man, but sorry. No way."

"Afraid of a guy hitting on you? Girls go to those clubs too, you know." He already knew his friend's answer.

Mark patted him on the back. "Oh man, I forgot this was in my hand." He handed Ethan a letter. "Your mom gave me your mail on my way up."

Ethan snatched it, looking at the return address. "Oh shit," he said, sitting up.

"What is it?" Mark leaned over to look at the envelope.

Ethan flipped it over. "Ashton Lake. One of the firms where I applied." He felt his nerves rise. What if it was a rejection? What if it wasn't?

"New York?" Mark asked.

Ethan ran his finger through the glued flap. "San Francisco." He'd only applied there on a whim. He thought he had no chance of getting a reply from that place, so his heart sped up as he tore open the envelope.

"That's really far, Ethan," Mark sat next to Ethan and read the letter out loud while Ethan's eyes scanned the words on the page. "Ethan Moore. That's you."

Ethan rolled his eyes.

Mark continued, "We have scheduled your interview for the junior account executive position at the Ashton Lake Advertising Agency for Monday, June sixteenth in our downtown San Francisco office. Please call to confirm..." He looked up from the letter. "Wow, Ethan, that's great."

Ethan grabbed the letter and finished reading. They were sending him an airline ticket and reserving a hotel room in his name for two nights. Ethan set the letter on the bed. "Hey, would you want to go with me?"

"I don't think they'll send you an extra plane ticket so you can bring a friend, Ethan." Mark laughed, slapping him on the back.

"No, but we could drive. Maybe take a detour to the beach?"

Mark's face lit up. "Doesn't Curtis live out there? Montega—rey or something?"

"Is that far from San Francisco?" Ethan wondered.

Mark shrugged. "Let's look it up." He texted Curtis, who confirmed he lived in Monterey. Then he added, "Get your asses out here so we can party."

Ethan reached for his laptop and Google-mapped directions from San Francisco to Monterey, California. Looking over his shoulder, Mark read, "Two and a half hours."

"We could go there first, and then I'd drive to my interview the next day."

"And hang out for a few days afterward?"

"Definitely." Ethan stood up and paced his room. California. Could he do this?

Mark handed Ethan his phone. "Get it over with, so you don't obsess about it all night."

Mark knew him so well. Ethan overthought everything. He'd finished top ten in his class because he obsessed about his grades—well, that, and he heard his parents' words in his ear saying "hard work will earn you respect." His mom always worried he'd get picked on. Another reason he hid his sexuality at school. It was bad enough he was smaller than most of the guys in his high school. He'd grown a few inches his senior year, but topped out at five foot eight and could eat a pound of pasta and not gain an ounce.

He sighed and took the phone from Mark's hand. "Here goes."

THREE DAYS LATER, Ethan and Mark packed up Ethan's old Corolla and took off for the West Coast, driving the better part of two days. After a good night's sleep, the boys spent the morning at the beach with their friend Curtis and his girlfriend. "You sure you don't want me to come with you?" Mark asked.

"Nah, stay and have fun. I'll be fine," he assured his friend.

Ethan spent the time alone in his car thinking about the upcoming interview, and asking himself possible questions out loud. He'd researched online how to ace an interview. "Mr. Moore. What is your best and worst quality?" he said in a deep voice, giggling. "I am very detail oriented and a hard worker." He smiled at his response. "Now, weaknesses." He'd read that you shouldn't say your weakness is actually a strength, and he didn't think telling them that he worried about everything would be a valued weakness. He'd get back to that one. "Next question, why do you want to work for Ashton Lake?" Why did he?

Before he knew it, Ethan arrived at the hotel. He parked in the circular driveway and handed his keys to the attendant. Then, he walked through the revolving doors into the impressive lobby of the Sir Frances Hotel. "Holy cow," he whispered, taking it all in. Ornate woodwork decorated the walls and huge chandeliers hung from the ceiling. He nearly tripped over a large pot of fresh flowers, looking at the walls instead of where he was going. Still gawking, Ethan stepped up to the front desk. A cute guy behind the counter politely asked for his name.

"Ethan Moore," the clerk repeated, typing on his keyboard. He smiled. "Your room's been prepaid, including all amenities," he said, as he handed Ethan two keycards. "Let me know if you need anything." He drawled out the words, giving him a seductive glance. Feeling self-conscious, Ethan turned away so the guy wouldn't see him blush. He thanked him and walked away, feeling the clerk's gaze follow him to the elevator.

The bellman met Ethan outside his room with the bag from his car, even though Ethan had told the guy he could carry it himself, and opened the door with a master key. Ethan peered inside. The spacious room was decorated in black-and-silver tones from the curtains to the furnishings. Ethan spotted the king-sized bed first. The fluffy black-and-white comforter called to him, but Ethan just walked inside and took in the rest of the room. The bellman followed Ethan with his luggage and placed it on the floor next to the bed. Then he retreated to the door.

"Thank you," Ethan said. The man stood with his hands folded, and Ethan realized he was waiting for a tip. "Oh." He reached into his wallet and pulled out a five-dollar bill and handed it to him.

The man bowed. "Good evening, sir. I hope you have a pleasant stay."

Ethan wondered if he'd given him enough money or too much, as he didn't know about things like that. He thanked the man again.

Once alone, Ethan turned toward the bed and grinned stupidly as he hopped on top of the cover, smoothing his hands over the soft material. He stood for a second, getting his balance, and then jumped up and down. The mattress was nice and firm with a little bounce. He jumped a few more times and then fell onto the soft comforter and laughed. Holy cow, this was some fancy room.

After unpacking his suitcase and hanging his suit in the closet, Ethan went back to the lobby to ask where he could find something to do.

The clerk leaned over the counter and in a soft voice said, "There's this club called Cruze. It's sooo hot." He gave Ethan another once-over, making Ethan nearly shiver.

"Gay club?"

He tilted his head like Ethan had spoken a foreign language. Of course, it was.

"I don't know." Ethan had never been to a gay club before. Not even in college. "What's here in the hotel?"

The guy, whose name tag read Cliff, rattled off the names of several restaurants and a lounge. Ethan was a simple guy. He wouldn't feel comfortable in a fancy restaurant or snobby cocktail lounge, so he decided to order room service instead. "Thank you."

"Any time." Ethan caught Cliff eying him up and down and felt his cheeks flush. "Good night." He scurried toward the elevator.

ETHAN GREETED THE man at the door, who pushed a silver cart with dome-covered dishes inside the room. "Good evening, sir," he said. "Where would you like me to set everything?"

Ethan pointed to the desk by the window and led him to the other end of the room. "It smells amazing," The waiter nodded as he placed the dishes on the table without saying another word. Ethan noticed the real silverware. This was by far the fanciest burger he'd ever ordered.

When he was finished, he nodded to Ethan and wheeled the cart to the door. Ethan thanked him, taking out a couple of bills from his wallet, and handed them to him. The man accepted the money and pushed the cart out the door into the hallway, shutting the door behind him.

Ethan sighed, once again taking in the aroma of his dinner. He sat at the table and lifted the lid off the main dish, revealing a juicy burger and a pile of steaming French fries. It was definitely the best-looking burger he'd ever seen. If it tasted only half as good as it looked, he was in for a treat.

Diving into the meaty goodness of his burger, Ethan moaned, not realizing how hungry he really was. After taking another delicious bite, he chased it with a fry and then a sip of beer.

After devouring every last morsel, he removed the smaller dome and chuckled at the single chocolate chip cookie lying on the fancy dish. It looked almost too good to eat—well, almost. His thoughts were confirmed as he took the first bite. Ethan was used to his mom's home cooking and the school cafeteria, but this was on a completely different level. After he finished every last bite, he placed the tray outside to be picked up.

Yawning, he dragged himself into the bathroom to shower and get ready for bed. Nerves overpowered him as he thought about the interview the next morning.

THE HALLS OF the Ashton Lake Advertising agency were intimidating, as men and women in sharp business suits hurried to their destinations, folders and briefcases in hand. Could he fit in at a place like this? A few people gave him polite smiles, but most ignored him, thankfully.

A man ran up to meet him in the lobby, looking winded, and shook Ethan's hand. "Bradley Parker," he said, leading Ethan down the hallway to a suite of offices. He seemed nice, but a little frantic. "Sorry, we're trying to land a new account, and everyone's a little crazy today," he said, bouncing. Ethan assumed he was always like that, but nodded anyway.

Ethan knew he looked good in the suit his brother let him borrow for his interview, but he felt like a little kid playing dress-up from his dad's closet. Bradley Parker was almost the same height as Ethan; however, he looked suave in his light-gray pinstriped suit. When would he be able to afford a suit like that?

Mr. Parker asked him every question he'd rehearsed, plus a slew of others. Ethan realized from the start canned answers wouldn't fly. This was a creative firm, and he needed to show he was worth taking a gamble on as a recent college graduate. He brought out his portfolio and showed him the few designs he'd done in school along with some more recent drawings. Ethan was pretty good at sketching, but his true strength was coming up with ideas. His little lightbulb went off. He'd need to remember to say that. He'd researched the company online and knew the types of clients they served, and their past successful and not-so-successful campaigns. He was prepared, and as much as Mr. Parker tried tripping him up, he felt pretty confident by the end of the interview.

After a full hour and a half of questioning, Mr. Parker walked him out to the lobby. "Thank you for coming, Ethan. You should hear from me within a couple of weeks."

"Thank you so much, Mr. Parker. I really appreciate your time," Ethan said, shaking the man's hand. Mr. Parker—he couldn't be much older than Ethan. And Ethan's gaydar pinged furiously at him—but this *was* San Francisco.

"I hope the hotel is satisfactory?"

"It's amazing. I had the best burger last night..." He stopped himself. He sounded twelve. "I mean, everything has been wonderful."

Mr. Parker chuckled. "They are good, aren't they? Have a safe trip home, Ethan."

"Thank you, sir."

"Call me Brad."

CALL ME BRAD? That didn't sound like a brush-off. Ethan knew he'd done well, but he wouldn't get his hopes up.

A car pulled up to return Ethan to his hotel. Brad Parker must have arranged it. They certainly did everything first class at Ashton Lake. Ethan melted into the leather upholstery and finally relaxed after his exhausting interview. Just as he began to nod off, the driver announced, "We're here, sir."

"Oh—thank you," Ethan said, yawning. He pulled out some money, but the driver put up his hand, stopping him.

"It's already taken care of."

"Thank you."

Ethan strolled into the lobby, catching the front desk clerk, Cliff, watching him. Ethan waved and Cliff smiled back. He thought about the information he'd given him last night. Gay club—what was the name? No, he couldn't. Should he? *No one knows me here.*

Back into his room, Ethan took off his suit and hung it in the closet, contemplating if he should go or not. When would he have another opportunity like this?

He showered, shaved, and dressed in black jeans and a blue button-down shirt while still arguing with himself. His adventurous side won in the end, and he went back to the lobby to ask the name of the club again.

"Cruze," Cliff told him. "You're going to love it. Best club in the district." He flashed Ethan a grin and then leaned over his counter like he wanted to tell him something.

Ethan gave him a funny look.

"I don't want to seem unprofessional or anything—but you are hot. Guys will pounce on you in that place."

Ethan blushed again. Is that what he wanted? What would Mark say? He knew exactly what his friend would say: "Go for it, buddy, just don't tell me the gory details."

Butterflies infiltrated Ethan's stomach as the cab pulled away from the curb, heading in the direction of the Castro district of San Francisco and Club Cruze.

Chapter Two

ETHAN

The taxi driver stopped in front of a plain brick building. A large gold plate that read Club Cruze in bold, plain lettering adorned the tall, wooden door. Ethan wouldn't have known this was a club at all except for the flamboyant boys and girls dressed like Hollywood starlets waiting in line for the doors to open. He glanced down at his own clothing and felt inadequate. *Maybe this is a bad idea.*

"That'll be twelve fifty," said the driver.

"Oh, yeah." Ethan reached for his wallet, pulled out his credit card, and slid it through the machine in the front of his seat. It even calculated the tip. He finished the transaction and put his wallet back in his pocket. "Thank you."

The man grunted good-bye as Ethan opened the door and slipped out of the backseat. As he shut the door, he looked over the sea of bodies again and changed his mind. *I can't do this.*

He turned around, intending to climb back into the cab, but caught it speeding off, leaving him stranded. He looked back at the daunting line and sighed as he walked to the end. He seemed to be the only person alone. Most were in groups of two or three. Some were kissing, others chattering, but everyone seemed excited to get inside. Ethan thought he might puke. He pulled out his phone to text Mark but stopped himself. He could do this. Mark would tell him to do it.

The line moved quickly, and before long he was inside the doors and immediately blasted by the pounding of the music. His eyes widened as rainbow strobes danced over his head to the beat, giving the room an eerie glow. It both excited and terrified. He spotted a long bar to the left, with strings of twinkling lights hanging across the top, a huge dance floor in the center, and another bar to his right.

The bouncer stopped him at the entrance, checked his ID, and gave him a thumbs-up and a wink. Ethan smiled as he brushed past the large, intimidating bear. He had no idea what gay bars were like at home, but this one was incredibly flashy. He thought back to what the front desk clerk had said to him. *They're going to pounce on you.* No one paid any attention to him at all. Was he relieved or disappointed?

Ethan spotted an empty stool at the end of the bar closest to the dance floor and headed straight for it. He sat and released a deep sigh. Now what? He was sure he looked as uncomfortable as he felt. He came here to have some fun after a long day, but now that he was here, he'd lost the small amount of confidence he'd had earlier. What if no one talked to him? God, what if someone *did*?

The bartender acknowledged him with a nod. He was tall, muscular, and rudely handsome in an intimidating sort of way, not unlike the bouncer. After serving another customer, the Herculean man made his way over to Ethan and set a napkin in front of him. "What can I get you?" he shouted over the booming sound system.

"Vodka tonic with a twist," Ethan replied. That sounded better than a beer. He'd drunk a few at a frat party last year and they went down pretty smooth. "Thank you."

The bartender nodded. "Never seen you here before. You new in town?" he asked, setting a tall glass with ice on the bar. He turned around, reached for a bottle of vodka, poured it into a small metal cup and then drizzled it over the ice. Ethan watched him take what looked like a hose and squeeze what was probably the tonic into the glass.

"I'm just visiting for a couple days—from Iowa." Why did he just tell him that?

The guy picked up a long, curled lemon peel and swirled it into in the drink. Then he placed a drink stirrer inside the glass and set it on the napkin. Ethan was impressed. The frat guys just threw in sliced lemons, letting them float in the pitcher.

"I'm Ethan," he added.

"Nice to meet you," the bartender grunted. "Let me know if I can get you anything else." He walked away to serve another customer.

Ethan picked up his glass and downed the liquid courage in a few gulps before flagging the bartender for another. Feeling a little more relaxed, he swiveled his stool toward the packed dance floor and watched the sweaty bodies grinding to the music. His gaze settled on a couple with their limbs intertwined, moving as one. Their eyes focused on one another as they touched. Ethan watched the explicit moves, getting a little turned on. *So, this is what a gay bar is like.*

While the couple gyrated on the floor, practically humping each other, Ethan wondered why he sat in a bar in a strange city a long way from home with a semihard boner, drinking alone. *Pathetic.* Taking his eyes off the public display, Ethan shifted his gaze to the entrance of the club.

CHANCE

Chance walked through the doors of his favorite bar, bypassing the bouncer as he waved him inside. "Hey, Chance," the man said, greeting him.

He nodded, giving him a smile and stopped just inside the door. His eyes scanned the club, looking for possibilities. He was getting too old for this shit. Had hooking up with strangers lost its appeal? Would he ever find someone he was interested in for more than just fucking? His mind wandered to his freshman year in college and the hot, young professor who'd stolen his heart—then stomped all over it. Chance blinked. No, it was better this way. He remained in control. He had no time for romance.

He straightened his posture and gave another glance around the club. Not seeing anything worthwhile, he headed over to the bar, spotting Andre behind the stick tonight.

"Hey, buddy," Andre shouted over the noise.

"Easy night?" The place was less crowded than usual.

"Not too bad yet. You're here early."

Chance shrugged. "I have meetings in the morning."

"You're a workaholic, man."

"Work hard, play hard. You know me." Andre grabbed the Chopin from the top shelf, Chance's favorite, and free poured it into the glass of ice, followed by a flow of tonic water. Then he took a hand-curled twist of lemon and let it slip into the glass, curling over the side. After setting the perfect cocktail on the counter, Andre laughed and turned his head toward the end of the bar. Chance followed with his eyes and landed on a sweet specimen sitting all alone nursing a drink, his wide eyes staring holes through the dance floor. He hadn't noticed him before. "Cute."

"Not sure he's for you, Chance. Small-town kid. Seems out of place at the meat market."

Chance looked him over head to toe. He had light-brown hair cut short and a petite, slender body. The guy turned his head, and Chance saw his face. He had big, brown eyes and pink, pouting lips curled into a shy smile. He was exactly his type. "What's he drinking?"

Andre smirked, shaking his head. "Same as you, except a house brand. He's had that deer-in-the-headlights look since he got here."

"Make me two more, with the Chopin."

"Right away, boss," Andre said, chuckling. He built the drinks and set them on the bar. After finishing his first, Chance picked up the other two and walked over to the cutie sitting alone.

ETHAN

Ethan watched as a gorgeous man with inky black hair wearing what appeared to be a dressy suit entered the club. As he came closer, Ethan realized the pants and jacket were leather—skin hugging, form revealing, black leather. His gaze moved up the man's long, sexy legs, landing on his crotch. Cheeks heated, Ethan looked away.

When he turned back, the gorgeous man was no longer in view, so Ethan returned his attention to the dancing. He couldn't expect someone that hot to notice him.

Ethan watched the couple plastered together in a slow dance like they were the only two people in the room and felt a little envious. When would he have a boyfriend? Maybe if he got the job and moved here? The pool of gay men was definitely larger than *his* hometown. He'd all but forgotten the sexy leather-clad stranger when he felt someone slide into the seat beside him. "Can I buy you a drink?"

Ethan started to say no, but he turned toward the voice. Oh, fuck. It was *that* guy. Ethan stared him up and down. With his lips slightly parted, he gulped as his gaze moved from the guy's face down to the outline of his crotch, which was very well endowed. Seconds passed as Ethan's gaze drifted up to a more appropriate location. The stranger had tanned skin and crystal-blue eyes. Ethan wondered if they were contacts, but didn't notice any outline in the irises. He'd never seen eyes so blue. Making a quick decision, he said, "Um—sure, I'll have a—"

"Vodka tonic with a twist?" the hunk interrupted, handing Ethan a glass while a little smirk formed at the edge of his mouth.

Ethan tilted his head and squinted his eyes. "How did you...?"

"Lucky guess," the man offered, his eyes twinkling. Ethan saw him turn and look at the bartender, who smiled, shaking his head before turning away.

Ethan looked back at the sexy man. Was it getting hot in here? If he still had on his tie from earlier today, he'd have loosened it. Then the velvet voice spoke again. "How long have you been here?"

"Just a couple of days. I'm staying at a hotel and—"

"No, babe." The man let out a throaty chuckle. "I meant how long have you been sitting in here all alone?" He placed his hand over Ethan's, his fingers stroking his skin, warming the area with his touch. Ethan thought he might pass out—or was he dreaming?

"Oh." Ethan's face heated as he looked away, certain he'd just turned three shades of red. "Not long." He couldn't believe this guy was paying attention to him. What the hell was he supposed to do now? Ethan was completely out of his league.

"What's your name, sexy?"

Sexy? God, the way the man looked at him while he said that word. Ethan *felt* sexy—and naked. "Ethan Mo—"

"Ethan," he interrupted. "I'm Chance."

"Chance?" Ethan raised his eyebrow.

"As in *take a chance.*" Chance winked. "Care to join me?" He motioned toward the tables by the dance floor.

Ethan nodded as Chance reached for his hand and tugged him off the stool, his feet wobbling as they hit the floor. He followed the man still holding his hand. *This is what you were looking for, remember?* Ethan reminded himself, feeling self-conscious as he glanced around the room. From couples dancing, to groups drinking and conversing, the place buzzed with energy. Ethan wanted to be a part of this.

As Chance led Ethan to an empty table in the center of the room, which Ethan thought was strange since every other one was occupied, his nerves took over again. What was he doing here with a stranger? But, as he looked around, no one seemed to care about that. *Relax.*

Chance pulled out a chair for Ethan like a proper gentleman, then slipped into the seat next to him and took his hand again. Chance liked to touch, Ethan realized. They sipped their cocktails and made harmless small talk. Ethan confessed his favorite artist was Katy Perry, so when "I Kissed a Girl" blared from the speakers, Chance grabbed Ethan's hand again. "Come on. Let's see what you can do."

Ethan couldn't do anything. Yet he followed the man, holding his hand until they stopped in the middle of the floor, and Chance wrapped his arms around him, pulling him close. Ethan shivered.

"Have you ever kissed a girl, Ethan?" Chance asked in a voice that could melt butter.

He shook his head, staring at Chance, wanting to kiss *him*. He didn't, but Chance must have noticed, because he licked his lips and stared directly into Ethan's soul.

The song changed into a heavy dance number, and Chance swiveled his hips to the music. Ethan stood there, not knowing what to do. Chance placed his hands on Ethan's hips and moved with him, letting Ethan follow along. "That's it." Chance inched closer until their crotches touched. Ethan's dick twitched from the contact. He remembered the couple from earlier and wanted to do that with Chance. Ethan looked around to see if they were still out there, but Chance put his hand on Ethan's chin, turning him back to face him. "You're the hottest guy in this club, Ethan." He knew that wasn't true. Chance was the hottest guy here, and probably everywhere, but he smiled and relocated his hands to Chance's shoulders as they moved to the beat, pretending to believe the obvious lie.

When the music slowed and Sam Smith's velvety voice came over the speakers, Chance wrapped his arms around him, letting Ethan's head rest on his chest. Ethan felt the man's heart pounding, and his own raced along with it. He looked up at Chance, who never took his eyes off him. Ethan really wanted him to kiss him. Maybe it was the third cocktail, but his inhibitions melted away in Chance's arms. Before Ethan realized what was happening, Chance raised Ethan's chin, and their lips met for the first time. His eyes widened as the warmth of Chance's mouth and his swirling tongue sent a zing of electricity through Ethan's body. He closed his eyes, and the scent of Chance's cologne mixed with the mild taste of citrus from the drink made him dizzy. Ethan pressed his body against Chance as they deepened the kiss, Ethan parting his lips to let

Chance inside. He actually moaned from the heat of Chance's mouth and feeling his erection pressed against his own. Ethan broke the kiss, breathing heavily. Chance opened his eyes. Ethan wanted to climb inside those crystal orbs. "Chance?"

"Hmm?" At some point, they'd stopped moving.

Ethan caught the rainbow strobes dancing overhead. "I, uh..." He really wanted to keep kissing Chance—or take care of his painful hard-on.

"Come on," Chance said, apparently reading his mind. He took Ethan's hand and led him through the club. They passed the bartender, and Ethan saw the man wink at him. *Oh great.*

He breathed again once they reached the street.

Chapter Three

CHANCE

Chance spotted a cab heading toward them, and signaled for it to stop. "Where to?" he asked the younger man. He never took a hookup to his own home, but Ethan wasn't his typical one-night stand. At least he didn't think so. There was something about him—half sweet, innocent kitten, and half minx just waiting to be unleashed. Ethan reminded him of someone—long ago.

"My hotel is just a few miles away." The shyness Chance first noticed about Ethan had returned. He was a mystery Chance couldn't wait to unravel. "Sir Frances."

"Perfect," Chance said as the cab pulled up. He opened the door, letting Ethan slide in first, before scooting in next to him. After telling the driver where to go, Chance took Ethan's hand again and rubbed his palm gently. Ethan breathed deeply, and Chance noticed the bulge pushing against his jeans. He placed his other hand on Ethan's lap, grazing his fingers against Ethan's erection. Ethan placed his own hand on top, adding to the friction. Chance leaned over and nibbled on his ear. "You like that, babe?"

Ethan nodded, arching into his touch as Chance's mouth made love to his lobe. Ethan moaned. They kissed and fondled each other the entire way. "We're almost there," Chance whispered. He knew the hotel where Ethan was staying.

When they arrived, Chance paid the driver and helped Ethan out of the car. "You doing all right, honey?"

"Perfect." He looked Chance directly in the eyes. Was that anxiousness or lust? He wasn't swaying at all, which was good. Chance would never take advantage of anyone. He wasn't a total shit. Ethan pulled out his keycard and Chance followed him through the lobby. Chance noticed the front desk clerk giving him a sour look. Feeling possessive, he took Ethan's hand and smirked at the guy, walking with Ethan to the bank of elevators. "Which floor?" he asked when the door opened.

"Six." Ethan stood against the back wall, his hands in front of his crotch, hiding the swell in his jeans. Chance smirked, turning around to push the button on the panel. He felt Ethan come from behind, rubbing Chance's ass with his crotch.

"Not a chance, babe," Chance said. He turned to face Ethan and kissed him, groping his backside. Ethan let out a giggle. Fucking adorable. The twinks Chance usually picked up were vapid little sluts looking for a mutually beneficial fuck, but this kid—he forgot to ask Ethan how old he was—had an innocence about him. Maybe Andre was right. But then Ethan ground their crotches together while giving him a searing kiss and Chance forgot his thoughts.

The elevator dinged, stopping on Ethan's floor, and Chance broke their kiss. He followed Ethan as he turned to the left and down the hallway. "I'm right here." He stopped in front of the door and fumbled with the key.

Damn, he had a fine ass. Chance nuzzled his neck as Ethan, giggling again, clumsily opened the door to his hotel room. Chance followed him inside and shut it behind them as he pressed Ethan against the wall and kissed him roughly.

Chance pulled away and noticed the lustful gleam in Ethan's eyes.

He moved toward the bed, removing his jacket. "Take off your clothes," Chance said, needy and demanding. Watching Ethan unbutton his shirt and reveal his nearly hairless chest, Chance kicked off his boots and slid his black muscle shirt over his head. His leather pants were skintight. He peeled them carefully down his legs so they wouldn't rip. These were his favorite pair. He paused when he caught Ethan staring at his legs. He bent over to reveal his ass, and heard Ethan gasp as he felt his eyes drink him in. Moments like this made his hours at the gym worth it. He turned around and licked his lips in anticipation, watching Ethan slide his T-shirt over his head and fling his pants to the floor, trying to be as smooth as Chance, yet not quite accomplishing the feat. Ethan looked at Chance with doe eyes and a shy smile, nervousness radiating from him as he locked his arms against his chest, as if he didn't know what to do next. Chance went to him and unfolded his arms and placed his hand on Ethan's cheek. "You're beautiful," he told him before devouring his soft lips.

Chance took his hand and led him to the bed.

He took in Ethan's gorgeous body splayed out just for him, and completely exposed. His cock was hard as stone, glistening precome, and twitching in anticipation of what Chance was about to give him. Ethan sucked in a breath as Chance knelt between his legs and swallowed his cock. His shaft was average length, but thick and straight. It was perfect. Chance wrapped his lips around the head and sucked him to the root, hitting the back of his throat. Ethan squirmed and made the most delicious sounds. While he worked Ethan's cock with his mouth and tongue, Chance caressed his balls in tiny circles, rubbing his thumb over the taint.

"Chance," Ethan breathed.

Chance drifted his fingers to Ethan's hole, circling and teasing his entrance. Ethan's body tensed. "I'll go nice and slow."

Ethan nodded, visibly relaxing while Chance opened the lube and spread it over his fingers. Then he pushed one inside, massaging the warm channel, and shortly after, added another. Chance's dick stiffened even more in anticipation of sliding into that tight heat.

As he slid his fingers in and out of a writhing Ethan, Chance licked across the tip of his cock. He tasted the creamy bead of precome at the tip, spreading it with his tongue, teasing the slit.

Ethan bucked his hips, pushing himself toward Chance to take him deeper. He let out a deep moan as his cock disappeared into Chance's mouth. "*Ahh* God, feels good."

Chance grabbed Ethan's butt cheeks, letting him fuck his mouth and control the rhythm. He hummed around his length, taking every inch sliding between his lips. Holding the shaft in his hand, he let it slip out of his mouth. "You taste amazing," he said, just before swallowing him again.

"Chance," Ethan moaned.

Chance released him, ignoring Ethan's groan of disappointment. He slowly licked up his body until he reached his mouth, claiming him. Ethan's breath was uneven as Chance felt his chest pounding.

"Please," Ethan pleaded.

"On your hands and knees," Chance instructed. "It'll be easier." Ethan flipped over and presented his ass, his scrotum dangling until Chance cupped him with his free hand, stroking the sensitive area. Ethan purred with delight at the attention Chance gave his balls. He spread Ethan apart and ghosted his lips across his puckered entrance, causing Ethan to shudder.

"What the...?"

"*Ssh*, I'll make this so good for you," Chance promised. He pressed his lips against Ethan's hole and kissed his most intimate spot, while he continued loving Ethan's balls. He knew his capabilities as a lover.

"Ah God, Chance," Ethan cried, as Chance worked him.

Chance moved his lips toward Ethan's sac and sucked one of the balls into his mouth. Chance swirled it with his tongue while he pressed two lubed fingers into the tight entrance. Ethan gasped when Chance curved his fingers and brushed against his prostate.

"Oh—my—fuck," Ethan said through uneven breaths. "That was—what was that?" Chance did it again, just for Ethan's delicious reaction to his touch.

Was he the first one to touch him there? Chance wondered just how much experience he had. "Good, babe?"

"Yeah—do that thing again." He stretched out each syllable.

Chance pressed two fingers inside Ethan's ass, brushing them against his special bump, drawing moans of pleasure from his receptive lover. "You look so good taking my fingers," he whispered in Ethan's ear, "I can't wait to fuck your tight hole."

"Do it," Ethan challenged, growing bolder. Something told Chance to take his time with this one.

"I need to get you ready to take me," Chance said, and kissed Ethan's left ass cheek. Then he slid a third finger into the warm, puckered cavity, stretching him.

Ethan looked up at him with wide, scared eyes.

"You'll be able to," he assured him. "We'll go slow." Chance was bigger than average. He could make a lover scream in pleasure, but he wanted to take care of Ethan. Make it good for him. Chance crooked his fingers again, hitting his spot repeatedly, as Ethan pushed back, begging Chance for more.

He rolled the condom onto his cock and applied a liberal amount of lube. He reached for Ethan's hips and positioned himself. "Ready, babe?"

He waited for Ethan's permission of a nod, then slid into Ethan's tight hole, stopping only a couple of inches in as he felt him clench. "You all right?" he asked, watching the expressions change on Ethan's face while he rubbed his back before sliding a little farther. He repeated this action until he was all the way in, his balls flush against Ethan's body. After giving him a moment to get used to his girth, he began to move.

Panting, Ethan pushed back, sinking Chance deeper into him. "Yeah, just—yeah—please," he begged.

"Babe, you're so hot," Chance grunted as he fucked him hard.

"Ethan," he corrected him. "My name is Ethan."

Chance never used first names. "Babe" was better than saying the wrong name, and they never cared, but this guy— "Ba—Ethan. You feel so good."

He pounded Ethan's ass, gradually increasing the rhythm as their bodies moved in sync with one another. Neither man spoke words, only sounds of panting and grunting. Chance reached for Ethan's cock, using his body fluids for lubrication. He looked far gone as he chanted, "Chance," and moments later Ethan came, shooting white spurts of stickiness into Chance's hand, his breath heavy through his body spasms. "God, that was...."

Chance released Ethan's softening cock, as he reached around his waist, slamming into Ethan's hot body. "Fuck, you're tight." After just a few more thrusts, Chance tensed as his body shook and he released into the condom, working Ethan's hole until he was too sensitive to move. He slumped over Ethan, slid out of him and then flipped him onto his back to kiss his lips, hungrily. Ethan responded although Chance could tell he was spent. "God, ba—Ethan, that was so fucking good." Through his orgasmic haze, he added, "Where have you been all of my life?" *Where did that come from?*

Ethan smiled and kissed him back. Chance slipped off the condom. He stood up to toss it in the trash on the way to the bathroom for a washcloth to clean up their mess.

Chance carefully wiped the washcloth over Ethan who gave him those doe eyes again. He didn't look like someone who just got what they wanted; he appeared shy and demure and incredibly sexy. Chance tossed the washcloth aside, and lay down next to the young man, spooning him, and kissed the back of his neck. He should really leave, but he was too exhausted to move. Chance cuddled his lover, something he never did, stirring old feelings he wished away as he fell into a deep slumber.

CHANCE'S WRISTWATCH ALARM awoke him the next morning. Ethan was firmly plastered against Chance's chest. He leaned down and kissed his cheek. Ethan stirred, but didn't awaken. Chance wasn't much for mornings after. In fact, he never spent the night with a hookup, but it felt nice sleeping with Ethan. He was cuddly and kissed in his sleep. Chance checked his watch. *Damn, I'm running late.* He had an early meeting with clients. He barely had enough time to run home and get a shower. He carefully lifted Ethan's arms and Ethan rolled over, hugging the pillow, his bare ass peeking out from the covers. Chance kissed him there before replacing the covers over his sleeping figure.

He quickly dressed in his clothes, noting the leather pants didn't feel as good on his skin this morning. Chance found a pad of paper on the desk. He wrote Ethan a short note and set it on the dresser. Then, he quietly left the hotel room. "Good-bye, ba—Ethan," he whispered, as he shut the door.

Chapter Four

ETHAN

Ethan woke the next morning disoriented and alone. He groaned. Had he dreamed the entire night? He pulled the covers away, revealing his naked body. When he shifted, the uncomfortable feeling in his ass made him realize that no, it wasn't a dream, but Chance was gone. He hadn't drunk enough to be hungover, but his mouth was dry and thoughts of last night hit him hard. What had he done? He got out of bed to take a much-needed piss and found a folded piece of paper on the dresser with his name scrawled on the top.

He opened it, his heart racing. *I had to get to work. Here's my number. Call me the next time you're in town. Luv, Chance.*

"Luv Chance?" Ethan wandered out of the bathroom and sat on the bed, clutching the note. *Chance gave me his number.* Ethan lay back, wincing as his naked ass hit the sheets. His cock twitched in memory of the best night of his entire life. Chance was an amazing lover. He held up the note and read it again.

With a couple of hours until checkout, Ethan ordered room service and then headed back into the bathroom for a long shower. Letting the hot water hit his back, he imagined Chance behind him scrubbing him, rubbing him, pressing his cock into him. He blinked, reluctantly bringing his mind back to the present.

Ethan had never hooked up with a total stranger before. He wondered what his mom would think if she knew, and he felt a twinge of shame. He hoped Chance didn't think he made a habit of sleeping with strange men. On the other hand, Chance was the one who approached him. *Maybe Chance is the slut.*

That thought didn't make him feel any better at all. But he couldn't bring himself to regret the encounter. He'd spent the night with a beautiful man and had the best sex of his entire life. What if he moved here? Would Chance want to see him again? He was getting ahead of himself.

Ethan soaped up his arms, rubbed the bar into his chest, and moved his hands down to his cock—*Chance*. He couldn't stop thinking about him. Chance kissing him at the club, Chance sucking his dick, Chance fucking him into the mattress—he wished they'd had more time together.

Ethan had had anal sex twice in his life. Both times were in college with sloppy-drunk partners as inexperienced as he was, and neither encounter was particularly great. Although he didn't have much to go on, Ethan was pretty sure sex couldn't get much better than last night.

Chance wouldn't have left his number if he didn't want to see him again, right? However, the note didn't say *call me when you wake up*; it said *call me when you are in town again*. Maybe Chance thought he traveled for work. Maybe Chance did this kind of thing often. Maybe Chance was accustomed to one-night stands. Maybe Ethan needed to stop overthinking before he drove himself crazy.

He finished cleaning off the remnants of his sexual escapade, got dressed, and ate his breakfast. As he repacked his suitcase, his cell phone rang. His eyes widened as he grabbed his phone, thinking it might be Chance. Then he remembered he had Chance's number, not the other way around. His phone rang again, and he sighed as he answered, "Hello?"

"Ethan, it's Mark," said the voice on the other end of the call. "Where are you, man?"

"Oh, it's you." He knew he sounded disappointed. "I'm still at the hotel, getting ready to check out."

"Were you expecting someone else?" Mark snickered.

"What? No, of course not," Ethan covered. "What's going on?"

"We're going to spend the day at Baker Beach. Meet us there."

ETHAN SPENT TWO more days in California with his friends at the beach. He thought about Chance the entire time. Should he call him? Would Chance even remember him? He kept his thoughts to himself and tried to enjoy his vacation.

On the long drive home the following day, Ethan told Mark about meeting Chance and their night together.

"Wait, he gave you his number and you haven't called him yet? What the hell are you waiting for, Ethan?" Mark seemed happy for him.

"I don't want to seem desperate, you know?" He shrugged. "Maybe he gives everyone his number, to be nice."

"Really, Ethan, just to be nice?" The sarcasm dripped from Mark's voice. "He could have left without leaving a note at all." He turned to look at Ethan, raising an eyebrow.

"Yeah, I guess." Ethan rubbed the back of his neck, a nervous habit he'd developed in high school. At least Mark wasn't judging him.

"Or don't call him, what the fuck do I care?" Mark smirked, knowing exactly how to push his best friend's buttons.

"Well, maybe I'll wait until I hear about this job," he said. "No sense starting something I can't finish."

Chance

Back in San Francisco, at the Ashton Lake Advertising Agency, the senior executive sat behind his desk fumbling through paperwork when his project manager, Bradley Parker, barged into his office. "Well, I've narrowed it down to three candidates," Brad blurted. "Take a look at this one, especially." He handed the exec a single sheet of paper.

Taking the resume from his manager's hand, the man glanced over it, reading the highlights: graduated with honors, participated in club lacrosse, Future Leaders of America, 3.9 GPA.

"He aced his interview," Brad said. "He was smart and had a little spunk. He would definitely fit in with this bunch."

The executive took the other two resumes, studying all three. They all looked excellent on paper. With college graduates, it was difficult to know what kind of employee they'd make. He took a few minutes before handing him the first one. "Hire him, Bradley."

"Don't you want to meet him first?" the man questioned.

"Nope, I trust you; get him in here. We need to start this project in a couple of weeks." Turning his attention back to his cluttered desk, he shooed the manager out of his office. Then he looked up at him with sparkling blue eyes. "Good job, Brad."

"Thanks, Chance—I mean Mr. Harlow." Brad chuckled. "I'll call him in the morning and tell him the good news." Then he left, shutting the door behind him.

Alone, Chance smiled to himself. He picked up one of the metallic darts on his desk and hurled it toward the dartboard hanging on his door. *Mr. Harlow is my dad.* He scanned the spacious corner office he'd occupied for the last three years. It still surprised him how this far he'd come in such a short time. At twenty-nine, he was the youngest senior executive in the history of the firm. He'd worked hard to get there and was proud of his accomplishments.

Chance graduated third in his class in college. He'd been accepted into graduate school when he got his break at the firm as a copywriter. Working his way to project manager in just over two years, he gained the attention of the vice president of marketing. He was offered an executive position at the same time he'd received his master's degree in marketing and management. He was known through the company as driven. He'd been that way since college after...He didn't like to think about Dr. Wesley Montague. That was a long time ago.

Chance was a green freshman when he enrolled in Dr. Montague's sociology course his first semester. The young professor courted him those first two weeks of class. Chance knew he was good-looking. He received a lot of attention from both sexes, but Wes made him feel like no one had before—special. He fell hard for the professor. They carried on a secret relationship throughout the term, consisting mostly of fucking in the professor's apartment six miles from campus. The good professor dumped Chance the day before finals. He was completely devastated.

He toughened up after he saw the guy courting some new meat at the beginning of the next semester. He soon learned Wesley Montague had a reputation, and he'd fallen right into his trap. He'd never let that happen again. The man taught him two things: never let your guard down and always be the one in control.

Chance gave his office a final look and nodded. He *had* come a long way. He turned out the lights and closed the door.

AFTER GOING HOME and changing, Chance headed over to Club Cruze, his favorite nightclub in the city. There wasn't anyone interesting tonight, so he hung out at the bar and talked to Andre. "You look down, my friend," the bartender told Chance, handing him his Chopin tonic.

"Is it me, or are the pickings getting slim around here?" Chance asked, sweeping the club with his eyes.

"You're getting pickier," Andre said, giving him a knowing look. Knowing what, Chance had no idea. He decided he'd seek out Kevin at lunch tomorrow. He was a parasite, but gave incredible head and eased his tension. He turned his head toward the other end of the bar at an empty seat. Blinking, feeling something like regret, he looked away.

He reached for his phone and called his buddy Brad. "Feel like dancing?"

Chapter Five

ETHAN

Six days after he returned home from his trip to California, Ethan received a call from Mr. Parker offering him the advertising job at the Ashton Lake firm in San Francisco. However, they needed him there in a week. They were sending a plane ticket and putting him up in the same hotel where he'd stayed before until he could arrange to rent an apartment. Ethan was ecstatic—then shitting bricks. He only had a few days to get ready and move his whole life halfway across the country. His mom and brother decided they would need an excuse to visit him soon, so they offered to drive his car out in a few weeks to help him get settled in and bring the rest of his things. What was he thinking, moving to a strange city where he knew no one?

But he did know someone. Chance. *Should I call him?* It had been two weeks. He'd probably moved on by now. *But he did say call him the next time I'm in town...*

Ethan picked up the phone at least a dozen times but put it down without dialing the man's number. He hadn't told anyone about him except Mark. He didn't know what his parents would think. Well, he knew what they'd say, and he'd get a big lecture. They'd known he was gay since he was seventeen—that wasn't the problem. But respectable young men didn't have one-night stands—with anyone. What did they know? He wasn't a girl. That was how gay men met, wasn't it? He shooed the unwanted voices out of his head and focused getting packed.

ETHAN HANDED THE gate attendant his ticket and boarded the plane headed toward his new life. He was terrified. He'd never left Iowa before two weeks ago, and now he was moving across the country—alone. He puffed out his chest. He could do this.

The plane landed a few hours later at San Francisco International Airport. After retrieving his bags from the moving carousel at baggage claim, Ethan walked through the revolving doors into the California air and hailed a taxi to the Sir Frances Hotel. He checked in with the same front desk agent from before, who recognized him. Then he remembered parading through the lobby with Chance as he tried hiding his erection, and he blushed, hoping that wasn't why the guy remembered him. No, the guy flirted enough with him the last time he was here.

Once in his room, Ethan dropped his bags and picked up a package with his name on it that lay on the king-sized bed. He opened it, revealing a bunch of employee forms to fill out, some information on the company, and a list of contacts for rental agencies near the firm. Tucked in the pocket of the folder was a business card for his direct supervisor, Bradley Parker, with instructions to call him when he arrived. Ethan read the material and made the call.

He thought about going back to that club to see if he could find Chance but decided against it. The odds he'd be there again weren't likely, and Ethan had no idea what he would say to him anyway. What if Chance didn't remember him, or worse, what if he was there with someone else? Besides, Ethan wanted to feel rested for his first day at work, so he ordered room service and settled in for a quiet dinner in front of the television. After flipping channels for a few minutes, finding nothing interesting, he fell asleep, dreaming about the man he couldn't get out of his head.

The next morning, Ethan showered, ate breakfast, and dressed in the brand-new clothes his mom helped him pick out after he'd gotten the news about the job. "You need your own suit now that you're a working man," she told him. He took a last look in the mirror and fixed his hair. Then, he smoothed the wrinkles his clothes had gotten from traveling in the suitcase. Once satisfied with his appearance, he rode the elevator down to the lobby and climbed into the waiting car the agency had arranged.

Ethan arrived at the building of his new place of employment fifteen minutes later. He thanked the driver and watched him pull away. Then, he took a deep breath, walked into the lobby to the bank of elevators, and rode up to the tenth floor.

Ethan stepped into the spacious lobby of Ashton Lake and stopped at the reception desk when nervousness suddenly overcame him.

"May I help you, sir?" asked the perky girl behind the desk.

"I'm Ethan Moore. It's my first day." Ethan's voice squeaked. This was his first real job out of college, and although he was excited and extremely lucky to have landed a position in his field, he had no idea what to expect. Before he broke out into a sweat and made a quick run for it, the perky girl at the desk answered him and put him at ease.

"Oh, Mr. Moore, Mr. Parker is expecting you. Please have a seat and I'll call him for you," she said, picking up the phone, dialing.

A few moments later, Brad Parker came bellowing toward him. "Ethan," the man called out to him. "Welcome back." He looked out of breath, like he'd been running.

"Thank you, sir. I'm glad to be here," he said, shaking Mr. Parker's hand.

"Please, call me Brad. Follow me, and I'll show you around."

They spent the next couple of hours touring the building, and Brad introduced Ethan to the team he'd be working with. "Sorry you missed the senior exec, Mr. Harlow, but he's, err, at lunch." He coughed.

Ethan looked over at Brad as the man glanced down, seemingly embarrassed. *That was weird.* Then it passed, and he was back to being perky. "Well, that's just about everyone, Ethan," he said, patting him on the back. "Let me show you to your office, and then we'll grab a bite to eat."

Brad took him to a little bistro down the street. "The crab cakes are excellent."

"Sounds great," Ethan agreed, closing his menu when the waitress came to take their order.

Brad told Ethan about the project he was hired for. "We're hoping this client will take our little firm to the next level. We've mostly had projects around California and a few in other scattered cities, but never international. It was a major feat getting them to meet us."

"I'm very excited to get started."

"Good. I will help you get up to speed. If there is anything you need or don't understand, I'm your main point of contact."

"Are you in charge of the project?" Ethan liked Brad. He was down to earth and approachable.

"You'll meet the senior exec this afternoon, Mr. Harlow. This is his show. He's amazing at what he does, so you'll learn a lot from him too."

Mr. Harlow sounded like a stodgy old hard-ass. He wondered why the guy wasn't there to meet him if they'd be working together.

Then Brad gave Ethan a funny look, almost a smirk. "What?" Ethan asked, wondering if he had something on his face.

"Oh, it's just—nothing. Mr. Harlow is a great guy to work for." Brad cleared his throat, obviously uncomfortable talking about the boss. Ethan found his words disconcerting. Was there something wrong with Mr. Harlow?

After they finished eating the best crab cakes Ethan had ever tasted— okay, the first he'd ever tasted—they headed back to the office. Brad led Ethan down the hallway to an office they hadn't visited that morning.

"Ethan, let's stop here for a minute," he said, knocking on a corner office door.

"Come in," Ethan heard from inside.

Brad opened the door and Ethan stepped inside. "Mr. Harlow, I want to introduce you to our newest employee, Ethan Moore. Ethan, meet our senior executive, Chance Harlow."

Chapter Six

CHANCE

Chance stood up, walked around to the front of his desk and folded his arms, giving the new employee a lavish once-over and wondering why he looked so familiar. Damn, he was cute. Why did he have to be so fucking cute? Chance never dated employees. Well, except for Bradley, but that was long ago, and they made better friends. Why was he even thinking about dating this kid? He straightened up and reached out his hand. He looked nervous with his mouth hanging wide open, and Chance noticed him actually shaking. Was he afraid of him?

"Nice to meet you, sir," the kid choked out as he shook Chance's hand.

Chance felt a little bad for him. Wanting to ease the tension, he sat on the edge of his desk and relaxed his body, hoping Ethan would do the same. "Bradley has nothing but amazing things to say about you. I'm looking forward to us working together. Welcome aboard, Ethan Moore."

"Thank you, sir. I'm very happy to be here." Chance heard his words but felt something was off. He looked terrified, and not just "I'm meeting the new boss" kind of nerves. Chance looked him in the eyes. *Ethan, Ethan...* Ethan looked away, a red glow spreading over his face. *Oh, my God, it's that Ethan. The little hottie I picked up at the club a few weeks ago. Well, fuck. This day just got interesting.*

"Please, I'm not 'sir' here, I'm Chance," he said, grinning at the blushing mess of hot boy in front of him.

"Mr. Harlow," Brad corrected.

"Right—Mr. Harlow. Mr. Parker, why don't you leave Mr. Moore with me so we can get acquainted? You can come back for him in—let's say twenty minutes," he said, checking his watch. "That all right with you, Ethan?" He patted Ethan on the back, and without waiting for an answer, he ordered, "Have a seat."

Ethan nodded, yet remained standing. His arms lay straight against his side, but his hands clutched the fabric of his pants and Chance noticed fear in those pretty brown eyes.

"Ethan..." he said, calmer this time, and motioned for Ethan to sit down again. "Bradley?" He glared at his second-in-command.

"Right, I'll just show myself out." Brad opened the door, muttering, "That was quick," while he exited the office.

Meanwhile, Ethan sunk into the large leather swivel chair in front of Chance's desk, while Chance paced in front of him, taking him in. "It is you, right, Ethan?"

"Chance, I mean, Mr. Harlow, I mean—oh God, I swear I had no idea who you were. I honestly didn't know you worked here," the poor boy babbled. *Damn, he was cute.*

"Why didn't you call me?" Chance cocked his head, arms folded. He'd never left his number for anyone before, but hadn't really expected a call from the guy.

"I'm so sorry. I picked up the phone so many times." Beads of sweat formed on Ethan's brow. He was clearly unnerved. Chance suddenly felt bad for the interrogation.

"Relax, Ethan, I'm just teasing you."

Ethan looked up at him with big, brown eyes and blinked. "I wanted to," he murmured.

They stared at each other for a moment before Chance broke their trance. God, he was beautiful. If they weren't at work, Chance would love to taste those lips again. Chance changed the conversation to business. "What do you know about the new client?"

Ethan explained everything Brad had told him and mentioned that he'd researched them on his own as well. Chance filled him in on the rest.

"I'm really looking forward to getting started."

"Good, this project means a lot to me." But, Chance was curious about a few things. "So, you moved here just for this job?" Chance leaned up against his desk, right in front of Ethan, peering into his eyes.

"Yes, of course, why else?" Ethan blurted.

"I thought, maybe—whatever..." *What did you think he was here for, you?* Chance hadn't spent that much time thinking about the cutie from the bar, but it had been the hottest sex he'd had in a long time. *Doesn't mean the guy moved his life out here for you.* He silently berated himself for having vulnerable thoughts. He had no time for those, or for Ethan Moore.

"Chance, I started to call you so many times, but I didn't know if you'd even remember me." Ethan looked small when he added, "I had no idea what that night even meant."

"It meant nothing," Chance snapped. One-night stands never meant anything. He ended the conversation by standing up and motioning for Ethan to do the same. "That'll be all, Mr. Moore."

At the same time, Brad knocked on the door and carefully pushed it open. A red-faced Ethan stormed past Brad and sprinted out of Chance's office.

Chance sat behind his desk, his anger burning. He stared up at Brad who looked confused. "Shut the door, Bradley," Chance barked.

ETHAN

Ethan stood outside the office, swearing to himself, when Brad shut the door and joined him. Ethan couldn't believe his dumb luck. How had this happened? He was thrilled and mortified at the same time. Now, he apparently pissed the guy off.

"Well, the boss seems to like you." Brad broke the awkward silence.

Ethan held his head down. He wanted to crawl under the closest table and hide, but that wasn't an option.

"Hey, man, are you all right?"

"Not really." He grimaced.

"Did...Mr. Harlow *do* something to you?" Brad asked with deep concern on his face. Ethan wondered what he thought Chance might have done to him.

"Oh, God no." He shook his head, as he recalled their meeting. He sat in that big, overstuffed chair, nervous as hell while the man circled him, undressing him with his eyes. Ethan had been intimidated and horny at the same time. He felt like chum in a beautifully decorated pond, about to be swallowed by a gorgeous shark. How was he supposed to explain that? Then, Chance shut down on him and he didn't understand why. "He was a perfect gentleman." Ethan swallowed the lie.

"Good," Brad said, relief washing over his face. "How about we finish the day and I'll take you out for drinks, and we can get to know each other."

"Yeah, okay, Mr. Parker," Ethan answered, rubbing the back of his neck. He wondered if Parker did that for all his new employees, or just the pathetic ones.

"Brad," he corrected.

"Brad—thanks." Ethan nodded before Brad took him to his new office so he could settle in.

Ethan didn't know what to think about the whole encounter with Chance. Was the man just playing him, or was he actually offended Ethan hadn't called? Would he still have been hired if he had? Would he be fired? Ethan had a million thoughts running through his brain. He was already mortified he'd had a one-night stand, but with his new boss? *Fuck me.*

He pushed all thoughts of Chance Harlow out of his mind for the rest of the day. He'd man up and call Mark tonight. Maybe he'd be able to help him through this, or he'd laugh hysterically at him. Ethan groaned. What if they fired him after only one day and he ended up on the streets peddling for cash—or worse, having to go back home as a complete failure. He let out a harried groan. How could he have fucked this up so soon?

After making it through his first day on the job, Ethan sat with Brad at a bar a few blocks from the office. With a drink in front of each of them, and one already ingested, Brad finally spoke up. "Well, Ethan, you met the great Chance Harlow. You know, he's the youngest senior advertising executive on the entire West Coast. He has a brilliant mind, but an insatiable thirst for cute boys. He's a player. I hope he didn't offend you this afternoon. I probably should have warned you; you're totally his type. But don't worry, he's not into sexual harassment— usually." Brad took a long swig and sat back with his arms folded, having finished his ramble.

"No, he didn't harass me." Ethan tilted his head. "He's a player?"

Brad nodded. "And he doesn't usually date within the workplace. It's not a rule or anything," he said, waving his hand, "it's just potentially messy, you know? Anyway, so what *did* happen in there? You looked really upset."

Ethan held his head in his hands. "Mr. Parker, I fucked up." He couldn't believe he was about to tell his new supervisor this, but he had to.

"First, it's Brad, and what do you mean, you fucked up?" Brad leaned forward with keen interest.

"Shit." He took a deep breath, then told Brad the whole sordid story, starting with being excited the interview had gone well, going to a club, meeting Chance, and taking him back to his hotel room. He left out the intimate details, obviously, and he finished the story with waking up alone the next morning and finding Chance's note. "Fuck, Mr.—Brad, I had no idea he worked here. I never would have done that. I'm so embarrassed," he groaned.

"No shit. Wow." Bradley shook his head, apparently enjoying Ethan's discomfort.

"Will you stop saying that?" Ethan's eyes went wide as his right arm shot to the back of his neck.

"Sorry." Brad sat back, still listening.

"Then to top it off, after meeting him today, he asked me why I didn't call him. He said he was just kidding, but then he told me it meant nothing to him and sent me away."

"He did what?" A look of anger shot across Brad's face.

"Well, I told him I didn't call him because I didn't know what that night meant," he corrected. "Then he said it meant nothing."

"Oh." Brad's face softened.

"Now I don't know what to do. Should I try to talk to him or just forget it ever happened? I really liked him. Will he fire me?" His voice got squeakier with every sentence.

"Let me talk to him," Brad interrupted.

"What? No way," Ethan shrieked, horrified at the suggestion.

"Look, Ethan, I know him better than anyone. I'll talk to him. In the meantime, you just learn your job—really well," Brad advised, looking determined.

Ethan raised his eyebrows. "Just how well do you know him?" The fact Brad and Ethan had many similarities did not escape him.

"We dated for a while," he said with a shrug. "It's totally over, though. Nothing for you to worry about," he insisted.

"I'm not worried." Ethan looked everywhere except at Brad.

"Sure thing, Ethan."

CHANCE

Chance stewed in his office the next morning, pacing, unable to get Ethan off his mind. *Well, shit, that hadn't gone well.* Sure, he hadn't spent *that* much time over the past two weeks thinking about the little hottie from the bar. *Was* he hurt Ethan hadn't called him? *No way.* Who was he kidding? He liked the kid—more than he cared to admit. And he was so good in bed. *But he* does *work here now and indirectly for me. Shit, this could get messy.* He made a rule of never dating coworkers. That rule came after Brad. Maybe it was a bad idea to pursue this. But Chance didn't always make good decisions when it came to cute boys.

A loud knock startled him, and he turned toward the door. "What the fuck, Chance?" Brad stormed into the room, slamming the door behind him.

"Well, good morning to you too, Bradley." Chance looked up, unimpressed.

"Seriously, Chance? You slept with our new employee?" Brad slapped his hand on his hips, glaring at Chance.

"Now, just wait a minute, Brad." Chance stood, giving it right back to his second-in-command. "He wasn't our new employee when we slept together," he said, louder than he meant to. Sitting back down, Chance calmed himself. "What did he tell you, anyway?"

"The poor guy is distraught; he thinks you're going to fire him."

"Why would I fire him? He's so pretty." He really was. And, what a lover.

"That's not funny, Chance. I like this guy. He's bright and gets along with everyone. He has real potential." Brad's threw his hands in the air.

"Do you have the hots for him, Bradley?" Chance batted his eyes in sarcasm.

"No, Chance, I don't. Do you?" No one got away with speaking to him like that except for Brad.

"No, I mean, yes, I mean..." Chance sighed, folding his hands. "Let me tell you my side of the story, okay?"

Brad sat down and glared at him, his big brown eyes reminding him of Ethan's sweet ones.

After a few deep sighs, Chance began. "I met him at Andre's a few weeks ago. He was drinking a generic vodka tonic with a twist when I walked in, and Andre pointed him out to me. He was so hot and sitting all alone. I brought him a Chopin and we started talking. We were dancing and kissing, and the next thing I knew, he was taking me to his hotel room. How could I say no?"

"You never do." Brad smirked.

"We had an incredible night together," he recalled, sighing. "He was so hot; begging me for it..." Chance closed his eyes, reliving that night. "Ethan was incredible. Sweet and shy at the bar, and then when I kissed him, he turned into a wildcat." Chance couldn't remember a more receptive and appreciative lover.

"No details, please," Brad said, rolling his eyes.

"Anyway, the next morning I had to leave for work, so I left him a note and told him to call me the next time he was in town. I never heard from him until I saw him yesterday." He leaned against his chair with his elbows stretched, hands behind his head, and waited for Brad's next tirade.

"You gave him your number?" Brad looked shocked. "You like him," he accused.

"Yeah, I like him; he's totally my type. But then so was that guy I had for lunch yesterday," Chance said dreamily.

"You're such a slut, Harlow," he accused. "What are you going to do about Ethan? Don't mess with him. He moved his whole life out here for this job." Brad's voice held warning.

"Yeah, I wondered if I had anything to do with his decision. I asked him that, you know. He said no," Chance said, annoyed.

"Well, I think he likes you, a lot. I told him all about you."

"Great, Brad. Thanks." Sarcasm dripped from his words. He didn't need this shit right now.

"I didn't want him getting his hopes up or anything."

"Nice chatting with you, Brad," Chance said, dismissing him.

Brad stood up. "What should I tell Ethan?"

"Tell him he has a cute ass."

"You're an ass, Chance."

"Yeah, I know."

Brad walked out the door and shut it.

Fuck. That did not go well.

Chapter Seven

ETHAN

Ethan found an inexpensive, one-bedroom apartment in the Lower Nob Hill district of San Francisco, not too far from the office of Ashton Lake. He could walk to work in nice weather but looked forward to having his car so he could get around the city. His mom and brother drove out a couple of days after he signed the lease, with the rest of his things, and helped Ethan move in. They took him to buy some furniture for his apartment, but Ethan insisted he'd get the rest after a couple of paychecks. Fortunately, he was able to divert questions regarding his social life. Not that he had one. He wasn't sure what to do about Chance. He was so attracted to the man, but dating the senior executive was probably a horrible idea. Besides, he had a lot to prove, to himself, Brad, and especially Chance. No, getting involved with Chance would be career suicide.

He drove his mom and brother to the airport a couple of days later. Without his family occupying his time, Ethan threw himself into his new job. Brad was a great mentor and becoming a friend too. He didn't have many of those yet.

The project Ethan had been hired specifically for was kicking off soon. Ethan knew he'd be working closely with Chance. He decided he needed to keep things strictly professional, even though he was distractingly attracted to the man. Fortunately, Brad hadn't mentioned Ethan's little problem to anyone, and neither had Chance, so at least no one else knew he'd slept with the boss.

Chance and Ethan were rarely alone, leaving almost no opportunity to talk since their first meeting in Chance's office. But there was clearly sexual tension between the two men. He just hoped no one else noticed. He was incredibly torn between his feelings and his conscience. Sleeping with the boss was a terrible idea, and dating didn't seem a possibility either. How would that look to the rest of the team? No, he was doing the right thing by staying away. It wasn't easy though, and Chance made it as difficult as possible.

Brad invited Ethan to go to a club one evening. Ethan recognized Club Cruze as soon as they approached the door. He stopped suddenly. "Brad, why are we here?"

"Huh? Oh God, Ethan, is this where—I'm sorry, do you want to leave?" Brad tilted his head forward and wouldn't look directly at Ethan. He'd obviously brought him here on purpose.

Ethan shook his head. "No, it's okay. Let's just get a drink." Ethan could do this. He needed to.

"Andre," Brad called over the bartender as they walked toward the bar.

"Brad, how are you, darling?" They exchanged air kisses over the counter.

"Beautiful, Andre, and you?"

"Oh, you know." He shrugged. "Who's your friend?" Andre glanced in Ethan's direction. After a moment's hesitation, his eyes widened and he smiled. "Hey, I know you. Ethan, right?"

"Wow, good memory." Ethan kind of hoped Andre wouldn't remember him, recalling the look on the bartender's face as Chance dragged Ethan out of the club a few weeks earlier, clearly with one intention. His face flushed.

"Chance is over there." Andre pointed to the dance floor. Brad and Ethan looked in the direction of the sweaty bodies pressed up against one another. They spotted Chance right away, dancing with some twink.

"He does have a type, doesn't he?" Ethan acknowledged with a pang of jealousy.

"You okay, honey?" Brad looked regretful, so Ethan let him off the hook. He figured Brad had brought him here to show him this side of Chance, but Ethan couldn't help feeling sad watching him fondle another man.

"Yeah, I'm fine." Brad placed his hand on Ethan's shoulder and led him to an open table near the back of the club. "I know what you're doing, Brad." The waiter came over with two more drinks, and Ethan concentrated on the clear liquid. When he looked up, the guilty expression on Brad's face had returned. "It's okay. You told me he was like this." Ethan sighed. "You know, I did come out here for the job. I mean, yeah, I was hoping I'd see him again, but I didn't have any expectations." Ethan took a long sip of the transparent liquid.

"That's good, Ethan. I'm not trying to hurt you, but I wanted you to see for yourself. Chance is a good guy—as a friend anyway. And he's great at what he does." He coughed. "Professionally, I mean."

Ethan choked, almost spitting out his drink. Both men laughed at the joke. He glanced up at Bradley Parker, who also knew how hot Chance was in bed and that twinge of jealousy returned.

They both looked up as the tall, dark, and gorgeous man approached their table. "What are you two girls giggling about?" Chance asked, expressionless, as he sat down.

"Oh nothing, big guy. Where's the twink?" Brad asked, looking behind Chance.

"I let him go. Not interested tonight," Chance said. He took a sip of his drink while staring right at Ethan. "Wanna dance?" He pulled Ethan out of his seat, not waiting for an answer.

"Sure," he said, looking back nervously at Brad, who played with the stirrer in his drink, shaking his head.

Chance pushed Ethan through the crowd to the dance floor and put his arms around him. "God, Ethan, I've wanted to do this ever since you walked into my office that first day."

"Um, Chance, I'm not sure this is a good idea." Ethan tried backing away.

"What? It's just dancing."

Ethan let Chance pull him in. He smelled so good. He could feel the combination of the music and the alcohol. He wanted Chance to kiss him right there. This was a bad idea, wasn't it?

"You feel nice," Chance said, pressing his body into Ethan and wrapping his arms around him. "You know, Ethan, I'm glad we're working together. I think we can do great things."

"I want to keep it professional, Chance. I need to prove myself." He knew he didn't sound at all convincing, least of all to himself.

"Not with me," Chance assured him.

"Chance."

"There's nothing wrong with dancing." Ethan knew Chance won this round. *Not that this is a game, is it?*

"You feel nice too, Chance." Ethan tightened his hold and let himself just feel. He'd missed this man.

"Mm," Chance purred into Ethan's hair. A few minutes later, the music sped up, and Brad danced over to them. "Can I be a third wheel?"

"Of course, Bradley." Chance released Ethan, who pulled himself out of his lust-induced trance.

They drew all sorts of looks dancing as a trio until a tall blond eventually swept Brad away, leaving Chance and Ethan alone again. "Well, he's occupied for the rest of the night; shall we?" Chance led Ethan back to the table.

They spent the next hour talking and drinking. Chance told Ethan how he became the youngest senior advertising executive in the firm, while Ethan listened in awe. "Wow, that's impressive, Chance."

"I was determined." Chance had a strange look on his face, and Ethan thought there was more to his story, but didn't want to ask.

Ethan told Chance all about his family in Iowa and going to college to discover himself. He also shared how he'd hidden his sexuality during high school out of fear because he'd seen another kid being picked on relentlessly.

"High school can be rough for gay kids," Chance offered.

"Were you bullied, Chance?"

"I was popular and good at sports," he said, shrugging. "And, I was bigger than most of the other guys, so they pretty much left me alone. I also had a lot of girlfriends."

Ethan shook his head. "Of course." It came out a little more sarcastically than he intended.

"What? I had my own set of problems, you know."

"Like what, both guys and girls throwing themselves at you?" Ethan snorted.

Chance shrugged again, obviously not wanting to finish this conversation. "Be honest; why did you want to move to California?"

"Well, I originally wanted to go to east to either Boston or New York, but then I received the invitation for an interview here. You guys have a great reputation. I'd be crazy not to even try. And then there was this beautiful man I met on my trip out here..." Ethan froze, staring wide-eyed at Chance. *Did I really just say that out loud?*

"Ha! I knew it." Chance pointed a finger at Ethan, smiling smugly.

"I mean..." *Fuck.*

"No, you already said it. Don't take it back," Chance said, folding his arms. "You know, I *was* hoping I'd see you again. I left you my number. I never do that."

Ethan smiled. He needed to hear that night had meant something to Chance too.

"Bradley tells me you're doing a great job," he said, changing the subject. "He can't stop talking about you. I'm looking forward to working with you, Ethan Moore."

"Thanks." Ethan blushed. "I am too."

"I have to go to a party tomorrow evening. Would you come with me?"

"Chance, I don't know. I think it's best if we keep this professional."

"Sure, Ethan. It's just a boring party, and I hate to go alone. Please?" He reached his hand out to hold Ethan's. "Just as friends, or coworkers, if you prefer." He batted his pretty eyes, trying to look innocent. "Coworkers?"

Ethan caved, taking Chance's hand. Damn, he wasn't making this easy. He wondered about the ethics of Chance's forwardness, but since he didn't report directly to the guy... Besides, he'd really hate it if Chance stopped pursuing him.

Brad bounced over to the table with the tall blond from the dance floor in tow. "Guys, do you mind if I...?" He turned around to gaze at his new friend, squeezing the guy's ass.

Chance and Ethan both laughed. "Sure, Brad, I'll make sure Ethan gets home," Chance said.

"Are you sure?" Ethan felt self-conscious. "I don't want to put you out. I can take a cab."

"Nonsense, Ethan. I'll drive you home. Have fun, Bradley." Chance waved off his friend. "I love Brad; he's a good friend and a great manager. You know we dated?" Chance looked directly at Ethan, swirling ice around his tongue. It was very distracting.

"He told me." Ethan looked down into his drink. God, the man turned him on.

"Jealous?"

"No, I know it's over." Ethan knew he didn't have any right to be jealous, especially of the past.

"We make much better friends." Chance looked thoughtful. "Is it all right if we call it a night, Ethan? I have to get up early tomorrow—meetings."

They finished their drinks and left the club. The drive back to Ethan's place was quiet. Ethan was lost in his own thoughts, wondering how it could be if he gave in to his heart. If he did, would Chance break it? Brad said he was a player.

Chance pulled into the parking spot in front of the apartment and turned off the car. "Good night, Ethan." He reached over and wrapped his arms around Ethan, then leaned forward to kiss him.

"Chance, I can't do this. We work together," Ethan protested unconvincingly, their lips mere millimeters away.

"So, we won't do *this* at work," Chance said, pressing his lips against Ethan's mouth.

"Chance..." But instead of pulling away from the man, Ethan let him in. Their tongues met inside his open lips, swirling together like perfect choreography in an erotic dance. Chance's lips were soft and plump, and they fit perfectly with Ethan's. He kissed with his entire body as he pressed against Ethan. They moved in perfect sync. Chance's scent was a mixture of musk and arousal. Ethan could feel his own heart beating out of his chest. As Chance deepened the kiss, Ethan let out a moan. Sensing Chance staring at him, he opened his eyes and pulled away. Chance licked his lips, and Ethan felt it in his groin. Chance slid his hand down Ethan's side and pushed up his shirt to touch the sensitive skin. Ethan shivered and another moan left his lips as Chance once again made their mouths one. His breathing quickened as Chance rubbed Ethan's aching cock, but then Ethan abruptly pulled away. "I gotta go." He couldn't let this go on any longer or he'd break his own rule.

"You sure, ba—Ethan?" Ethan cringed. Babe—for some reason he didn't like Chance calling him that.

"I'm sorry. I'll see you at work tomorrow." Ethan instantly regretted his decision even though he knew it was the right thing to do. *Stupid conscience.*

"Okay." Chance pecked him on the lips. "Good night. See you in the morning."

"Good night, Chance. Thank you for the ride home and for— everything," Ethan said dreamily while shutting the car door.

Ethan walked up the front steps to his apartment. As Chance sped away, Ethan turned around to stop him. He shook his head. *It's for the best.* Then silently berated himself and headed inside his apartment, alone and horny.

Chapter Eight

ETHAN

Chance called Ethan into his office the next morning. "Hi, Chance." The man sat behind his desk looking absolutely gorgeous. *Why* didn't he let Chance come home with him last night? "What's up?" he asked instead.

"The party tonight is a black-tie affair." Chance looked him up and down, frowning. "Do you have a tux?"

"Oh, no I don't." Ethan tilted his head to the floor. Was he getting uninvited? "Sorry."

"Good."

Ethan lifted his head to find Chance grinning at him. "You and I are having lunch together and I'm taking you shopping," Chance announced.

"Shopping? You're going to buy me a tux?" Ethan questioned.

"We'll rent you a tux, but you'll need shoes and some other things." Chance looked as if he'd just won the fucking lottery.

"Chance, you don't have to do that." Ethan glanced away shyly.

"I can't take you without something to wear. Besides, I want to, all right?" He gave Ethan a reassuring look. "I promise you'll have a great time."

"Shopping or the party?"

"Both," he said, as if it was an obvious conclusion.

As Ethan walked to his office, he thought about the impending shopping trip, hoping Chance wasn't trying to buy him. He was pretty sure Chance didn't take any of the other employees shopping—or to parties. What was he doing?

"Morning, Ethan." Ethan looked up and saw Brad heading toward him.

"Morning, Brad."

"Follow me." Brad waved Ethan over to him and walked him toward his office. "We have a lot to do today to bring you up to speed, so prepare to work through lunch."

"Oh, I can't today," Ethan blurted without thinking.

"I'm sorry, Ethan?" Brad snapped. "It wasn't a question." He glared, and Ethan shrank back against the reprimand.

"Sorry, Bradley, Ethan is having lunch with me today." Ethan hadn't realized Chance had followed him, but he was glad for the intervention. "We have some errands to run. You can have him before and after, but I get him for the hour," he said, sitting on the chair in front of Brad's desk. He put his feet up and folded his arms behind his head, looking smug as fuck. God, he was beautiful.

Ethan looked back at Brad who appeared livid. "Well then, I guess we'll have to work that much harder this afternoon." Brad glared at Chance.

"Jealous, Bradley?" Chance said, winking at Ethan, who wanted to crawl under the desk. He never wanted to get between these two.

"Hardly." Brad cleared his throat.

CHANCE

Chance took Ethan to his favorite lunch hangout several blocks from the office. It was kind of a seedy bar and cafe, but they had great food. He rested his arm on Ethan's back as he led him inside. He sensed a familiar pair of eyes follow them. *God, why did he have to be here today?* He moved his arm to Ethan's waist and steered toward the host, hoping Ethan didn't notice.

"Good afternoon, Mr. Harlow." The man spoke to Chance with a note of surprise. "Table for two?"

"Yes, please; a quiet one in the back," Chance answered. They followed the host to their seats, and he handed them menus. The waiter came over a few minutes later to take their order, outwardly flirting with Chance. Ethan scooted his chair closer to Chance. Ethan was jealous— interesting.

After the waiter took their order, Chance excused himself. "Little boys' room," he announced. "Be right back." He stood up, leaving a bewildered Ethan, and walked into the restroom, knowing he was being followed.

"Chance," the small man breathed once they were behind closed doors. "You didn't come alone today."

"I have a lunch date." He folded his arms, hoping the guy would get the point.

"Date? How about just a quickie, then?" He pressed himself into Chance, groping him, but Chance backed away.

"Seriously?" He knew the guy was an ass, but offering sex while someone was with a date? "Knock it off," he said, pushing past the other man.

The guy seemed extremely annoyed. "Sure thing, Chance. You don't know what you're missing," he spat.

Ignoring him, Chance fixed himself and walked out of the bathroom alone. A few seconds later, Chance saw him come out, glaring at them as he passed their table and stormed out of the bar.

Chance noticed the odd look on Ethan's face. He didn't want to explain Kevin to Ethan.

"That was strange," Ethan said, looking from the door to Chance. "You know that guy?"

"Yeah, well, I come here for lunch a lot, and he—and—um…" Chance stammered. He wouldn't lie about it, but…

"Oh my God, Chance, you hook up with guys during lunch?" Ethan blurted, then quickly covered his mouth.

Chance shot Ethan a wicked look. He didn't have to explain himself to Ethan. He wouldn't understand. He silently berated himself for bringing Ethan here in the first place, good food or not. For the first time, he felt embarrassed by his casual hookups. He blamed Ethan. The kid made him want different things, and he found it unnerving.

"Never mind, I don't really want to know."

Fortunately, their food arrived. "Dig in, Ethan." He hoped Ethan would put it out of his mind. After all, he didn't actually know anything. Then why did Chance feel so guilty?

While they ate, he refocused their conversation on areas for Ethan to explore in San Francisco. "I should take you to Fisherman's Wharf. They have excellent seafood down there. Oh, and you definitely need to ride a cable car."

Ethan shook his head. "Chance, we're not dating."

"It's not a crime to help you get to know the city. Besides, I like hanging out with you." He shrugged. He didn't like Ethan pushing him away. It wasn't something he was used to. The sounds Ethan made as he devoured his crab cake sandwich were as delicious as the food. It made Chance horny. Taking his mind off Ethan's mouth and other interesting body parts, Chance continued telling Ethan about places in the city they should visit.

Ethan looked up from his sandwich with those big brown eyes. "Okay, Chance. I'd like that."

"Good." His greatest skill was that of persuasion.

When the check arrived, Ethan reached for it, but Chance grabbed it first, smirking.

"You always get what you want, don't you?" There were several innuendos in Ethan's statement.

"I've worked hard for everything I have," Chance snapped. People always thought things came easy for him because of his looks. They didn't.

"I just meant you usually win an argument." Ethan sighed, obviously not intending to offend him.

"I can be very persuasive, Ethan." Chance relaxed again and noticed the sparkle return to Ethan's eyes. He could get lost in those pools of loveliness.

After lunch, Chance drove them to the men's store to rent Ethan's tuxedo.

"Mr. Harlow," the sales clerk greeted eagerly as they walked inside the store.

Ethan shot Chance a look, and Chance shrugged. "I come here a lot," he mouthed.

"How may I help you today, gentlemen?" the well-dressed man asked, looking back and forth between the two men.

"Ethan needs a tux for a party this evening."

"Very good. Follow me, please." He led them to a back wall lined with a dozen different styles of tuxedos.

"Wow, these are gorgeous." Ethan walked to the one on the far left, and Chance scoffed at his selection. Chance knew the prices went up from left to right. No way was Ethan wearing a cheap tuxedo.

"That one." Chance pointed to a classic, yet elegant black tuxedo with long lapels and simple, slender pants. Chance had impeccable and very expensive taste.

"It's too much," Ethan said, holding the price tag.

"Nonsense. You'll look amazing. Besides, we're only renting it."

"I'll give you a good deal, sirs," the sales clerk assured them. Chance was a good customer.

Ethan looked defeated, yet pleased, as the man nodded and went into the back room.

While he retrieved a tuxedo in Ethan's size, Chance and Ethan looked for a shirt and accessories. Chance wanted Ethan to be happy so he let him pick the color, but he picked the brand.

The man returned and took them to the dressing rooms. Chance tried following Ethan into one, but Ethan pushed him away. "Not a chance, bad boy."

Chance smirked. He knew him too well. The things he'd like to do to Ethan in there. He cleared his throat. "Fine, but you have to come out and show us."

Chance heard Ethan in the dressing room peeling his work clothes off. Picturing him naked, he had to adjust his own pants.

"You two make a fine couple," the salesman noted.

"Tell *him* that," Chance said.

The guy gave him a funny look but stayed on task. "How's it coming along, sir?" he called inside the dressing room.

"Good," Ethan yelled back. "How does this go on?" They heard him struggling with something.

"Let me help you, sir." The salesman knocked on the door, and Ethan, peeking around to make sure it was only the salesman, then let him in.

Chance scowled, folding his arms.

"Oh no, sir, that's not how…"

He heard Ethan giggle. *God, he's adorable.*

They came out a minute later with Ethan grinning. "Thanks."

"That's what I'm here for, sir." He pointed Ethan toward the mirror. Chance couldn't take his eyes off him. The jacket fit perfectly, like it was made for Ethan's slight frame, and the pants hugged his ass just right. He swallowed while taking in the sight.

Ethan twirled around in the black tuxedo. He looked classy and adorable at the same time.

"You look incredible, Ethan. I could just eat you up." Ethan snorted as Chance fixed his bow tie and placed a lavender handkerchief in the jacket pocket to match the shirt.

The salesman appeared satisfied with his customer's nearly finished look. "May I show you to the shoes?"

They both nodded and followed the man to the shoe section. He held up two pairs of black dress shoes complementary to the rest of the outfit. Both Ethan and Chance pointed to the same one.

"Very good." He looked down at Ethan's feet and left again to retrieve the shoe in his size.

"Chance. I don't know what to say."

"My pleasure, Ethan." And he kissed him on the cheek. Chance liked doing things for Ethan. It was a strange feeling.

Their attentive salesman returned with the shoes and took them out of the box for Ethan to try them on. Chance got there first and picked them up. Then he kneeled and helped Ethan put them on his feet. "They're perfect." He looked up at Ethan and thought the same thing about him.

Chance paid for everything, ignoring Ethan's argument he was spending too much money on him. He just smiled and handed Ethan the bags as he grabbed the tuxedo, now hanging in a plastic bag. They left the store and drove back to the office to face the wrath of Bradley Parker.

Chapter Nine

CHANCE

Chance jogged up the steps to Ethan's apartment and hesitated in front of the door. Why was he nervous? He ran a hand over his hair. Because he didn't date. Not in a very long time. But this wasn't a date. He took a deep breath and rapped on the door. Ethan answered immediately, looking like something out of a fairy tale. "Damn, Ethan, I really *could* eat you up." Chance licked his lips, forgetting his nervousness, and stepped toward Ethan to fix his tie and handkerchief again. "There."

"Thanks, Chance. I'll never get that."

He planted a small kiss on Ethan's lips when he noticed Ethan blush. "You look incredible."

"Thanks. You look amazing too."

Chance cupped his hands over Ethan's face and kissed him again. Ethan opened his mouth, letting their tongues greet each other.

"Chance," he cooed, "I thought we were just going as friends." He didn't seem like he minded, though. *Interesting.*

"We are, Ethan. I like to kiss my friends, especially when they look so tasty." Chance shrugged it off as if it was a perfectly normal thing to do.

"I guess I need to keep my guard up with you." Ethan shook his head, giggling.

"No, you don't, baby. Just let go," Chance whispered into Ethan's ear, still holding on to him.

"I like working with you, and I don't want to mess this up. Besides, you like to play around too much. I wouldn't be okay with that if we were together," Ethan deadpanned.

"So, you think you can tame the great Chance Harlow?" Chance smirked, mocking his nickname.

"Nah, I wouldn't even try."

"I bet you could do it," Chance muttered, and Ethan gave him a funny look. "Come on, Ethan," he quickly covered. "I'm going to show you how the snobby rich get their party on." He chuckled, leading Ethan out to his car. He hated these kinds of get-togethers, but it was expected of him at his position.

Twenty minutes later, they pulled into the crowded parking lot of a fancy country club on the outskirts of the city. They passed a white Bentley, black Porsche, and several Mercedes and BMWs as they walked toward the entrance of the club. Chance watched Ethan gape at the garish display of wealth in the parking lot.

Once inside the country club, they walked around and Chance introduced Ethan to various heads of companies with their wives or girlfriends. There were clients of the firm, business acquaintances of Chance, and some future business opportunities, he hoped.

Ethan looked bored, so Chance asked him to get them a drink while he talked to a CEO of one of their clients.

ETHAN

When he returned from getting their drinks, some twink was hanging all over Chance, who looked as though he was enjoying it. Ethan coughed to get his attention. When he finally noticed him, Chance abruptly pulled away from the guy. "Blaine. It was nice seeing you again." He brushed off the front of his tuxedo jacket as if to wipe away the guy's handprints. *What the hell?*

Chance turned around toward Ethan and reached for his drink. "Thanks for rescuing me." He took a long sip as the twink slinked away. Ethan noticed the similarities again. He really did have a type. Ethan felt a little nauseous.

"You didn't look like you needed rescuing, Chance." Ethan snorted.

"Well, I did," Chance retorted, with a hint of annoyance in his voice. He signaled for Ethan to come closer, and he whispered, "I used to date that guy. He was a total nightmare."

Ethan looked back at the guy. He was definitely Chance's type. Why was he jealous? He was the one who told Chance they could be nothing more than friends.

"I'm glad you're with me tonight." Chance put his arm around Ethan. "Let's mingle. I want to show you off. You look so hot."

Ethan raised an eyebrow. *He makes it sound like we're dating.* He *would* like to show Blaine who Chance belonged to. *But he doesn't, does he?* He groaned at his self-inflicted circumstance, and gazed at the man driving him crazy.

Ethan decided not to leave his side again in case there were any other flirty ex-boyfriends on the loose. Instead, he stayed close to Chance while he spoke with clients and business associates. Chance introduced Ethan as the new star of Ashton Lake, making him blush. In spite of his earlier doubts, he had an amazing time. Chance was well respected in this circle, and Ethan felt proud to be with him.

"Over there, Ethan,"—Chance pointed—"is the COO, Grant Masterson, and the guy next to him is the chief financial officer, Mr. Carpenter. I don't know him very well. He keeps to himself."

Ethan was impressed that he knew them at all. "Should we go over and talk to them?"

"No, I'm here to mingle with clients." He looked back over at them. They were standing together, turned away from most of the crowd, speaking with the CEOs from one of Ashton Lake's clients. "I wonder why they're here." Just then, an older couple came over and the man greeted Chance. He introduced him to Ethan as a client.

A couple of hours of mingling and a few cocktails later, Chance walked Ethan toward the exit. "Well, I think I've had enough of this."

"Okay," Ethan replied, yawning. "We have a long day tomorrow."

"Brad's a real slave driver, isn't he?"

"You run the show, Chance," he reminded him.

"But Brad keeps me in line." Chance winked. Ethan doubted that.

Chance put his arm around him and led him back to his car. He opened the passenger door, but before Ethan could get in, Chance reached out and put his arms around him and pressed him against the car. "God, Ethan, you feel so good."

Chance put his lips to Ethan's mouth, and Ethan found himself kissing him back. Chance pushed Ethan's mouth open with his tongue and licked inside his mouth. "Mm, Ethan, too good."

"Chance," he complained unconvincingly, still kissing the man.

"Let me take you home." Chance backed up, sighing, and let Ethan in the car. He walked around to the driver's side and got in, holding out his hand for Ethan, who took it and gave it a squeeze.

"I had a nice time, Chance. But you promised we'd just go as friends," he reminded him.

"Do I make you uncomfortable, Ethan?"

"No." Ethan wished he could give in to his obvious feelings for the man, but this job was important to him and he didn't want to screw it up. He figured sleeping with the boss was right there at the top of major fuckups. It was bad enough he already had.

"Okay." Chance smiled, pulling his hand away so he could drive.

Once they arrived at Ethan's apartment, Chance jumped out of the car and walked around to open the door for Ethan, who started laughing.

"What's so funny?"

"I almost think you're a gentleman, Chance."

"I am." Chance batted his eyes. "May I come in? I promise to behave."

"Sure you do." Ethan rolled his eyes, opening the door wider.

Chance followed Ethan into his apartment. He closed the door behind him, wrapped his arms around Ethan, and kissed him. "I've wanted to do this all night."

"Chance..."

"What?"

"You're not behaving," Ethan scolded through uneven breathes, his semi hard-on from kissing in the car turning into a full-out erection, straining against his pants.

Chance reached down to rub Ethan's cock. "Do you want me to, Ethan? Do you want me to leave you alone?"

"No." Ethan sighed in defeat, kissing Chance with a passion that could only lead to one thing.

"Take me to bed, baby," Chance said in that wispy, sultry voice of his, melting the rest of Ethan's inhibitions away.

Ethan took Chance's hand and led him to his bedroom. *What could it hurt?*

ETHAN

Clothes scattered on the floor, Chance pulled Ethan's naked body into his. He placed his hand behind Ethan's head and kissed him while lowering him onto the bed. Then he crawled on top of him and pressed their cocks together to create much-needed friction.

Chance caressed Ethan's chest and arms and kissed along his biceps. Chance moved his lips over to his bare nipples as he licked and sucked each one, his teeth scraping the bud. It felt amazing. Ethan couldn't remember why he wanted to keep this man away. He was perfect—they were perfect. Chance scooted down to Ethan's thighs and roamed his hands everywhere but the spot where Ethan wanted him the most. "Feels good," Ethan said, hoping to encourage him.

Chance pushed Ethan's legs open and knelt between them. He brought his mouth to the inside of Ethan's thigh and sucked hard enough to leave a red mark before moving to the other one. Ethan raised his ass off the bed to get closer to Chance's mouth.

"You like that."

He liked everything this man did to him.

Ethan gave a satisfied groan as Chance pushed Ethan's knees into the air. He squirmed, willing Chance's mouth closer to his cock. Teasing, Chance caressed his balls, his tongue making its way to Ethan's perineum, but leaving Ethan's hard cock standing at attention against his stomach, leaking a tiny bead of precome, aching to be touched. "Please, Chance."

"What do you want me to do?" He had a way of looking at Ethan that melted him to his very soul. *Everything*.

"Please, just..." He sighed in pleasant agony. "Anything," he breathed.

Chance smirked, his lips getting closer to the target. Ethan bucked his legs, aiming closer to Chance's teasing mouth. "Tell me what you want, Ethan," Chance demanded as Ethan felt his lips curl into a smile.

"God, I want your mouth." Ethan's cock leaked in agreement.

Chance licked across the slit of his cock and teasing Ethan with his breath. He swirled his tongue around the slit, licking the precome pooled around the head, before taking it between his lips. He sucked and licked along the sensitive area underneath the mushroom tip. "Chance," Ethan whined.

He was incredible at this. He licked a stripe from tip to base, and then he took the entire length, sucking it firmly into his waiting mouth.

"Fuck, finally."

Chance laughed, closing his lips around the base again, drawing in his cheeks like a small Hoover. With his hand, he massaged Ethan's balls and perineum while Ethan writhed in response. "Fuck."

Chance reached his hand behind Ethan's cheeks, searching for his pretty, pink hole. He licked one finger until it was wet and dipped it inside the warm canal, hitting the special spot and driving Ethan wild. "Oh, God, Chance, please, I want..."

"I know what you want. Lube, condoms?"

Ethan pointed to the dresser. Chance snatched both, tossing the condom on the bed and popping the top on the lube. He poured a generous amount on his finger, nudging it all the way inside Ethan, reaching again for his spot. Ethan moaned, deep and gruff, when Chance found it.

"That's it, baby; you're so hot for me, aren't you?" He inserted the second finger, hitting Ethan's prostate with every brush of his fingers. Ethan bucked his hips as Chance added the third finger with a scissoring motion, stretching him. Ethan wanted to say something about the new nickname. It was better than "babe," he decided.

"Chance, please. I need you," Ethan begged, pushing back on his fingers, fucking the digits.

Chance threw him a wicked grin and swiftly pulled them out. He slid the condom over his engorged member and smoothed the lube over the stiff shaft. Ethan groaned at the loss of contact but started to roll over, eager for what was coming next.

Chance stopped him. "I want to see you this time." His voice was smooth as velvet.

Ethan pulled his knees up and wrapped his legs around Chance's waist as Chance leaned over him, cock at attention and aimed at its target. "Ready?"

Ethan nodded, and Chance breached his entrance, pushing inside, inch by inch, and feeling the tension as Ethan tightened from the hot missile entering his body.

"You okay?" Chance asked with genuine concern. "Just relax, Ethan." He pushed a little farther.

Ethan obeyed as the pain subsided, easing into pleasure. "I'm good—fuck—keep going." Ethan's expression said he was all right and ready for more, so Chance pushed in deeper, kissing Ethan at the same time. Ethan couldn't kiss back, though, as his head rocked back and forth.

Chance slid the rest of the way in, but stilled for a moment, letting Ethan get used to him. "Chance, please, move."

"You feel so good." Chance slowly fucked Ethan. "God, I've missed this. I've missed you." He picked up the pace, sliding into Ethan's tight heat.

"Fuck, more, fuck—oh God—Chance..." Ethan lifted his hips to meet each thrust.

Chance reached down with his still-lubed hand and stroked Ethan's cock, bouncing between their sweaty bodies. It didn't take but a few strokes before he yelled Chance's name and milky ribbons shot from Ethan's cock, landing on their chests and over Chance's hand.

After a few more grunts and thrusts, Chance released inside the condom. "Fuck, Ethan," he said, collapsing on top of Ethan as they both lay panting from the intense spasms of their orgasms. "You are beautiful." Chance lowered his head to Ethan's chest.

Ethan looked up and smiled. "I want to stay like this forever."

"Mm, not just yet." Chance pulled out of him and tied off the condom, and went into the bathroom for a washcloth. He returned to the bed and cleaned Ethan up. *He's so considerate.* After wiping away their mess, Chance climbed back into bed and wrapped his body around Ethan, holding him tight as they fell asleep in each other's arms.

Chapter Ten

ETHAN

Ethan sat up in bed and stretched his arms, recalling the previous night. Chance taking him to the party; Chance bringing him home; Chance fucking him. *Oh shit, not again.* He groaned, looking at the empty side of the bed. *And he left—again.* Ethan got up and headed into the bathroom, expecting another note. Then he smelled it—coffee brewing. *Could Chance still be here?* He flew out of the bathroom and into the kitchen, forgetting he was still naked.

Chance looked him up and down, smirking. "Nice, Ethan."

"Oh, fuck." Ethan looked down, cock coming to attention at the sight of Chance. He started to bolt out of the room, but Chance grabbed him and pulled him into a hug, kissing him on the lips.

"Morning, baby. Sleep well?"

"Yeah—I'm glad you're still here," Ethan said, rubbing the back of his neck.

"You thought I took off?" Chance looked mildly offended.

Ethan nodded, and Chance kissed him again until Ethan relaxed into the man and kissed him back.

"It's a good thing I keep a change of clothes in my car, or we'd be late for work. Here's your coffee. Jump in the shower 'cause you smell like sex," Chance teased, threading his fingers through Ethan's hair. "I like it," he whispered into his ear. "But Bradley won't." He smacked Ethan on the ass.

"I'll finish making breakfast," he yelled. Ethan could feel Chance's stare on his naked butt as he walked away.

Ethan just smiled. *What does this mean, though?*

They drove separately to the office, but walked into the building together and unfortunately caught the same elevator as Brad. He looked over at both of them, shaking his head. Then he knitted his brows together, giving Chance a look that said, *I hope you know what you're doing.*

And Chance returned it with an innocent look. *What, Bradley?*

To which Brad responded with a stern glare. *You know what. Be careful.*

Brad got off the elevator first, stomping away, and Chance shrugged in response to Ethan's look of *What the hell was that all about?* Ethan walked toward his office, confused by the unspoken conversation they'd just had.

Ethan worked all morning with Brad and the rest of the team in the large workroom. Occasionally, Chance peeked in and smiled at him. No one else noticed except Bradley, who would shake his head.

At lunchtime, Chance came by and announced he was going out. Brad shot Ethan a quick glance while Ethan stared back with wide eyes and willed tears not to fall. Seriously, he was going to hook up right after they'd spent the night together? He tried to pull it together and not let it get to him. He didn't actually know if that's what Chance was doing.

"Come on, Ethan. Let's get some lunch too." Brad put his arm reassuringly around Ethan and led him out of the building in the other direction from the sleazy bar he knew Chance was most likely headed.

"He might just be eating lunch, you know," Ethan blurted when they were sitting down.

"I know that, honey." Brad looked thoughtfully at Ethan. Ethan felt like someone just ripped out his insides. Lunch was a long hour spent brooding and consoling.

Chance was already back when Ethan and Brad returned to the office. He walked between the two men, putting an arm around each one. "Have a nice lunch, gentlemen?"

"As a matter of fact, we did, Chance. You should join us next time. Right, Ethan?"

Ethan nodded, searching Chance's eyes and hoping to see something in there that said, *"I did not just have sex for lunch."* That would be nice. Ethan coughed. "I mean, yeah, you should come with us tomorrow."

"I don't like to mix work with lunch, so no shop talk, all right?" Chance replied, obviously oblivious to Ethan's concerns. Maybe he *did* just eat lunch.

CHANCE

Brad walked into Chance's office later in the afternoon. He leaned against the doorjamb with his arms folded, scowling.

Chance looked at him and started laughing. "What's wrong with you?"

"You know, I think he's in love with you."

"Who?" He knew who.

"Ethan, you idiot."

"I like him, Brad, but it's no big deal, you know?" He heard the words coming out of his mouth but wasn't sure he even believed it anymore. Ethan was gorgeous, interesting, creative, and amazing in bed, but was it more than that? It couldn't be. He didn't do that anymore. Too dangerous.

Chance hadn't had anything more than one-night stands since he and Brad dated a few years ago. Fortunately, they'd figured out they made better friends before anyone got hurt. And no one had interested him for more than a night, until Ethan came along. Chance couldn't get him out of his head, and it was affecting his casual sex life, which just pissed him off.

"Yeah, maybe for you, but not for him." Brad stormed out, leaving Chance to his own thoughts.

The next day, Chance barged into Brad's office where he and Ethan were busy working. "Well, are you two coming?" he asked. They both looked up, confused. "Lunch, remember? My treat."

Brad and Ethan looked at each other. "Yeah, I'm starving," Ethan said.

Brad chuckled at Ethan's enthusiastic nod. "Come on, big guy."

Chance took them to the same place he had taken Ethan the day of the party. He liked this restaurant, but noticed Ethan's uneasiness at the stares the trio received as they walked inside. Ethan spotted Kevin at the bar watching them and nudged Brad. Chance saw the recognition in Brad's eyes too.

"Excuse me; little boys' room," Chance announced. Kevin wouldn't dare come over with both Ethan and Chance there.

"Me too." Ethan rose out his seat and followed Chance into the bathroom, striking up a conversation along the way.

"Can't stay away from me, huh, Ethan?" Chance put his arm around him as they walked to the restroom.

"Nah, I just really have to pee."

"Oh, okay, Ethan." Chance chuckled, looking back at Bradley, who had walked over to Kevin. He wondered what he was up to. At least he didn't need to worry about Kevin coming in here and messing with Ethan. Chance wouldn't like that at all.

Ethan went into a stall instead of the urinal. "Don't trust me, huh?" Chance teased.

They met at the row of sinks to wash their hands." Can I ask you a question, Chance?"

"Of course."

"Did you come here for lunch yesterday?"

"No, I had an errand to run." He didn't want to tell Ethan he had gone but changed his mind when he saw Kevin at the bar and walked out before he noticed him. Ethan had caused him to completely lose interest in his occasional lunch hookup. Nah, he didn't need to tell Ethan that.

But he saw the smile form on Ethan's face that said he knew. Ethan walked over to him and placed a kiss on his cheek. Then opened the door and walked out with a grinning Chance behind him.

Brad was at the table when they returned. Chance noticed Kevin drinking at the bar. Brad looked over at him smugly, and Kevin downed his cocktail and stomped over to their table, glaring at Brad. "Cock blocker!" he spat, storming out of the restaurant.

Brad bowled over laughing, Ethan gave Brad a thankful look, and Chance just stared blankly at both of them, shrugging. Situation diverted. He needed to find a new lunch hangout. *Too bad the crab cakes are out of this world.*

"Thanks," Ethan whispered to Brad, who just nodded in triumph.

"Anytime."

Chapter Eleven

Ethan

Ethan planned to sleep in late and spend Saturday watching television in his pajamas all day. He was sitting in his tiny kitchen, sipping coffee, when his cell phone rang. He answered it to a very chipper Chance on the other end.

"Oh, hey, Chance. Is everything all right?" Chance was the last person he'd expected to hear from on the weekend.

"Are you dressed?"

"Yeah…" He wondered why Chance would ask him that. He looked down at his pajamas and blushed. "Why?"

"I'm fifteen minutes from your place."

"What?"

Chance chuckled into the phone, causing Ethan's cock to twitch. "I'm taking you sightseeing and then to lunch at the wharf. Be ready. You sound like you're wearing pajamas."

"You can tell that?" Ethan scratched his head.

"I bet you look cute. Maybe you should stay like that until I get there." Ethan could hear the lust in his voice.

A flush rose in his cheeks. "I'll be ready." He hung up the phone, quickly showered, and dressed in a pair of tan shorts and a black tank. He was just coming out of his room when Chance knocked on the door.

Ethan opened it to find his gorgeous not-exactly-boss grinning at him.

"You changed."

"Chance."

"Come on, Ethan, I have plans for us today." Chance tossed him a wicked glance, making Ethan shudder and adjust his shorts as they felt a little tighter.

"Where are we going?"

"You'll see."

Ethan pulled the door to his apartment shut, and Chance put his arm around him, leading him to his car. Chance drove a black Lexus sedan. Ethan sank into the leather seat while Chance shut his door and walked over to the driver's side. "Have you been to the wharf?"

He shook his head. "I wanted to bring my brother and mom there, but we never got around to it."

"Well, you're in for a treat." Chance smiled at Ethan.

Ethan sat back as they drove. Chance pulled into the office garage and parked the car, surprising him. "Why are we stopping here?"

"You'll see," he said again. "Come on."

Ethan followed Chance out of the car and took his hand as Chance led him across the street and another block over to a cable car stop. They waited just a few minutes before they saw it coming, and Chance waved for the car to stop. When it did, Chance grabbed Ethan's butt and helped him up. Ethan turned around and scowled, but Chance just smirked, and Ethan had to giggle. He was insufferable.

There were plenty of seats, so Ethan strolled down the aisle to an empty one and sat down. Chance scooted next to him and draped his arm around him. He explained the history of the cable car and gave Ethan a guided tour as they rode through the neighborhoods. They had taken the California Street Line which ran west to east through the city.

"Chance, look. Chinatown." Ethan pointed as they entered the colorful neighborhood. "I love Chinese food."

"I'll take you there for dinner one night."

"Chance," Ethan said in a warning tone.

"What?" Chance had an innocent look on his face Ethan knew really meant he wanted to devour him.

"Do you think this is a date?"

Chance shrugged. "Only if you want it to be."

"Humph." Yeah, he shouldn't date the boss. It was a bad idea. Today, though, he should just relax and let it be. It wasn't a date, he decided. Just two friends hanging out.

They continued east and ended up at a large white structure. "This isn't the wharf, is it?" he asked, looking at the large white structure.

"No, we'll take the ferry to the wharf."

"Wow, on the water?"

Chance chuckled at Ethan's excitement, and Ethan blushed. "Have you ever been on a boat before?"

Ethan shook his head as he grabbed Chance's hand and followed him out of the car and over to the ferry dock. They watched as the cars were loaded onto the parking deck and then boarded the ferry. Ethan ran to the side of the boat to watch as the ferry pulled away from the shore. "This is awesome, Chance."

"Glad you're having fun."

"I am," he said. Whether he admitted it or not, this felt like a date and he was having a nice time. Chance stood next to him and placed his arm around him. Ethan leaned in as Chance kissed the top of his head.

Chance pointed out landmarks as they sailed along the bay. "You should see the skyline at night, Ethan. It's gorgeous." All Ethan could think about was how gorgeous Chance was. "You still with me, babe?"

"Huh?"

"I want to take you on a night cruise, Ethan."

"Chance," he reprimanded gently. He was persistent; that was for sure. Ethan asked himself if it would be so bad. He was beginning to question his choices where Chance was concerned.

"You can always say no," Chance challenged him.

"You're hard to say no to."

"I know," Chance said, smirking.

"Hey, what's that?" Ethan pointed to what looked like a small island, his excitement resuming.

"Alcatraz."

"The prison?" he squealed as he gripped the rail and leaned forward to get a closer look.

"It has an interesting history. I'll take you there sometime too."

"We can get on it?"

"The island? Sure, there are tours there." Chance laughed.

"What's so funny?"

"I like seeing these things from your eyes, Ethan."

"Oh." Ethan knew his enthusiasm made him seem like a kid. Chance wasn't making fun of him, though. The ferry pulled into Pier 41 and they waited for it to dock, then exited along with the other passengers.

"Is this the wharf?" Ethan asked as they started walking along the boardwalk aligned with stores and restaurants.

"This is the ferry terminal, Pier 41," Chance explained. "The wharf is just a couple blocks away. On the other side is Pier 39. There are a lot more restaurants and nightlife over there, but the wharf is famous." Chance took Ethan's hand and led him through the streets to the historic Fisherman's Wharf.

Ethan nodded, making a mental note of places he wanted to explore.

"It has great seafood, Ethan. You have to try the Dungeness crabs. We'll stop by a stand and pick some up to take home."

"Look," Ethan interrupted, "the cable car."

"This line will also take us back to the office."

There was so much to do and see in one visit. Chance kept hinting at future "dates," but Ethan hmphed, arguing it wasn't a date. He was losing his argument, even with himself.

They walked along the Portwalk lining the water and watched the fishing boats. The breeze blew, and Ethan couldn't take his eyes off Chance. When Chance looked over at him and caught him staring, Ethan looked away.

"Hungry?" Chance asked him as they neared a run-down building.

"Starving."

"Great, come on." Chance led Ethan farther down the street to what looked like a typical grungy storefront seafood store. Ethan gave Chance a funny look as he followed the taller man inside.

"Ethan, you are in for a treat. This is the best place for seafood at the entire wharf."

He trusted him, but he seriously thought Chance would try to impress him with some overpriced, upscale, pretentious waterfront establishment with fancy waiters or some shit. Then he remembered Chance's lunch spot. *Maybe he just likes places like this.*

They walked through the store into a casual dining area with wood-trimmed booths and antiques of nautical history. Ethan couldn't keep his head still. The host brought them to a booth overlooking the water.

"Wow, is this the bay?" Ethan asked, looking out the circular window. He turned around, catching Chance smiling at him.

"The lagoon," the waiter answered as he handed them each a menu and a glass of water. "Welcome to the Lighthouse, gentlemen."

"What?" Ethan asked as the waiter turned away."

"I like watching you experience things for the first time."

"This place is great, Chance," Ethan's said, ignoring the comment as he looked around the modest surroundings.

"You sound surprised."

"A little," he replied with a smirk.

"It's not much to look at from the outside, but..."

"It's perfect," Ethan assured him.

The two men enjoyed an excellent meal, beginning with Dungeness crab cocktail and cups of lobster bisque with homemade sourdough bread and a bottle of white wine. Ethan was practically full with just the appetizers, but his mouth watered when the waiter brought their entrees.

Chance ordered for both of them. Cioppino, a San Francisco specialty of fresh-caught seafood with an herbed tomato-and-wine sauce. Ethan dug into his, enjoying himself. This day was certainly a surprise.

"Mm, God, this is as good as sex," he said, giving a moan.

Chance raised his eyebrow, laughing.

"What?"

"Nothing. Glad you're enjoying it."

"Thank you, Chance. This has been a lot of fun."

"Well, there's more if you stick with me, Ethan."

"Chance, I like being with you, but..."

"Yeah, yeah, I know. Well, let's not waste my one opportunity to show you the town. Ready for the next stop?" Chance had this confidence about him. It wasn't arrogant or anything, but it *was* sexy as hell.

Ethan nodded as Chance paid the check. Afterward, they walked to Pier 39, and Chance pointed out the Aquarium of the Bay. "You definitely need to see it one day, Ethan. It's an incredible display of local marine life." Ethan peeked over as they walked past.

They passed street performers, and Chance pointed out a couple of his favorite nightspots.

"Oh look," Ethan shouted, "an arcade."

Chance shook his head. "They have laser tag too."

"I love laser tag," Ethan said, enthusiastically. "My brother and I used to play." He'd love to get Chance in there. Then, he reminded himself they weren't dating.

After Pier 39, Chance led him back to Fisherman's Wharf and the pier, where there was nothing but boats and water. The breeze had picked up, and Ethan was getting chilly. Chance put his arm around him and let Ethan snuggle into the warmth of his neck and chest. Chance kissed him on the top of the head. "Come on, Ethan. Let's get you home."

They caught the cable car from the wharf back to Union Square. It was crowded, so they didn't get a seat. Instead, Chance showed Ethan how to jump on and grab the poles lining the outside of the car. Ethan held on tight and let the wind blow through his hair while gazing at Chance. This was the best day he'd had since he moved here—possibly ever.

They arrived back at the garage, and Chance drove Ethan home to his apartment. "Do you want to come in for a minute?" Ethan asked.

Chance tumbled out of the car a little too enthusiastically, causing Ethan a fit of the giggles. "Anxious, huh, big guy?"

Chance shrugged. "I'm not ready for the day to end yet."

Ethan laughed. He was certain Chance had more nefarious reasons for wanting to come inside.

"Me either," Ethan confessed. It really had been a pleasant day.

Chance followed Ethan inside, attacking his mouth before the door closed. "God, I wanted to do this all day."

"Chance," Ethan attempted to argue, but couldn't remember why.

"Do you want me to stop, Ethan?" It was a challenge.

He really didn't, so he shook his head and kissed Chance back. "Take me to bed, bad boy."

Chapter Twelve

CHANCE

The Bali project was progressing nicely, and it was time for Chance to decide who to accompany him on this important opportunity for the firm. He knew who he wanted to take. Ethan, although the newest member of the team, showed real talent, and he contributed so much to the project. He was driven like Chance, but softer around the edges. They needed that balance—Chance needed that balance. The clients wouldn't be able to resist him. And, as much as Ethan argued, he couldn't keep his eyes off Chance. He'd catch Ethan staring at him. and just smirk, saying, "*Come and get it.*" Ethan would blush and look away. They played this game nearly every day, and although Chance always enjoyed a good game, he liked winning more. And nothing got past Bradley Parker, who gave him death stares at every given moment. Good thing he was harmless.

After his weekly board meeting where he was given the greenlight to proceed, Chance walked into the workroom and made an announcement to the group. "Okay everyone, the next step is the trip to Bali. I'm taking one person with me." Chance looked around the room at the varied expressions from the team. Everyone already knew that. "Since I want the best person for the job, we're going to have a little competition," he continued, surprising everyone including Brad. "Each of you will come up with a pitch for our client in Bali and present it to Brad and me at tomorrow's staff meeting. Get to work." Chance walked out of the room with Brad following him.

"Pretty ingenious, Chance."

"I thought so too, Bradley." Chance, proud of himself, patted Brad on the back and strutted off to his office, while Brad reentered the workroom with a new mission at hand.

CHANCE PASSED BY Ethan's office the next morning and found him leaned over his presentation board in deep concentration. He must have gotten in early. He liked the kid's enthusiasm and wondered about his motivation. Smiling, he continued to his office and shut the door to get some work done before the staff meeting. Brad had put together a great team, but Chance didn't have the same relationship with any of them that he had with Ethan. He scoffed. What relationship? They were coworkers—nothing more. Ethan made that very clear.

Chance watched the staff file in with their presentation boards. "Should I do Ethan a favor and not pick him?" Brad asked quietly, not wanting to be overheard.

"What the hell, Brad?" Chance spat. Chance was a professional first, and disliked being doubted, especially by his department manager.

"Sorry." Brad shrunk back, knowing when to back off.

"Just choose the best one. I hope it's him, but this project is important to me and to the firm. I need the best man for the job."

Brad just nodded.

One by one, each staff member gave their pitch. Chance was not only looking for the best idea but the perfect presentation. He wanted someone who was comfortable with speaking to a large group and would make a good impression with the client, and also able to brainstorm ideas incorporating their needs. He sat chewing on his pen, watching intently while each took their turn. There were some good ideas, but none blew him away.

The last presentation was Ethan's. Chance wondered if Bradley did that on purpose. Chance looked away from Brad and turned his attention to their star employee.

Ethan stood up and walked to the front of the room. He carefully set up his presentation board, then addressed the group. He presented his pitch perfectly. Chance couldn't take his eyes off him. He was polished and confident. And so much like Chance at that age, it was scary. When he finished, Chance and Brad looked at each other, reading the other's thoughts.

"Okay, everyone, well done. Brad and I will discuss, and we'll meet here after lunch." Chance stood, and walked out of the conference room.

"Well, I know what I'm thinking. How about you?" Chance asked Bradley once they were alone.

"I knew the kid was a superstar when I hired him," Brad said, grinning.

"Good job, Bradley." Chance patted him on the back. "Let's go get him. I'm starving."

"Huh?"

"I want to take you both to lunch."

"I pick the restaurant this time?" Brad insisted.

Chance rolled his eyes. "Sure thing."

Brad took them to a little French bistro out of the way from the office. The waiter came over and took their drink orders, casting lustful glances at Chance the entire time. When he came back for their meal order, Chance noticed Ethan glaring at the guy before turning to Chance. He raised his eyebrow. "Do men always throw themselves at you?"

Brad snorted.

"What? He's just being friendly." Chance shrugged, uninterested. The waiter had nothing on Ethan. Too bad he didn't know it.

"How do you think you did today, Ethan?" Brad asked.

"No shop talk, remember?" Chance took a sip of his drink, playfully glaring at Brad as he put the gawking waiter out of his mind.

He changed the subject to Club Cruze, and invited both of them out Friday night. Ethan accepted the offer a little too enthusiastically.

"Awesome, Ethan." He expected resistance from the younger man. "Bradley?"

"Sure, I'm up for it." He gave a sour look toward Ethan, who just shrugged, taking a sudden interest in his glass of water.

When they returned to the office, Chance called everyone back into the conference room. Once everyone was situated, Brad stood up. "I want to congratulate all of you on a job well done. Everyone had terrific ideas, so you all should be proud of yourselves." He stopped for a moment and led the group in a round of applause. "We took a number of things into account. It's important to make an excellent impression on our client *and* deliver the best product. After much deliberation..."

Chance looked up at Brad and practically snorted. Brad glared back. "After much deliberation," he repeated, "Chance and I have made our decision."

Everyone sat quietly, some wringing their hands. Ethan rubbed the back of his neck, not looking at either Chance or Brad.

Chance stood up and took over from Brad, walking slowly around the large table, pausing at each person. "I—we felt one of you stood out from the rest. Not only did he present a fantastic idea, he delivered it superbly." Chance finally stopped just behind Ethan, who still wasn't looking at him. "Ethan Moore, I would be proud to have you accompany me to Bali."

Ethan's eyes grew wide in stunned silence.

"Congratulations, Ethan," Chance said, shaking the shocked man's hand. Ethan outdid everyone, and most of the others seemed to recognize that. Some actually looked relieved, Chance noticed, scoffing. One guy rolled his eyes. He'd keep his eye on that one. Brad walked over to Ethan and shook his hand. "Congratulations, Ethan. You did a fine job."

"Thank you, Brad, Chance." Ethan seemed genuinely surprised and pleased.

Chance dismissed the group and watched everyone give Ethan their congratulations. He was a gracious winner. Once they were alone, Chance walked over to Ethan again. "I'm proud of you, Ethan." He kissed the top of his head and walked out of the room.

ETHAN

As the day went on, Ethan began to worry. He hoped he'd won honestly and Chance didn't choose him just so they could... Ethan shook that nagging feeling away as he packed up for the day.

Brad peeked in his office. "Ethan," he called to him, interrupting his thoughts.

"Brad. Can I ask you a question?"

"Sure, ask me anything."

"Which one of you picked me?" Ethan searched his eyes for an immediate reaction.

"Ethan, you blew everyone away. Both Chance and I knew it the minute you finished. Don't worry about anything. I know for a fact Chance wouldn't jeopardize a project just for sex, okay?" Brad reassured him.

"Thanks, Brad."

"You'll have a great time in Bali." He winked as he walked away. *That's what I'm worried about.*

As soon as Brad left, Chance strolled into his office and leaned against the doorjamb. "Come on, let's get out of here."

"Huh?" He looked up from his desk, startled. Chance always made quite an entrance. Even in a business suit, he was a very sexy man. Ethan couldn't help but stare at the guy.

"We're taking you out to celebrate." He stepped in closer to Ethan and pecked him on the cheek.

"Um, Chance?"

"What's up, baby?"

The nickname caused Ethan to look up and twitch. "I just wanted you to know I'm honored you chose me to go with you. I take it very seriously, and I will do my very best."

"I know that, Ethan," Chance interrupted. "But you totally earned this. I didn't just give it to you." He sounded angry. Ethan would have felt bad, but he needed to stay focused on his next thought.

"So, I think we need to keep this professional. No more sleeping together." Ethan rubbed the back of his neck.

Chance lifted Ethan's chin and looked him square in the eyes.

"Okay, no sleeping together, I promise," he said, holding two of his fingers up in the Boy Scout Promise. Ethan snorted, imagining Chance as a Boy Scout.

"I still want to celebrate." He ignored Ethan's outburst. "Brad is joining us."

"Did I hear my name?" Brad peeked around the corner, obviously not having gone far.

Chance put an arm around each of them. "Let's go, gentlemen." And they walked together out of the building to the parking lot. "Ethan, I'll pick you up in an hour. Bradley, we'll meet you there."

Both Ethan and Brad raised an eyebrow. Ethan walked to his car thinking about the talk he'd had with Chance. Would Chance respect his wishes? Was that even what he wanted? Or was he just being completely stupid?

Chapter Thirteen

ETHAN

Ethan followed Chance inside Club Cruze. The bouncer greeted them, giving Ethan an eager once-over. He turned to see Chance giving the guy a *back the fuck off* look and couldn't help the inward smile. They headed over to the bar to say hello to Andre. "Chance, Ethan." The bartender smirked at Chance. Ethan rolled his eyes. He felt completely exposed, like everyone knew his business.

"Hey, Andre, is Brad here yet?" Chance asked him, grabbing the two Chopin tonics Andre had prepared for them, and handing one to Ethan. He took a sip.

Andre pointed to the dance floor, where Brad was hanging all over some tall guy.

"See what happens if he's left alone too long?" Chance chuckled. "Let's get a table."

He chose one close to the dance floor. "Tomorrow we'll start working together on our strategy for Bali."

"I thought you didn't like talking shop outside the office?" Chance was such a hard guy to figure out.

"I don't talk shop at 'lunch,' Ethan," Chance said, sarcastically, making air quotes with his fingers.

Ethan scowled at the thought of Chance eating "lunch" but then forced that thought down as they were "keeping things professional." He was such a fucking idiot. "I have some great ideas."

"Shoot." Chance listened to Ethan while he sat back and sipped his cocktail, giving him his undivided attention. He made Ethan feel special and important, and seemed to value his opinion. Some of his doubts melted away.

They were deep in discussion when Brad arrived. "Hey, boys, what took you so long?" The same tall guy from the dance floor was hanging all over him.

"We've been here, Bradley. Didn't want to disturb you," Chance answered as he looked over at Tall Guy.

"This is Stephen. Isn't he pretty?" Brad introduced his new friend.

"Hi, Stephen. I'm Chance. This is Ethan."

"Nice to meet you both," Stephen said, taking a seat, pulling Brad onto his lap. While Stephen talked about himself to Chance and Ethan, Brad looked the other way, uninterested in conversation, nibbling the man's ear.

"Let's dance." Before Ethan answered, Chance pulled him from his seat and dragged him to the dance floor. "I wanted to be alone with you," Chance said, as he wrapped his arms around Ethan. He placed his hands on Ethan's hips, guiding his moves.

"Chance..." Ethan couldn't resist Chance when they danced. He was doomed.

"You know, you're the prettiest boy in this entire place," he whispered into Ethan's ear.

Ethan blushed. Chance always knew just what to say. "You're making this no-sleeping-together thing really difficult."

"Your rule, not mine," Chance reminded him as they moved to the beat. Ethan laid his head on Chance's shoulder while Chance pulled him close, their crotches touching. Ethan felt Chance's arousal and he smelled of sweet sweat and musk. What this man did to him. Chance leaned closer. "You feel so good against me, Ethan."

Ethan didn't argue; Chance placed his lips over Ethan's and kissed him. Ethan closed his eyes and took him in.

The music sped up and Chance took Ethan by the hand and twirled him around. Laughing, Ethan spun and landed back in Chance's arms. It felt right, but he knew it was wrong.

Ethan noticed Brad and Stephen watching them from the table. Close enough to just make out their conversation, Ethan startled when he heard Stephen ask, "How long have those two been together? They are totally in love." Brad just hmphed. Ethan froze at the thought.

When Ethan and Chance returned to the table, Brad and Stephen were still all over each other, making things even more awkward. Ethan fidgeted in discomfort.

"We're leaving, Brad." Ethan nodded at Chance.

"Okay, have fun, you two. I'll be fine." Brad went back to making out with Stephen while Ethan and Chance exited the club.

Chance drove Ethan home and parked the car in front of his building. He reached out for Ethan's hand and turned his head to look at him. "I had a nice time, Ethan." Chance stared at his lap.

"Me too, Chance." Ethan leaned over to kiss Chance. "Walk me to my door?"

Chance practically fell out of the car, and then ran over to Ethan's side to open his door. He grabbed Ethan's hand and helped him out of the car, closed the door, and walked Ethan up to his front door.

Ethan used his key to unlock the door as Chance pushed him inside, pressed his body against the wall, and then kissed into his mouth. "Ethan, God, you are so hot."

"Um, Chance—we're not supposed to..." Ethan didn't even try to sound convincing.

"No sleeping with you. I remember, Ethan." Chance shot him a sly grin. "Can I do something else?" he asked while palming Ethan's cock through his pants. Ethan couldn't remember for the life of him why he didn't want to have sex with Chance as the man played with Ethan's dick through his clothing, right there in the hallway.

With his hand still cupping Ethan's erection, Chance locked his lips with Ethan, letting their tongues wrestle each other's. He released him quickly and unzipped Ethan's pants. He pulled them down to the floor and sucked his cock through his underwear. Ethan was at full attention, tenting the white cotton. "Fuck, please."

Chance smirked, clearly knowing he'd won this round. He freed Ethan from his drawers and wrapped his hand around Ethan's cock, stroking the base while licking the head, smearing the precome pooled around the tip. Ethan moaned Chance's name, glad for the wall holding him up.

Chance sucked earnestly, up and down the hard shaft, tugging and squeezing the base while giving his jaw a workout on the shaft. "I love the taste of you, Ethan."

"Chance..." But then Chance increased his suction, and Ethan gave up. He bucked his hips, thrusting into Chance's mouth, fucking the wet entrance. Chance licked two fingers and pressed them into Ethan's hole. The men slid to the floor, Chance now on top of Ethan with his fingers still inside him. "Fuck, Ethan. I need you," Chance pleaded.

"Not here," Ethan said. "Bedroom." Chance pulled Ethan from the floor and followed him to his room, pulling his pants and underwear off along the way. He reached for lube and a condom in Ethan's bedside drawer and prepared himself while Ethan scooted onto the bed watching him. "Fuck, just fuck me."

Chance entered Ethan in one smooth stroke. They both lay still for a moment until Ethan relaxed. "Move," he whispered.

Chance kissed Ethan as he began rocking inside him. "God, you feel so good, ba—Eth." They had a beautiful rhythm going as they glided together. Nothing felt better to Ethan than Chance's cock buried deep, filling him completely.

"Chance," he said, through panted breaths as he came, without Chance ever touching him.

"You're perfect, Ethan," Chance told him before they fell asleep, wrapped in each other's arms.

THE NEXT MORNING, Chance and Ethan arrived at work together again. Brad saw them, and just shook his head. "So, Ethan, have a good night?" he said, patting Ethan on the back.

Ethan blushed, taking a sudden interest in the floor tiles. Last night, he'd woken up in his own bed with his head foggy from the alcohol and the sex... *Fuck, not again*, he'd groaned. He lay there for a minute then rolled over on his side. He blinked twice, realizing the sight in front of him was real.

"Chance," he whispered. The vision before him stirred and threw his arm over Ethan's chest. *I broke my own rule.* Ethan nuzzled against Chance and fell back to sleep as Chance's warm arms enveloped his smaller body.

But today was a new day and he needed to do better at not sleeping with Chance. He sighed. Easier said than done. Apparently, he had no willpower when it came to the man. But he had something to prove, not only to himself, but his team. There was one guy, Cliff, who always gave him dirty looks whenever Chance was nearby. He didn't want anyone thinking he was sleeping with the boss, so he'd better not be—anymore. He groaned at himself.

ETHAN

A couple of weeks had passed since Chance had slept over. Ethan refused to go to the club, and he always knew when Chance went out the previous evening by his mood. It was on the days he didn't go out the night before that Chance was in a hurry to go to lunch alone.

Ethan had no right to be upset. They weren't dating, and Ethan had made the no-sex rule, not Chance.

The team spent the rest of the week and the next getting ready for Chance and Ethan to go to Bali. This project was a huge deal that would put the company on the global map, and everyone knew how important it was. Tempers flared, and Chance looked like he needed to blow off some steam. That wasn't good.

"I'm going to lunch," Chance announced as he stood up from their meeting with Brad and walked out of his office. Ethan glared at him, willing himself not to cry.

Brad looked from Chance to Ethan and obviously noticed Ethan's face fall. "You okay?" Brad asked when Chance was gone.

"It's my own fault, you know."

"How is it your fault?" Brad stared daggers at Ethan.

"I told Chance I wanted to keep it professional and not sleep with him, but I keep screwing up and sleeping with him."

"He *is* hard to resist." Brad smirked.

"You resisted him."

"But I'm not in love with him."

Ethan chose to ignore that remark. "Now that I'm finally keeping my word, I can't help wondering if he's out with other guys. I don't expect Chance to go without. It's not as if we're a couple."

"Ethan." Brad looked into Ethan's eyes, growing serious. "Do you want to be?"

"I want to be taken seriously." Ethan sighed. "And if I'm sleeping with the boss..."

"Yeah, I get it."

"Maybe after the project is over, it'll be different?"

"So you're going to a gorgeous resort in Bali, and you think you'll be able to resist him?" Brad raised an eyebrow.

"I'm fucked, aren't I?"

"Yup." Brad chuckled. "Pretty much." After a few awkward moments where neither spoke, Brad finally suggested they get something to eat.

It was a quick lunch because there was a lot of work in the office. They beat Chance back, and when he walked in, he was in the same bad mood as when he'd left.

"Looks like lover boy didn't get any," Brad said, nudging Ethan.

Ethan looked over at Chance and smiled, feeling somewhat victorious.

"Back to work, everyone," Chance shouted and slammed his office door.

Chapter Fourteen

CHANCE

What the fuck is wrong with me? Chance yelled at himself. *I'm turning down eager prey.* He sat down and pondered that thought at the same moment Brad walked in.

"You all right, boss?" Brad tried to contain his smirk, but Chance didn't miss it.

Chance scowled before shaking his head. "Can I ask you a question?"

"Shoot."

"What's the matter with me?"

"You mean other than the fact you're an idiot?"

"Fuck you, Brad."

"You wish," Brad retorted, to lighten the mood. It might have worked until he added, "Can't you see it? You, Ethan...?"

Missing the point and caught in his own fantasies of the man, Chance replied dreamily, "Ethan is so hot."

"And he works indirectly for you. He's doing the right thing, you know. I'm glad he's being the professional one."

"Take his side, why don't you? I'm professional." He pouted.

Brad held up his hands in surrender. "I know you are, but when it comes to Ethan, you're thinking with the wrong head."

Chance grumbled under his breath, but Brad was unfazed. "You know you love me," Brad added, walking out the door, chuckling.

"Ethan!" Chance yelled from his office a few minutes later.

"Chance?" Ethan stepped into his office and stood at the entrance, looking amazing.

"Ethan, sit down. We have a lot of work to do, and I'd rather we do it alone, all right?" Chance sighed, certain his exhaustion showed on his face.

"Um, okay," Ethan said with a shaky voice, shutting the door behind him.

"Don't worry. I'm not going to molest you in the office, Ethan." Chance rolled his eyes. He was so frustrated.

"Oh, I didn't—um—I know that," Ethan stammered, sitting down on the leather chair in front of Chance's desk.

Chance just laughed, the frustration boiling out of him. "Sorry I'm being a bitch, but we have a lot of work to do and we leave in three days."

"We'll be ready," Ethan said as he got comfortable in the chair.

"Can you work late tonight? I think we can get a lot done."

"No problem, Chance. I'm all yours," Ethan said, then blushed when he realized his slip.

Chance smirked but retained his professionalism as he pulled out the files and began reviewing their pitch. They worked late into the evening until Ethan yawned and Chance took pity on him. "I think we can wrap it up for the night. Thanks for staying, Ethan. Your hard work means a lot."

Ethan stood up, stretching, showing a little bit of skin from where his dress shirt rode up.

Chance licked his lips. "I mean it, Ethan." Chance leaned over to Ethan and kissed him on the lips.

Speechless, Ethan held his finger to his lips and walked out of the office.

Chance watched him leave, wondering when he'd completely fallen for the younger man. He shut down his computer and locked up for the night. Then he realized what Brad had been telling him. *Fuck.*

ETHAN

Two days before Chance and Ethan were leaving for Bali, tension was thick. Ethan held to his no-sex rule, Chance was in a perpetual bad mood, and Brad was acting like the new diva in charge, ordering everyone around. Ethan was certain he'd made the right decision about Chance, even though he frustrated the hell out of himself. After another long day at the office, he went home to pack, thinking about Chance, the plane trip, Chance, the gorgeous resort, and how he was going to resist

Chance. He was deep in his thoughts when the doorbell rang. Ethan stumbled through his living room, tripped over the clothes he had strewn over the room, and practically fell on top of Chance after he opened the door.

"Well, hello to you too, Ethan." Chance held on to Ethan so he wouldn't topple over, chuckling.

"Oh, hi, Chance. What are you doing here?" Ethan was genuinely happy to see him.

"I wanted to apologize for the way I've been behaving at work."

"It's all right. Everyone understands how important this trip is. We've all been a little tense."

"It's not just the trip. I've been without..." Chance didn't finish his thought, staring down at his feet looking embarrassed. It was a new look for him.

"Is that why you're here, Chance?" Ethan folded his arms and glared at the other man.

"God, Ethan—no," Chance stammered, face turning red. He sighed. "May I come in?"

"Sure," Ethan said, holding the door as Chance walked into his apartment. Ethan followed him into the living room. "Can I get you something to drink?"

"Thanks." Chance sat on the sofa, looking around at Ethan's living room. There was nothing more than a couch, a coffee table, and television. "You need more furniture, Ethan." Chance had been there twice but had only seen the hallway, kitchen, and Ethan's bedroom. He obviously hadn't noticed how little furniture Ethan had.

"Well, I just moved here and I have this slave driver of a boss, so no time for decorating." Ethan snickered as he walked back with two glasses of wine and handed one to Chance.

"Thank you." Chance took the glass and patted the seat next to him for Ethan to sit. "Ethan, if we didn't work together, would you date me?"

"You want to date me?"

"I asked you first," Chance challenged, taking a sip.

"I thought you didn't date."

"I never said that." Chance looked over at Ethan.

Ethan knew Chance used to date. Brad had told him as much, and he'd met Chance's ex, Blaine. Then there was that lunch hookup guy Ethan had seen, and God only knew how many others he hadn't. Man,

Chance's personal life was fucked up. Ethan didn't judge him. He wanted to understand him. Neither man spoke, as each was deep in his own thoughts. Chance finished his drink and suddenly stood up.

"Are you leaving?" Ethan got up too.

"Do you want me to stay?" Ethan noticed the glimmer of hope in Chance's eye when he asked.

"Chance, I—"

Chance put his hand up. "It's okay, Ethan. I'll see you tomorrow. I just wanted to apologize for the tension at work." Chance leaned over and kissed Ethan on the cheek. "Good night."

Chance walked to the door and opened it while Ethan stood still and put his hand up to his cheek. "Good night, Chance. See you in the morning."

Then he was gone. *God, that man's frustrating.* Ethan finished off the rest of the wine before heading up to bed. He still felt Chance's lips on his cheek, and it made him horny. He took off all his clothes and got into bed, pissed he hadn't asked Chance to stay. What would it hurt?

Ethan reached for the lube on his nightstand and poured some on his hand. Still thinking of Chance and how sexy the man was, Ethan reached for his cock and stroked himself hard. He thrust into his hand and then built up speed until he was panting and his dick was throbbing and leaking. With his other hand, he poured some lube on his fingers and pressed one into his ass. It was kind of a weird angle, and he thought about how Chance stretched him. Stroking his finger in and out, adding a second, he crooked them just so to hit that spot inside himself.

Driving himself closer, he tensed. "Ahh, fuck." Just like that, Ethan came with thoughts of Chance. Then he lay there, coming down from his orgasm, wishing he wasn't alone.

CHANCE

"You see that guy over there?" Andre said, handing Chance his usual. Chance hadn't wanted to go home after seeing Ethan, so he went to Cruze instead to see his friend.

"Which one?" Chance looked around the bar, not seeing anyone intriguing.

The bartender pointed to a cheesy-looking twink dressed in a silk shirt and bell-bottomed pants, dancing alone, pawing at himself.

Chance choked on his drink. "Seriously, Andre?"

"I only point him out because he's been asking about you," he said in defense.

Chance turned away from the twink. "Not interested."

"Since when?" When Chance just stared down at the bar, avoiding his friend's gaze, Andre answered his own question. "Oh, since that cutie with the brown hair."

"I tried to get laid the other day, and all I could think about was Ethan. What the hell is wrong with me?"

"Is my playboy friend ready to settle down?" Andre teased.

Chance just rolled his eyes and gulped down his drink.

He'd always treated guys like objects. It was easier that way. Professor Montague had taught him that. Especially guys like his lunch hookups and the twinks. They weren't looking for relationships and neither was he. Then there was Ethan. Sweet Ethan wasn't like those guys. He didn't deserve to be just a hookup.

The twink suddenly noticed him and bounced over to the bar. "Hi there, I'm Dwayne," he said enthusiastically, reaching his hand out to shake Chance's hand.

"Hi, Dwayne," Chance said, looking him over and trying not to laugh. He didn't offer his own name since he knew the twink already knew it. He didn't shake his hand, either. No reason to string the guy along.

"Can I buy you a drink, Chance?" Dwayne offered, eyeing Chance with lust in his eyes but not paying attention to the fact Chance was uninterested.

"No thanks, Dwayne, I'm good." Chance turned around to face the bar again, rolling his eyes to Andre.

"Well, that was rude," Dwayne whined, stomping off.

"Nicely done, Chance. I think you hurt his feelings." Andre snorted.

"I think I need to go home." He downed the rest of his cocktail. "Thanks for the heads- up on that guy; wouldn't have wanted to be blindsided by all that silk." They both shared a laugh. Then Chance stood up and walked out of the bar and headed to his car.

He thought about driving back to Ethan's, but he was probably sleeping by now, so he drove home thinking about Ethan, the twink, and how fucked up and complicated his life had become since Ethan came into it. He couldn't imagine Ethan not in it.

ETHAN

Last day in the office before their trip and because Ethan and Chance had worked hard the day before, today was just fluff and packing up. There were meetings until lunchtime, to wrap up last-minute details, leaving Ethan and Chance as prepared for the trip as possible. Ethan felt good, and knew that their hard work would pay off.

Chance asked Ethan and Brad to join him for lunch. Ethan readily agreed and Brad just snickered, following them out of the office.

Chance made an exception to talking shop at lunch. He told them about the gorgeous resort where they were staying, and what to expect from the client. He explained to Ethan how to behave in return, honoring their customs. "You don't want to offend them," he warned. "The Balinese custom when greeting someone of high social class is to bow, and others, just nod." How would he know who's of high social class? He'd follow Chance's lead. Hopefully he wouldn't do anything to completely disgrace them.

Ethan listened intently to every word Chance said, but internally, he was freaking out, and not just because of the customs of the country they were visiting. He was going to a beautiful resort with this amazing man in front of him, and he'd told him he didn't want to have sex with him. *I'm such a fucking idiot.*

"You listening, Ethan?" Chance asked unknowingly, while Brad snorted, shaking his head.

"Ethan must be thinking about who to bow to and when to just nod," Brad said, covering. Ethan needed to thank him later.

Back at the office, Chance told Ethan to go on home and finish packing. "The limo will pick you up at nine p.m. sharp." Then he added, "Don't forget your bathing suit."

Ethan was nearly packed, so he decided to take a short nap before Chance picked him up. He fell asleep almost immediately, and dreamed of Chance, Bali, the flight, and amazing sex...

Chapter Fifteen

ETHAN

Ethan had just enough time to jump in the shower before Chance arrived in the limo taking them to the airport. He thought about the dream he'd had as the hot water ran over his body. He stroked his hand over his semihard cock and was deep in thought when he heard the phone ring. It brought him out of his trance and he quickly rinsed off. He shut off the water and towel-dried himself as he walked into his bedroom to get dressed. He pushed the button on his answering machine to find out the call was from Brad, wishing him luck and adding, "You'd better be up by now." Ethan chuckled and finished dressing.

He shoved the rest of his things into his suitcase and carried it to the front room just as the bell rang.

Ethan opened the door to the most beautiful sight he'd ever seen. Chance leaned against the doorframe, looking so sexy in black trousers and crystal blue button-down shirt matching his eyes. Ethan's mouth hung open as he openly gawked.

"Good evening, beautiful," Chance said, staring back. "You look amazing, ba—Ethan." Chance waltzed through the door and gave Ethan a quick peck on the cheek. He'd told him ahead of time to dress nice but comfortable for the long flight.

Ethan blushed. "You always manage to look gorgeous."

"Ready for our adventure?"

Ethan's head bobbed as Chance took his hand and led him outside. He was getting used to Chance's embraces. Chance never did it at work, but outside the office, he always reached for Ethan's hand or touched his shoulder. It was nice, Ethan admitted to himself. When Ethan reached for his suitcase, Chance said, "The driver will get those," and walked him to the car as a guy slightly older than Chance, tall, with light-brown wavy hair grabbed Ethan's bags and brought them outside. Ethan wasn't used to this special treatment.

"Wow, Chance. This is incredible," he said, climbing inside the large backseat of the company car.

"Would you like a drink?" Chance asked, scooting next to Ethan and reaching for the cocktails already prepared in two chilled glasses.

"Sure, I guess." He felt the nerves begin to rise as the trip was now happening. He was going away with his gorgeous boss to a beautiful resort halfway around the world. *Fuck, I'm so fucked.*

"It'll calm your nerves before the flight," Chance assured him, like he knew exactly what Ethan was thinking. He seemed to do that a lot too.

"Thanks, Chance," Ethan replied, taking the glass from him and settling into his seat.

The driver, who Ethan noticed had pretty green eyes, finished putting his bags into the limo and pulled the door shut. Once he'd climbed into the driver's seat, he opened the partition to the back of the limo. "Ready, sir?"

"Onward, Alex," Chance replied to the driver in a familiar tone. "Alex has been with me for three years," he told Ethan after Alex had pulled the partition shut again. "He's become a good friend," he added.

"He's cute," Ethan said into his drink.

"You think Alex is cute?" Chance choked.

"Well, yeah, don't you?" Ethan asked innocently, taking another sip.

"Okay, you got me there, Ethan." They both chuckled as "cute Alex," pulled away from the curb. "He also has a wife and two adorable kids," Chance added with a grin.

They chatted quietly on the way to the airport. Ethan was a bundle of nerves that, yes, the cocktail helped with tremendously. He had one more before they arrived at the airport.

Alex stopped the limo and walked around to open the door for Chance and Ethan. He walked to the back and opened the trunk before taking out the luggage. They did curbside check-in so they wouldn't have to carry their bags through the airport. Chance waved good-bye to Alex and put his hand behind Ethan's back, guiding him inside the terminal.

There was plenty of time left before their flight, so Chance took Ethan to a private members-only club. They walked through the darkened glass double doors, and Chance showed the man his card. There was a huge bar and scattered tables with large, overstuffed chairs. They could view the flight schedules from anywhere in the room and hear the speaker with arrival and departure announcements so they could relax while in the club without fear of missing their flight.

Ethan looked around the lounge in awe as they followed the maître d' to their table. All the furnishings were in tasteful black leather and dark cherry. "Wow, Chance." The fine wood and thick, red carpeting gave a warm respite from the bright lights and bustle of the airport. "This is amazing," Ethan said, sitting on one of the cushiony chairs, and pawing the soft leather arms. It reminded him of the chair in Chance's office. "Do you always travel like this?"

Chance shrugged, obviously enjoying Ethan's reaction.

"I'm impressed," Ethan said, looking at all the important-looking businessmen and women who seemed perfectly at ease lapping up the luxury. He felt like a fish out of water, and hoped he didn't look too out of place.

Chance laughed at the comment. "Don't be. They're just people, Ethan."

They ordered a nice dinner and had another drink. Ethan felt sated and happy when he heard their flight called for the first time.

"Ready to go?" Chance said, standing up and reaching out for Ethan's hand.

"Yeah, I guess." Ethan groaned, reluctantly peeling himself out of the oversized chair and petting the upholstery one last time. "I could live in this chair."

Chance laughed and grabbed Ethan's hand to help him up. "Should I get you one for your office?"

"I'd never get any work done." He wasn't entirely sure if Chance was just kidding.

They went over to their gate, handed their boarding passes to the agent, and then walked through the bridge where they met the friendly flight attendant who showed them to their cabin.

"First class?" Ethan murmured as they strolled to their seats.

Chance placed their carry-on bags in the storage area on top and ushered Ethan into the window seat. The flight attendant offered them pillows and blankets, which they both accepted. They settled into their seats while the rest of the plane boarded, waiting for takeoff. Ethan was a little nervous for this part but was comforted when Chance held his hand. The flight attendants did their safety talk, and once the plane was safely in the air, they walked the beverage cart down the aisle, taking the passengers' drink orders.

"Two vodka tonics with a twist, please."

"Certainly, sir."

Ethan smiled, recalling the first time he'd met the gorgeous man sitting next to him.

"You don't have Chopin, do you?" Chance asked. Ethan wasn't sure it tasted *that* differently, but Chance liked things expensive and classy. He kind of loved that about him.

"I'll check, sir."

She returned with two bottles of vodka that Ethan didn't recognize, but it definitely wasn't what the bartender poured at Cruze. Chance looked at the label and nodded. "Thank you." The flight attendant placed a bottle on each of their trays with a cup of ice and a clear liquid Ethan figured was the tonic.

After she left, they cracked open the lids on the vodka, poured it inside the plastic cups that sported a lemon wedge on the side, and stirred it with the tiny straws. With their matching cocktails, Chance made a toast. "To a successful trip."

"To us," Ethan replied, ignoring the double meaning of what he'd just said. They clinked their cups and Ethan stifled a chuckle, watching Chance take a long sip. Damn, he was gorgeous.

Once he'd finished his drink, Ethan leaned back and closed his eyes, in anticipation for the long flight.

CHANCE

Taking advantage of the quiet, Chance pulled out his laptop and began working. At one point, Ethan unknowingly rested his head against Chance's chest. Chance stroked his hair and kissed the top of his head. Ethan opened his eyes, startled, and tried to pull away, but Chance held on to him. Ethan drifted back to sleep, a soft smile on his face as he snuggled closer. Chance could get used to this. Ethan was special; like no one else he knew.

He put his computer away and let himself fall asleep, resting against Ethan. Chance kissed the top of Ethan's head again as he dozed off, feeling more relaxed than he had in weeks.

He woke when the flight attendant came around with dinner menus for the first-class passengers. Chance nudged Ethan awake to order his dinner. While they ate, the two talked about arriving in Bali and debated what they would do for the rest of the day. They had nearly two full days to rest and enjoy themselves before meeting the clients on Monday morning.

"I asked the front desk to make us appointments for a massage in the spa," Chance stated.

"Um, that sounds nice, but..." Ethan sounded unsure of himself.

"Ethan, this is a business trip. It's all paid for," Chance said, patting him on the knee.

Chance read him well. He knew Ethan wasn't used to this kind of treatment. He still looked uneasy. "Ethan, let me take care of my new star employee who deserved his place on this trip, all right?" He wanted Ethan to relax, so maybe they could both enjoy their trip.

"Okay, Chance." Ethan perked up, and Chance kissed him on the top of his adorable head.

"Good, it's settled."

Once the plane arrived in Hong Kong after a fourteen-and-a-half-hour flight, they had a two-and-a-half-hour layover before the next one that would take them directly to Denpasar International Airport. Chance took Ethan to a private club, similar to the one in San Francisco. Since they'd already had breakfast on the plane, they just ordered coffee.

Ethan took right to the club this time. He also seemed more comfortable with Chance, who was making an effort to be attentive so Ethan could imagine them being more than just coworkers. The waiter paid way too much attention to Chance, which had never bothered him in the least, but with Ethan glaring at them, it became more of an annoyance. Chance didn't want to give Ethan the impression he needed the attention.

The waiter took their order and walked away, and when Chance looked back, Chance caught Ethan staring longingly at him.

"See something you like, Ethan?"

"You," he said, before stopping himself. "I mean..."

"You do like me, don't you?" Chance said, victoriously.

"Of course I do. That's never been the problem."

"We're not at home; we're not at the office..."

"No, we're going to be with clients."

"Not right now. We're in a strange airport where nobody knows us or cares what we're doing," Chance replied.

Ethan scooted closer to Chance. Chance felt him relax against him. "Okay, Chance. You win, for now."

Chance gently kissed Ethan on the lips. No one in the club even noticed. They sat close together, holding hands and stealing kisses until they heard their flight called.

They boarded the plane for the last leg of their journey which would land them in Bali in about eight hours. They needed to get some rest if they wanted to have any fun when they arrived. Chance made Ethan comfortable with a blanket and pillow, then got himself situated. He scooted closer to Ethan, letting Ethan put his head on his shoulder. They kissed one last time and fell asleep in each other's arms. Chance felt optimistic. He needed to convince Ethan they should be together. He hoped he could.

Ethan woke up and needed to use the restroom. "Do you want me to come with you, Ethan?" Chance asked.

Ethan gave him a funny look. "Why would I need you to come with me to the bathroom?"

Chance leaned over Ethan and looked him right in the eyes, smirking. "Have you ever joined the Mile-High Club?"

"Chance!" He watched Ethan turn six shades of red. "No, of course not." And then he crawled over him and practically ran down the aisle to the bathroom. Chance laughed, watching him.

When he came back, Chance smiled sheepishly. "I was just kidding, Ethan."

"No, you weren't, bad boy." Ethan scowled at the man. "But that's what makes you so—Chance."

Chance rolled his eyes. He wasn't wrong.

The airplane touched down in Indonesia in the late afternoon. They went through customs, which took quite a bit of time as security didn't think much of Chance's leather jacket, which he put on after the flight, and searched all his bags—for what, he had no idea. Annoyed with the delay, Chance showed them his business visa, and they ushered him through with muttered apologies. Ethan, on the other hand, breezed right through customs.

Chance chuckled at their situation. "You have that innocent, boy-next-door look, Ethan."

"And you look like a rock star."

Once they'd both gotten through customs, they walked toward the exit and spotted a man holding a sign with their names. After brief introductions, they followed the man outside to the stretch limousine that would take them to the resort.

Chapter Sixteen

CHANCE

The limo pulled up to the hotel entrance, and the driver helped them with their bags. As they walked inside the lobby, the hotel manager greeted them. "We've been expecting you, Mr. Harlow," he said, walking them to the front desk so they could check in.

Chance was pleased with all the personal service. He smiled as he watched through Ethan's eyes, who was clearly mesmerized by the lobby alone. It was richly decorated in tones of brown with tasteful bamboo furniture, ornate paintings on the walls, and intricate rugs, with live plants sparsely placed to give it an outdoorsy feel. His mouth hung wide open as he walked around the lobby, Chance following him.

"It's beautiful," Ethan said.

"It really is," Chance agreed, sharing Ethan's enthusiasm. The client wanted them to "experience the best" of Bali.

The desk agent gave Chance and Ethan each a key to their two-bedroom suite. Chance made a comment under his breath about hoping they'd only use one of them.

The bellhop took their bags, put them on a luggage cart, and pushed the button for the elevator. Chance and Ethan followed him inside, and Chance made small talk as they rode the elevator to their floor. The man used his passkey to open the door to their luxurious suite on the seventh floor. The foyer opened into the living room area, where the bellman placed their bags on the floor. Chance tipped him, and he nodded his thanks before he shut the door behind him, leaving the two men alone.

Ethan looked like a child in a candy store. "Chance, this is incredible." He ran from room to room and eventually back into the living room. "Which room is mine?" he asked innocently.

"Whichever one you want, Ethan." Chance chuckled as he enjoyed Ethan's enthusiasm. He walked over to kiss him, but Ethan tensed.

"Chance," he said in a warning tone with little venom. Then he was off, running into the kitchen.

Chance laughed, watching Ethan explore their surroundings.

"I love this place," Ethan said, bouncing back into the foyer.

Chance was amused by Ethan's childlike behavior. Although there was just a few years' difference between them, they were worlds apart. He wanted in Ethan's world. While he gave him time to take it all in, Chance called down to the front desk and confirmed their massages and spa treatments. "Come on, babe. Let's have some fun."

Ethan looked around the place again and nodded. "Okay."

ETHAN

Ethan followed Chance into the elevator and down to the lobby of the hotel. They walked through winding hallways toward the spa. The hostess looked up when they entered and greeted them right away. "We've been expecting you, Mr. Harlow; Mr. Moore."

Ethan looked over at Chance, feeling out of place, and Chance just smiled at him as if to say, *"You belong here, Ethan."* He read him so well, it was scary. Why was he fighting this again? Sometimes he couldn't remember.

The hostess led them into separate private massage rooms, handed them each a large bath towel, and instructed them to undress. "You can either take off your underwear or leave them on," she told them. "It's entirely up to you."

Ethan rubbed the back of his neck, wondering if Chance would take his off. *Probably,* he laughed to himself. This was his very first massage and he felt nervous. Who would enter that room and put his hands on him? He finished getting naked, and climbed on top of the massage table, then draped a sheet over himself. He was relieved when the masseuse turned out to be a woman, then doubted his choice to go in the buff. *Well, at least I won't get hard during the massage,* he thought, while the masseuse went to work on his tight muscles. All he needed was some hot guy massaging him and embarrassing himself. He wondered how Chance was doing in the next room. *God, don't think about him naked, you'll get hard for sure.* "You all right, sir?" the young woman asked when he'd tensed up.

"Oh, fine." He stifled a snicker.

An hour and a half later, Chance and Ethan emerged from their rooms rejuvenated and relocated to the changing area of the spa to retrieve their clothes. Ethan felt much more relaxed as Chance walked up to him and gave him a hug and kissed the top of his head. "Enjoy yourself, Ethan?"

"Chance, that was incredible. I feel completely amazing."

Ethan watched Chance stretch his arms, tightening his abs as the towel shifted, revealing the top of his pelvic muscle, which formed a sexy V, leading to his pubic hair and dangling goodies. He quickly looked away when he noticed Chance lick his lips. "Yeah, me too. I wish we could..." he whispered.

"What was that, Chance?"

"Nothing, Ethan. Let's have dinner in our room and get a good night's sleep. We've had a long couple of days."

"Sounds good," Ethan answered happily.

They dressed back in their sweats and went back to the room. Ethan quickly unpacked his clothes and put them away in the closet and dresser while Chance called room service.

Ethan put on his pajamas and met Chance in the living room. The calming effects of the spa treatments were still with him as he sighed and plunked himself on the sofa next to Chance. "Want to watch a movie?"

"Sure. Pick something out." The television had a large online selection. Ethan finally chose a comedy.

"Are you having fun, Ethan?"

He bobbed his head up and down. "I could get used to massages." He'd never felt so relaxed, yet energized at the same time.

A few minutes later, their dinner arrived. Chance left to answer the door, and returned with the dinner cart. "This smells delicious. I hope you like it."

"We came all the way to Bali for burgers?" Ethan chortled, when Chance lifted the metal lids to reveal two American-style hamburgers on thick sesame buns with handmade potato chips and a pickle on the side. They reminded him of the burger at the hotel in San Francisco the night before his interview.

"Don't worry. We'll have plenty of time to experience the local delicacies."

"This is perfect," Ethan assured him. He brought the thick and juicy burger to his lips, and took a bite. He moaned at the delicious taste. He was hungrier than he realized.

They barely made it through the movie before they were asleep. Ethan woke to the sound of Chance nudging him awake. "Ethan, let's get you to bed."

"Huh?" Ethan opened his eyes to the beautiful sight of Chance leaning over him, and before he realized what he was doing, Ethan reached up and kissed him.

"Don't tempt me, babe, or I might drag you to my bed and have my way with you."

Ethan's eyes flew open as he realized his sleep-deprived action. "Sorry."

"Don't ever be sorry, Ethan." Chance smirked and his blue eyes twinkled, causing Ethan's cock to swell. *The way that man looks right through me.*

After a brief but awkward moment, Ethan pulled himself off the couch. Chance followed him and kissed him on the cheek. "See you in the morning," he said, parting at their adjoining rooms.

"Good night, Chance," Ethan said with a yawn. Not having been fully awake, he immediately fell back to sleep in the king-sized bed, curled up to his pillow.

THE NEXT MORNING, he padded into the bathroom to freshen up, then dressed in his swimming trunks and polo shirt. The plan for today was to bake in the sun and have cocktails by the pool. He met Chance in the kitchen who handed him a cup of much-needed coffee. They went outside to the patio restaurant for breakfast and feasted on seasonal fruit and toasted ciabatta.

Afterward, they walked around the resort grounds to enjoy the lush gardens and bright greenery. Passing the entrance to the exercise room, both men expressed their interest in testing out the equipment later that afternoon.

"I have to work on my figure, you know." Chance jokingly batted his eyelashes at Ethan.

"Your figure is perfect," Ethan muttered.

"So, you have noticed."

"Of course I have. You're gorgeous. I—it's just—I need to stay professional. I'm too new on the team. What would the others think of it, or me...?"

"Do you find me unprofessional, Ethan?" Chance interrupted, frowning.

"No." He didn't mean that at all. "But I'm just starting out and I need to be taken seriously at my job, and if you and I—you know. I don't want the team thinking I get special treatment because I'm your plaything."

Chance stopped walking and took a deep sigh, like he was contemplating what to say. "I'm sorry, Ethan. I'll stop. I never meant to give you that impression." His expression was remorseful, and Ethan nearly felt bad.

"No, you won't," Ethan replied with a sly grin. "I'm not even sure I'd want you to."

"Well, then. I accept your challenge." He returned the grin and a wink.

Ethan just shook his head. Why did he keep encouraging him if it wasn't what he wanted? It was a lot to think about.

They ended their stroll at the pool area and found an empty table and deposited their towels and sunscreen. Chance took off the shirt he'd worn at breakfast, and Ethan couldn't help staring at his muscular chest and arms. He wasn't the only one who noticed, as the poolside waiter promptly came over and offered to bring them a drink. Ethan snorted at the attention that Chance didn't seem to notice.

Chance ordered bottled water for them both, as they wanted to stay hydrated in the hot sun. After a quick swim, they laid towels on nearby chaise lounges and took turns applying lotion to each other's backs. It was very intimate, like a massage, and Ethan imagined Chance on the bed, naked, while he rubbed him all over. His heart raced, and he stopped.

"You all right, Eth?"

"Um, yeah." Chance didn't need to know what he was thinking.

"My turn." Chance jumped up, and let Ethan lay down. He tried thinking of anything other than Chance rubbing lotion into his body. Getting hard out here would be mortifying.

For lunch, they swam up to the bar on the other side of the large, irregularly shaped pool, ordered sandwiches, and had their first cocktail of the day. Instead of their usual, Chance asked the bartender to give them a Bali specialty.

"How about I mix you a pitcher of my signature frozen mango margaritas?" he asked, already putting ingredients into the blender.

"Sounds perfect. Ethan?"

"Yeah." He was still thinking about rubbing sun tan lotion over that gorgeous body, and Chance's hands all over him. How was he supposed to make it through the next nine days?

The bartender put two glasses in front of them, poured the frozen concoction into each glass, and left the pitcher for them.

"Thanks," Chance said.

Ethan took a big gulp. It went down very smoothly. "Man, this is good." The bartender smiled at them, appreciative of the compliment.

"Let me know if I can get you anything else," he said, walking over to another customer.

When they'd finished lunch, they wandered back to their chaise lounges with another round of frozen cocktails.

After swimming a few laps, they checked out the exercise room. Chance raced for the weight bench while Ethan opted for the elliptical machine.

Ethan watched Chance as he worked up a sweat. Sweaty Chance was incredibly hot.

Chance looked over and smirked, moving to the universal machine where he did standing biceps curls. He never took his eyes off Ethan who only knew that because he hadn't taken his attention from Chance since they entered the gym.

A couple of hours later, both energized from their workout, they went back to the room for a well-earned shower.

Ethan pulled out a pair of tan slacks and a short-sleeved, button-down shirt to wear for dinner in the main restaurant. He was looking forward to a nice meal after the long day in the sun. He finished dressing first and walked into Chance's room to find him standing in front of his closet, nearly naked. Ethan stood in the doorway for a moment just staring at Chance's muscular back and cotton-covered ass. He stayed a little too long, and Chance turned around. "See something you like, Ethan?"

"Am I frustrating you?" Ethan asked.

"Yes," Chance replied, his smile not quite reaching his eyes. "But I understand." Chance sighed, and Ethan knew he didn't really understand. If Ethan was honest with himself, neither did he.

Ethan grabbed a beer from the refrigerator. While standing at the kitchen counter, he mumbled to himself. *Why am I acting like this? What is it getting me, anyway? What if I resist him too much and push him away? God, would I want that?* He already knew the answer. *Maybe this trip was a bad idea. Or maybe it's perfect.*

Chance quietly wandered into the kitchen and put his arms around Ethan, who jumped, startled. "Shit, Chance, didn't know you were there."

"I know, Ethan." Chance backed up and stood smirking at Ethan with his arms folded.

"What?"

He pressed Ethan against the refrigerator, kissing the breath right out of him.

"Chance..."

"Hmm, baby. No clients here, just you and me," Chance said, caressing Ethan's hair. He pulled him closer with his other hand, resting it on his ass.

They kissed for what seemed like several minutes until Chance abruptly stopped the kiss and backed away. "I'm starved, Ethan." He winked and turned toward the door, leaving a bewildered and debauched Ethan following behind, rubbing the back of his neck.

"I am so fucked," Ethan mumbled, needing to adjust his trousers.

"What's that, Ethan?"

"I'm hungry too."

Chapter Seventeen

ETHAN

Ethan and Chance entered the foyer of the swanky hotel restaurant. In comparison with the open lobby, this was more elegant with dark red and brown tones and rich wood furnishings. There were huge paintings of the Bali landscape. A wealthy guest had commissioned the largest painting hanging in the center of the room, Ethan had learned from the welcome packet in their room. The restaurant had a romantic ambience, or maybe it was the man standing next to him. Chance looked sinfully delicious in his black suit. He would wear practically anything and still look like a rock star.

They were immediately greeted by a handsome Balinese host. He eyed Chance up and down with a lustful stare. Chance was completely unaware of his effect on men; or at least it appeared that way to Ethan. "This way, gentlemen," he said, looking directly at Chance. Ethan snorted and walked closer to Chance.

Chance held out his hand for Ethan to grab, which he eagerly did, wanting to stake his claim on this man. Or at least make it look that way to the vultures. *Why am I acting jealous?* Hell, it was no act.

The man seated them at a quiet table in the back. Chance ordered for both of them, starting with two glasses of a local white rice wine. He was charming to the waiter, yet sweet and attentive to Ethan, making him feel like they were on a date, not a business trip.

Ethan daydreamed of the two of them together while Chance talked about their day so far and what he wanted to do after dinner. He was so deep in thought that Chance startled him with his next words. "And I think I'll pick up the first guy I meet at the pool. Beautiful Balinese man, what do you think, Ethan?" Chance looked over at Ethan innocently.

"What?" Ethan raised his voice, not believing what he'd just heard. He thought of the host leering at him, and jealousy seeped through his body. His face heated as it reddened with anger.

"Jeez, I was just trying to get your attention. Where did you go?"

Ethan ignored his question. "Do you mean that, Chance?"

Chance picked up his glass of wine and took a long sip. Then he leaned forward and looked Ethan in the eyes. "In all seriousness—yes, we are here on business, but I plan to enjoy myself too. Don't you think I, or rather we, deserve it after all the hard work we did to get here?" Then he sat back.

Ethan's eyes widened. Chance had just laid it out for him. It was his to take. Why didn't he take it?

"All I'm saying is it shouldn't be a problem for you if I have some fun, and you should too, you know?" Chance said, through bites of food.

Ethan knew he was right. Who was he to deny Chance sex? If Ethan wasn't willing to go there with him, it was unfair of him to hold Chance back. But he couldn't bring himself to give in to the man, or worse, let him go. But what if he did? What if he gave in to Chance and they spent the week fucking each other's brains out? Then what? *We go back to work and pretend like nothing happened? Chance goes back to his lifestyle of sleeping with random men and I return to ignoring my feelings for the man so I can build a reputation as a hard worker, not an office pet?*

Chance obviously noticed Ethan's frustration. "Let's drop it, all right, Ethan? I was just thinking out loud." He changed the subject to work until they finished their magnificent Balinese meal. They had the nasi goreng, a spicy version of fried rice with garlic, and a staple Balinese dish, chicken satay. The side dish was gado-gado, crispy vegetables with peanut sauce. They'd also drank a couple more glasses of wine by then, and Ethan was feeling more relaxed.

After the dessert of black rice pudding, bubur sumsum, Chance signed the room check, and they returned to the suite to change into bathing suits.

Ethan couldn't shake what Chance had told him earlier. "Did you mean what you said at dinner?" he asked, walking into the living room. "You know, about having fun on this trip?" He rubbed the back of his neck.

"Of course I did." Chance shrugged. "Oh, you mean about meeting men here? Well, that sort of depends on you, Ethan."

Ethan squirmed uncomfortably.

"Look," Chance said, clutching Ethan's shoulders, "I'm not trying to be a dick here."

"I know that." Chance was actually being very straightforward. Ethan couldn't have asked for more. *He* was the one being a dick.

"I like you, Ethan. I mean, I really like you." Their eyes met and locked and Ethan melted a little bit. "Before I met you, I had every intention of going on this trip and having an excellent time meeting men and playing around. It's perfect. I'm far from home, and afterward, no one will remember me."

"Oh," Ethan said, moving his gaze to the floor.

Chance picked Ethan's chin up. "Then you came along," he said softly.

Ethan looked up and almost smiled.

"And, honestly, you've given me a lot of mixed signals. But I'm not going to pressure you into anything when I'm not even sure what I want."

There went Ethan's smile.

"You want to keep this professional to prove your worth as an employee. I totally get it, okay? But yes, I'm also here to have fun, and I think you should too. What goes on here, stays here." Chance winked.

This was all Ethan's doing. He couldn't have it both ways, and Chance was right. Ethan was so confused with the situation he had put himself into, he felt like throwing up. "Okay, Chance." Chance was giving him the space he'd basically asked for. *Great job, Ethan.*

Chance let him go, and they left the suite with towels in hand.

Walking through the lobby, Ethan sensed the stares again on Chance, who was sexy as hell in his snug swim trunks, ignoring the looks he received. Ethan rolled his eyes and kept walking alongside him. They made their way outside to the main pool. It had two bars, one on the deck near the hot tub, and other on the far side that you could swim to. It was like a totally different world out here with all of the greenery and hot bodies.

"I've never seen so many gay men in one place before, and they all seem to notice you." Ethan snorted.

"Bali attracts many gay couples on vacation, as well as businessmen," Chance explained.

"Huh," Ethan answered. "How did you know that?"

"Research; I like to know where I'm going. I like being prepared. Besides, I saw a few looking at you too."

Ethan doubted that. Everyone paled next to Chance.

They dropped their towels on the grass and walked over to the poolside bar. They sat down, and the bartender greeted them with a smile and placed two napkins in front of them. "What can I get you, gentlemen?"

Chance ordered their cocktails, and chatted with the bartender. Chance was very sociable, and although Ethan knew he wasn't flirting with him, the guy definitely gave it back. Chance downed his drink and then announced, "I'm going for a swim. Want to join me, Ethan?"

"I'll stay with our drinks," Ethan told him. Chance walked to the edge of the pool. He stopped for just a moment, rubbing his hands together before reaching his arms over his head and diving in.

Ethan watched him. He was graceful, as his long legs cut through the water. Then he stood up, exposing his upper body, wet and glistening. Chance carded his hands through his hair, bending his head back, eyes closed. *He's so fucking sexy.* Ethan looked around and found several pairs of eyes from the bar also fixated on Chance, including those of the bartender. Who could blame them? Ethan shook his head.

A man from the bar dove into the pool and landed just inches from Chance. "Hey, sexy," New Guy said to a seemingly surprised Chance.

"Hey yourself," Chance flirted back.

Ethan felt a pang of jealousy but fought it off because Chance swam toward him at the deck, ignoring overly forward New Guy, thankfully.

"Come in with me, Ethan," Chance coaxed. "The water feels amazing."

Ethan stood up and jumped in without argument, splashing Chance. New Guy swam away, glaring back at Ethan. He smiled, victoriously.

Chance splashed him back, then yelled, "Race to the swim-up bar, loser pays," and took off toward the other bar. Ethan instantly caught on and started chasing after him, laughing.

Chance barely made it ahead of Ethan. "Two vodka tonics with a twist, please," Chance said, as Ethan caught up to him. "Do you have Chopin?"

The bartender nodded, reaching for a bottle on the top shelf.

"Here, Ethan." Chance handed him a drink. "You know," he said to the bartender, "when we first met, Ethan was drinking a no-name brand."

The bartender raised his eyebrows, looking at Ethan, who just shrugged.

"I thought it tasted fine."

"Yes," Chance agreed. "But this tastes much better."

"Chance has expensive taste," Ethan told the bartender who nodded in agreement. "He's raising my bar."

"You deserve the best, ba—Ethan." That earned raised eyebrows from the man behind the counter.

After a couple of drinks, they jumped back into the pool and swam. Ethan was relieved Chance wasn't hitting on other guys, but those stupid voices in his head kept him from doing what he really wanted. Besides, they were meeting the client tomorrow, and he had to be on his best game. He knew that for sure, but still...

They eventually headed back up to the suite to get ready for bed. Ethan went directly to his room, but he could hear Chance rummaging around in his own room. He climbed into his bed and thought about the day: Chance, tomorrow, Chance, the clients, Chance...

He'd settled down, ready to fall asleep, when he thought he heard noises from the other room. Ethan panicked briefly, thinking Chance was with another man. But that was impossible. They'd returned to the room together, so Chance must be...

"Ahh, fuck... Ethan."

Chapter Eighteen

ETHAN

Ethan woke to the smell of breakfast and saw the covered tray in the living room. He heard the shower running, reminding him of what he'd heard last night in Chance's bedroom. He tried to put it out of his mind, but visions of Chance masturbating invaded his thoughts. And did he hear that right? Did Chance say his name? Was Chance thinking of him when he came?

Ethan was still thinking about it while he ate his breakfast when a very naked Chance walked into the room, toweling off. "Hey, Ethan, you're up. Good, you're eating. I'll be out in a minute." He turned back toward his room, displaying his naked ass while Ethan stared, eyes wide, and he gulped, imagining for a second eating his breakfast off those perfect buns.

A few minutes passed, and Chance joined Ethan again, this time fully dressed. "Sit down and eat, Chance. This is amazing," Ethan said through mouthfuls of over-easy eggs and breakfast meats, accompanied with Balinese croissants.

Chance kissed the top of Ethan's head and sat down to eat. "Are you ready for today?"

"I think so." They were ready. They'd worked very hard preparing, and Chance had confidence in him. That helped, a lot.

"Glad to hear it." They finished their breakfast in mostly silence after that. "Finish getting ready. The limo will be here to pick us up in thirty minutes."

"I *am* ready." Ethan laughed, sitting on the sofa in his suit.

Chance shrugged. "It takes me a little longer than you to get beautiful," he said, walking back into the bathroom to finish dressing.

Ethan rolled his eyes and went back to his room for one last look in the mirror, satisfied he wouldn't insult their clients with his attire.

Chance reemerged ten minutes later, looking stunning in a black suit with a light-blue shirt the same color as his eyes. Ethan swallowed, taking the man in. They picked up their briefcases and presentation and headed for the lobby to wait for the limo which pulled up to the curb moments later.

The trip downtown took nearly twenty minutes, but it was a gorgeous ride through the countryside with its lush greenery and interesting architecture. Ethan and Chance stared out their windows, admiring the landscape the entire way to the client's office.

The driver pulled up to the driveway of a huge office building. "Thank you," they both said, and stepped out of the limo as their driver tipped his hat.

A small group of men stood waiting outside to greet them. One gentleman introduced himself as the vice president, Mr. Salomayer, and served as the spokesman. "Mr. Harlow, Mr. Moore. Welcome to Bali, gentlemen." Ethan thought the man looked more European than Balinese, from the locals he'd already met.

"Thank you, sir. It's a pleasure to be here." Ethan remembered everything Chance had told him about proper Balinese etiquette. However, when Chance went to bow, Mr. Salomayer reached out his hand, and Chance, ever smooth, shook his hand instead. Ethan sighed in relief and shook everyone's hand as well, as they all introduced themselves before leading Ethan and Chance inside the building.

They spent the morning with the heads of the company, discovering what they were looking for from the advertising firm. Right after lunch, they met with the rest of the group and were in small strategy meetings for the rest of the day. The VP provided a spacious private office for them to work in. They had three days to come up with their final presentation, which they would deliver at the beginning of the next week. They were under a lot of pressure to do well, but Chance had very realistic expectations. They hoped their months of preparation would pay off.

After a long but productive day, Chance and Ethan rode their limo back to the resort. "See you tomorrow morning at eight, gentlemen," the driver said, tipping his cap.

"Thank you," they chimed. "See you in the morning."

They climbed out of the limo and walked together into the lobby. Once they were inside, they were finally able to relax.

"God, Chance. Today was incredible."

"You should be proud of yourself." Chance wrapped his arms around Ethan and kissed him on the mouth as Ethan tensed. "Sorry. I just like doing that to you," he said, smirking.

"I like it too." Ethan blushed, walking past his impetuous but persistent boss toward their suite. Chance opened the door, and Ethan went directly to his room to change his clothes.

"Ready for dinner?" Chance yelled from his room.

"Yeah, I'm starving," Ethan answered back. It would be easy to give in to his feelings for Chance. *I can't. I have to stay professional—don't I?* Ethan struggled with himself, and for once Chance finished dressing before him.

"What are you thinking about so hard?" Chance leaned up against the wall, grinning at Ethan, who was standing by his closet in his underwear.

"Oh, nothing, just today and stuff..."

"Well, as gorgeous as you are half-naked, Ethan, I'm hungry. Get a move on," Chance said, leaving him to dress.

Fuck, get a grip. Ethan pulled on a pair of jeans and a button-down cotton shirt, and the two left their suite to go downstairs for dinner.

"Let's celebrate a successful first day." Chance grinned at Ethan as they ordered their drinks from the same waiter as the night before, who still couldn't keep his eyes off Chance.

Ethan rolled his eyes and scooted his chair closer to his dinner partner. Chance snorted. "Jealous, Ethan?"

Ethan lowered his head so he didn't have to meet Chance's eyes. "No."

"I'm ready for a swim after dinner."

"I think I'll turn in early tonight." Ethan wouldn't even look at Chance.

"Suit yourself," Chance said.

After their meal, they went back up to the suite and Chance changed into his bathing suit, while Ethan put on pajamas. Once he heard Chance leave, Ethan grabbed a beer out of the refrigerator. He turned on the television in the living room to watch a movie by himself and think about Chance, and not think about the men he was most likely flirting with.

CHANCE

Chance dropped his towel on a chair and jumped into the lukewarm water and swam over to the bar for a drink. As he climbed out, the bartender came right over to take his order.

"Hey, man, you alone tonight?" the bartender asked.

"Yeah, my business associate went to bed early."

"Business associate, huh?" The bartender raised his eyebrows with interest, but when Chance offered no explanation, he took care of another customer, leaving Chance with his thoughts.

Chance wasn't alone for long, as a nice-looking gentleman scooted into the seat next to him. "Hey, gorgeous. You all alone?"

Seems to be the question of the night. Chance laughed to himself. "Yeah, I am."

The man took Chance's response as an invitation to sit down. "What are you drinking?"

"Vodka tonic with a twist, but I think I'm done for the night." Chance stood up, downed his drink, and walked away before the man had a chance to react.

"Man, that guy's hot," Chance heard the man say to the bartender. "Is he here with anyone?"

"Um, sort of? Not exactly sure with that one." The bartender shrugged.

Chance wasn't sure either as he dove into the pool and did some laps. He could have let that man buy him a drink. What was his problem? *Ethan.*

He swam a couple more laps and made up his mind. *Fuck this. He's not interested.* Chance climbed out of the pool and walked back to the bar. He took the seat next to the man who'd spoken to him earlier. He reached out to shake his hand. "My name's Chance."

"Hi, Chance, nice to meet you. I'm Doug." He shook Chance's hand.

Chance settled in the seat. "Nice to meet you. I think I'll take that drink now," he said, winking at the bartender.

They sat at the bar and talked for a while. Doug was here on vacation by himself from Southern Florida. He had recently split from his ex and was here to rejuvenate and have some fun. The two men got along splendidly. Chance was feeling a little more relaxed as they talked and sipped on their drinks.

"Let's move this party to the hot tub," Doug suggested a little while later.

Chance nodded, following Doug with a fresh round of cocktails. He hung on to the side as he sunk into the bubbling jets, letting the steamy water envelop his body. Doug scooted next to him, never taking his eyes off him. They leaned back and enjoyed the heat of the jets while sipping their drinks. Doug, making a bold move, leaned toward Chance. Just as his lips were about to touch Chance's in a simple kiss, Chance could feel another presence and stopped. He looked up and saw Ethan standing right behind Doug with wide eyes.

"Ethan—I thought you were going to bed," Chance stammered, startled at his presence.

"I changed my mind." Ethan shrugged. "I didn't know you were busy. I'll go." He looked sad.

"It's all right, come on in." He wanted him here. Why? He was about to be kissed by a good-looking guy who wanted him. "Doug, this is my business associate, Ethan. Ethan, this is Doug." *Because I'd rather kiss Ethan.*

Chance noticed the put-off expression on Ethan's face as he sat down very close to Chance, looking quite possessive. *Interesting.*

Chance felt a little bad disappointing Doug, but he was enjoying this, as Ethan scooted closer, his leg touching Chance's. He listened to Doug talking about his plans for the next day, but felt the energy buzzing from Ethan. He was definitely interested. Chance just needed him to relax and go with his feelings. He was a challenge, for sure. Chance yawned. "Well, we have a big day tomorrow. Doug, it was very nice meeting you. Will we see you tomorrow?" Chance flirted shamelessly, which just seemed to piss off Ethan further.

"Definitely." Doug stood up. "Ethan, it was nice meeting you too," he said, shaking Ethan's hand. Then he gave Chance a quick peck on the cheek.

When they got back to their suite, Chance opened the door and went right to his room. He shut the door behind him. He was a little pissed at Ethan. Doug wasn't exactly his dream man, but he was there and quite willing until Ethan had cock-blocked him. On the other hand, Ethan was so cute, being all possessive. But he couldn't have it both ways. Chance stomped around the room, tossing off his clothes. Chance was painfully hard as he lay naked on the top of the bed and grabbed his cock. *Fuck, I come all the way to Bali, and the only action I get is my own hand.* He worked up a rhythm trying to image Doug's lips on him, but the only image that came to his mind was the frustrating man lying in the next room. He came, saying Ethan's name for the second time in two nights.

ETHAN

Ethan ordered room service in the morning while Chance took a long shower. They ate quietly together, but Ethan could feel the tension and knew he was the reason for it. "Chance?" he finally asked.

"Yeah, Ethan?"

"Is everything all right?" He looked over at the man shoving bites of food into his mouth like he was pissed off at it and cringed.

"Of course it is; why wouldn't it be?" Chance answered rather sharply.

"It's just, last night—I'm sorry I ruined your evening; I didn't mean to." He hoped Chance believed him.

"I wasn't into that guy," he answered, never looking at Ethan. Chance took another bite of food, a little more gently this time.

"It looked like he was about to kiss you."

"So?" Chance shrugged again, sighing. "Ethan, we have a lot of work to do this week. We need to focus all our attention on the project. No more tension between us, all right?"

"Okay, Chance."

"Good." Chance bent down to kiss Ethan lightly on the cheek. Then he walked back into his room to finish getting ready, leaving a conflicted Ethan placing a finger to his lips.

The limo picked them up promptly at eight to take them to the office. This time, they walked directly into their private office and got right to work. They had two more days to finalize their presentation. They worked so well together. They were completely in sync as they bounced ideas off each other. The day went by quickly, and soon it was time to head back to their home away from home.

The drive that evening was much more pleasant than the morning as they chatted happily about their day. Chance called Brad from the car to update him on their progress. After Chance relayed all the details, he handed Ethan his phone. "He wants to talk to you.

"Hi, Brad, what's up?" Ethan asked nervously.

"Did you give in to the playboy yet? He sounds awfully happy."

"What?" Ethan blushed, mortified. "No—I haven't," he said into the phone, not able to look at Chance.

He could hear Brad take the phone away from his mouth and speak to someone. Then he heard whoops and cheers in the background. "Told you, man," someone yelled through the telephone.

"Willpower, Ethan," Brad said to Ethan. "Put Chance back on." Ethan handed the phone to Chance, leaned back into his seat, and groaned.

"What did you say to Ethan? He's blushing several shades of crimson right now." Chance snickered.

Ethan didn't know what Brad told Chance, and he probably didn't want to know.

"Bye, Bradley."

Ethan shook his head. "I think they have a pool going or something," he mumbled.

"What's that, Ethan?"

Nothing. "Dinner? I'm starving." Ethan turned his head toward the window, taking sudden interest in the passing scenery.

After dinner, they took their nightly swim. Ethan couldn't help noticing how Chance stared at him as they were drying off on the deck with their oversized towels.

"What are you looking at, Chance?"

"You." Chance swept his tongue across his lips unconsciously.

"Chance."

"Ethan?" Chance smirked, obviously unembarrassed at being caught ogling his business associate.

"Nothing," Ethan said, giggling. They quietly headed back up to their suite. The sexual tension was unbearable, and Ethan knew it was better not to spend time alone with the man or he wouldn't be able to control himself. He decided to turn in. They had to be up early the next day, anyway.

Chance used the bathroom first, and Ethan could hear him rummaging around. He sat on his bed, muttering about how stupid he was.

"Ethan, the bathroom is all yours," Chance yelled from the other room.

After cleaning up, Ethan climbed into bed in just his boxers, his legs stretched out with his hands resting behind his head. He wasn't tired anymore. He was horny as hell. How easy would it be for him to go into the other bedroom and give himself to Chance? His argument to remain professional was waning with the distance between them and their coworkers. He thought about what he'd heard from Chance's room the two nights before. Chance had said his name as he came.

He reached under his shorts and pulled out his cock, wiggling the material down his legs. He spat in his other hand and wrapped it around his aching dick, making long strokes and tugging it just so. Then he rubbed his thumb across the leaking tip. God, he wished there was a mouth nearby. He giggled at the ridiculousness of that thought. *There is, and he wants you and you're being a big stupid idiot.* He pumped his dick with the same harshness as the words in his thoughts. His orgasm built, and his breathing got heavier.

"Fuck, fuck," he whispered. Then the first ribbon shot from his cock as he kept stroking it. "Fuck—Chance."

After his breathing returned to normal, Ethan washed himself off before returning to bed, not bothering with his underwear this time. He pulled the covers over his naked and sated body and drifted off to sleep.

Chapter Nineteen

ETHAN

At the end of the third day in their temporary office, they were ready to present to the board. Chance called the vice president's office, asking him to come in and take a look at their progress. He brought two other executives with him, and Ethan and Chance gave them a sample of their presentation. They seemed impressed and told Chance and Ethan to enjoy their weekend in Bali and they would see them first thing Monday morning when they presented to the entire board.

On the ride to the resort this time, there was a bottle of wine in the back of the limo with two chilled glasses. Ethan sat back while Chance poured them each a glass. Offering a toast, he held up his glass. "To our success."

They ate dinner in the hotel restaurant with the same waiter serving them as the night before. Ethan disliked the guy for some reason. It may have been because he was ogling Chance during every meal. No, it was definitely because of that.

"Do you find the waiter attractive, Ethan?"

"No." Ethan snorted. "Why would you ask that?"

"Because you keep staring at him," Chance said, looking through the glass of wine perched at his lips before taking a sip.

Ethan's eyes got wide for a minute, but he didn't want to tell him it was because he was jealous. Chance hadn't even noticed the guy's eyes were all over him until he paid attention to Ethan's reactions.

"What are you having tonight, Chance?" he asked, ignoring the question.

Just as they were about to order, Doug strode over to their table. "Hey, Chance. Hi, Ethan." He sounded perky. It was annoying.

"Doug, would you like to join us for dinner?" Chance said without asking Ethan.

Ethan looked down at his plate, playing with his fork to avoid Doug's stare, willing the man away. "Oh thanks, that's all right. I already have a table." He pointed to the other side of the room.

"Okay, see you around, then?" Chance looked befuddled.

"Absolutely. Have a nice dinner, you two." To Ethan's disbelief, he winked and walked away.

"That was strange." Chance went back to scanning his menu.

"You don't notice the way men look at you, do you?"

"I'm not an idiot, Ethan," he snapped. "I'm just being polite."

"Huh?"

"It would be kind of rude to flirt with someone right in front of you even though we're not together. I'm not a total shit."

"Oh—yeah—I know that." Ethan remained focused on his menu.

They talked about the impending presentation, then Chance brought up the phone conversation with Brad the other day. "What did Brad say to you in the car?"

Ethan nearly choked on his wine. "Why do you ask?"

"You turned bright red, and I heard laughing through the phone. I'm sure Brad is up to something." He looked pointedly at Ethan.

Ethan put his glass down and looked up at Chance. "I think they're taking bets on whether—or rather when—we sleep together," he croaked, grimacing.

Chance laughed. "That sounds like Bradley. Well, it does take away one of your obstacles."

"What do you mean?" Ethan raised an eyebrow, watching Chance smirk.

"You didn't want people at work thinking you were sleeping with me." He took a long sip of wine, then put down the glass. He sat back, resting his arms behind his neck. "It seems they already do." He had an annoyingly triumphant look on his face.

Ethan took a bite of his blackened fish. *True*, he groaned inwardly.

"Let's go out tonight." Chance quickly changed the subject. "I want to hit the town. We've hardly seen anything outside our hotel." His blue eyes sparkled and Ethan didn't have the heart to disappoint him. Besides, they always had a great time out together. *And how does that usually end up?* He knew the answer to that one.

"Okay, sounds like fun."

Back in Ethan's room, Chance pulled out clothes from his closet, making all sorts of huffing sounds.

"What?" Ethan lay on the bed, trying to ignore the mess Chance was making around him.

"Don't you own any clothes, Ethan?"

"Yes, I own clothes." Ethan got up, reached into his closet, and pulled out a nice blue and black striped polo shirt. He tossed it to Chance.

He looked at it with disdain. "No way; absolutely not." He threw it on the bed and abruptly left the room. Ethan heard him rummaging in the closet in his own room, cursing. He came back a few minutes later. "Here, put this on." Chance handed Ethan a black, tight, silk-knit shirt. Ethan took it, staring at the garment. Chance walked over to Ethan's dresser and pulled out a pair of black jeans, and handed those to him too. "Okay, try these."

"Where did you get this shirt, Chance? It's not yours." Ethan raised his eyebrow at the garment, which looked very expensive and three sizes too small for Chance.

"Brad," he stated, like it was perfectly normal.

"Brad gave you his clothes for our trip?"

"In case you hadn't brought anything to wear," Chance replied innocently.

Ethan lay back on the bed and groaned. "Of course he did."

Chance walked out of Ethan's room, and when he returned a few minutes later with two cocktails in his hand, Ethan was wearing the jeans and tucking in Brad's shirt.

Chance whistled. "Wow. You look fantastic." Chance handed Ethan a drink.

CHANCE

"You look so good, I could just…" He stopped himself. Ethan had made it clear enough times that nothing would happen on this trip. He should really stop torturing himself. "Come on."

He led Ethan out into the street and they jumped into a waiting cab. Chance directed the driver to the nearest gay bar which he told Ethan had been recommended. Climbing out of the taxi, Chance grabbed

Ethan's hand, and they walked inside the large dance club. The floor was hopping; bodies dancing together; hot lights, hot men.

"Fuck, this place is awesome," Ethan exclaimed.

They walked over to the bar and flagged down the bartender. "Two Chopin tonics with a twist, please," Chance yelled over the music.

"American?" the bartender asked, handing them their drinks.

Chance nodded. "California."

"Welcome to Bali, gentlemen."

Chance looked over at all the men watching them. "All these guys are staring at you, Ethan."

"Maybe a couple, but the rest all have eyes for you, Chance."

"Why don't we drive them all crazy?" he said, leading Ethan onto the dance floor. He placed one hand on Ethan's shoulder and the other on his ass, moving both of them to the music. What Ethan lacked in natural rhythm, he made up for in enthusiasm. Chance felt him melt against him. He leaned forward and whispered in his ear. "You're the hottest boy in this whole place." He sensed Ethan smirk against his chest.

The music slowed, and Chance pulled Ethan closer, pressing his face against Ethan's. He brushed his lips against the soft skin of Ethan's cheek in a delicate kiss.

"Chance..."

"Ethan," he whispered back. He'd like nothing more than to kiss him. He raised his hand that was touching Ethan's butt, and moved it to his other cheek to turn his head. Just as he was about to taste Ethan's lips, a drunken man nearly Chance's height and build fell into them, before straightening up and leering at both of them.

"You two are so fucking hot. Let me cut in."

"Nah, he's all mine," Chance informed him, not sure which of them the guy was referring to. He held Ethan against him, ignoring the guy. Another drunken guy about three inches shorter and much stockier than his friend wedged in between them and pawed Ethan, dancing him away from Chance.

"You and me, gorgeous," said the tall guy, having pulled Chance away from the others. Chance looked back at Ethan who seemed to be enjoying the attention, or maybe it was shock. He wasn't pulling away though. *Maybe this is what we need.* He placed his hands on the guy's shoulders and moved his hips to the music, letting the guy grind him.

"I noticed you two right away," the guy told him. "You and your boyfriend swing?" He wasn't great at sweet talk, but had some great moves.

"Oh, we're not..." He was interrupted by the feel of hands rubbing his crotch. Chance was horny as hell, so he let the guy fondle him through his jeans. It felt amazing and he was rock-hard. He only wished it was Ethan touching him. Ethan was such an enigma. He was clearly into Chance, but fought him at the same time. Was it just because of work? He felt the same tinge of rejection as in college. But Ethan was nothing like the professor. If Chance was honest with himself, Ethan reminded him of himself at that age. When he was still innocent with so much love to give. Chance bucked into the guy's hands as he kneaded his crotch. He threw his head back.

"We have a table," the guy said after a few dances, pulling Chance out of his thoughts. He looked around and there were no empty tables. They might as well, or they'd be standing at the bar all night. "Sure." He had no intentions of doing anything more with this guy, but they might as well have some fun. He watched Ethan still dancing as he followed the guy to a table at the back of the club and scooted into the circular booth, mere inches separating them. Ethan and the other guy joined them moments later as the waiter came over and took their drink orders.

After a couple of cocktails, Ethan excused himself to the restroom, and when he returned, he looked awful. Chance started to ask what was wrong.

"Can we go? Now!" His eyes were wide with fear and he was trembling. The expression on Ethan's face was sheer terror. Concerned, Chance stood up from the table and led him out of there immediately, leaving the other man looking bewildered at the sudden departure of his catch for the night.

"Please let's go back to the hotel," Ethan said once they were outside. He was shaking. It was a little chilly, yet Chance was certain that wasn't why. He put his arm around him and Ethan didn't argue.

Chance hailed a cab and helped Ethan inside. He held his hand the entire way back to the resort. Thinking of a way to make Ethan feel better, Chance suggested they go for a swim when they got back.

He nodded, "Sounds good." His tone didn't match his words. Chance wanted to ask what happened, but Ethan's arms were folded over his stomach, his head turned to the window. Ethan had been fine until he went to the restroom. Chance panicked. "Ethan, did something happen to you in the bathroom?" Oh God. He had a horrible thought.

Ethan turned his head with the same look on his face he had in the club. "I don't want to talk about it." That did nothing to alleviate Chance's fear of what might have happened. Chance should have gone with him. Was he attacked, mugged, worse?

Chance paid the cab driver and led Ethan back to their room. He didn't push him any further.

Ethan was ready before Chance, waiting for him in the front hall with his bathing suit and holding a towel. They walked quietly to the pool. Chance noticed Doug at the swim-up bar again. "Hey, you two," he yelled from the other end.

Chance waved to him before turning his attention to Ethan. "Can I invite him over?"

"Why would I mind?" He sounded short.

Chance nodded to Doug, and the man walked over to their end of the bar. "Hey there." Doug kissed Chance on the cheek. "Ethan," he added.

Ethan just nodded and took a sip of his drink. He looked exhausted, and after a while, he got off his barstool. "Chance, I'm tired. I think I'm going to turn in."

"Sure. Are you sure you're all right?"

"Yeah, you and Doug have fun. I'll be fine."

Chance watched Ethan swim away, worried about him.

"What's wrong with him?"

"We were at a club. Honestly, I'm not sure," Chance said, still watching Ethan.

When Ethan was out of sight, Chance turned his attention to Doug. They talked for a while at the bar and ended up in the hot tub with a new set of drinks.

After a few minutes of quiet relaxation, Doug spoke up. "May I ask you a question?"

"Shoot." Chance's eyes were closed, and he leaned his head back against the ceramic edge of the tub.

"Are you positive there's nothing going on between you and Ethan?"

"Yes," he said, sighing. "He works with me and wants to keep things professional between us." He tried not sounding disappointed, yet failed.

Not seeming to notice, Doug replied, "Then can I kiss you?" He scooted closer to Chance and put his arm around Chance's back.

Chance leaned over and let Doug kiss him on the lips. He felt all the sexual tension from the past few days build up and explode. He attacked Doug's mouth, and soon they were panting with want. Doug fondled Chance through his swimming trunks. He slipped his hand inside the waistband, but Chance stopped him, pulling away. *God, he cock-blocks me even when he's not here.* But it wasn't just Ethan. It was him too. *Fuck.*

Annoyed with himself, he abruptly stood up. "I'm sorry, Doug. I need to check on Ethan." He sprang out of the hot tub, grabbed his towel, and jogged back to the suite, leaving a most likely bewildered and frustrated Doug. His heart just wasn't in it. No, frustratingly, his heart was in their hotel suite with Ethan.

When Chance entered the suite, he could hear Ethan's even breathing. He walked into his room and just stared at the sleeping man. *He is so beautiful.* Before he realized what he was doing, he'd slipped off his bathing suit and climbed into bed beside him, spooning the back of Ethan, kissing the top of his head.

Ethan stirred briefly, snuggling into the warm body while Chance held him close and fell into a deep sleep.

Chapter Twenty

CHANCE

Chance woke up early and eased his way out of the bed without disturbing Ethan, who looked so peaceful, sleeping. He left his room and jumped in the shower, allowing his thoughts to drift to the previous night. He wouldn't let himself think about how much he'd wanted to wake Ethan and touch him. That took an incredible amount of willpower, if he did say so himself. He wrapped his hand around his cock, stroking, wishing it were Ethan's mouth. He moved his hand up and down his shaft, faster and faster, imagining Ethan bobbing and sucking him. He moaned, trying to keep quiet and not wake Ethan. When he came, he imagined Ethan licking him clean before standing up, the come dripping from his mouth as he kissed Chance, letting him taste himself. *Fuck.*

As Chance came out of the bathroom, Ethan began stirring. He stretched and sat up. Chance saw him look over at the pillow with the indentation from his head. In his sleepy state, Ethan looked confused. Chance walked into the room, toweling off. "Get up, sleepyhead. We have a full day ahead of us."

"It's Sunday." Ethan groaned.

"Yes, it's Sunday. We're going to have a nice breakfast, and then go sightseeing. The company limo is taking us on a private tour of Bali," Chance informed him.

"When did you have time to set that up?" Ethan asked, looking fully awake now.

Chance just winked and walked out of Ethan's room, dropping his towel. He could feel Ethan's lustful stare boring into his backside, and he smiled. *See what you're missing?* Then he got dressed and waited for Ethan in the foyer.

They rode the elevator down to the lobby and walked over to the breakfast buffet in the hotel restaurant. The weekend host led them to their table. They walked over to the large buffet filled with American-Bali breakfast dishes. The aroma of carved meats and homemade breads permeated their nostrils. After filling their plates, they sat down at their table, where a steaming pot of coffee and two glasses of freshly squeezed orange juice had just arrived.

"Our driver will give us the complete tour of Bali, and he said we can stop and get out anywhere we want. Is there anything special you wanted to see?" Chance was excited to share the experience with Ethan. He wanted the day to be memorable, but Ethan was only half listening. "You still with me?" He still appeared a little shaken from the previous evening, and Chance wondered again exactly what had happened.

"Yeah, just sleepy," Ethan said. "It sounds great, Chance. Anything you want to do is fine with me." Chance let it go for now, but when they returned, he was going to find out what was going on with him.

After breakfast, they ambled into the lobby, where Chance spotted Doug at the front desk. He walked over and chatted for a moment, giving him a quick pat on the back while Doug kissed his cheek. They briefly hugged, and then Chance walked back over to Ethan, who looked like he was trying not to watch the casual farewell.

"Doug said to tell you good-bye, Ethan," Chance said when he'd returned to Ethan's side.

"Oh, he's leaving? What a shame."

Chance let Ethan's sarcastic tone go. He was prepared to do whatever it took to have a good time today, and it was his mission to make Ethan enjoy himself.

Outside, the limo waited to take them on their private tour of Bali. The same driver who'd been ferrying them back and forth to the office greeted them as they climbed in the backseat, where a pitcher of mimosas and two chilled glasses waited for them.

"Now, this is the life," Chance said, handing a glass to Ethan, who began to perk up a little.

Their driver took them to all the major tourist spots. Chance enjoyed watching Ethan's building excitement as they drove through the city. The driver pointed out interesting landmarks and gave them some history of the area. Chance finally asked him his name, since they'd be spending the entire day together.

"It's Putu," he told them. Then, he explained he was the first child in his family.

Chance asked him many questions, while Ethan sat back, mostly listening to them talk. They learned that, in Bali, children are named by the order they are born. "My sister is Made, and our younger brother is Nyoman." Putu went on to explain that all families name their children the same names as his.

"Do you have friends also named Putu?" Ethan asked, fascinated.

He nodded. "Yes, only one, though. The more common first-child name is Wayan, and I have several friends with that name." Putu was a wealth of knowledge in history and culture. It was almost more interesting just talking with him than taking in the sights.

The first stop was the village of Batubulan in the Gianyar Regency, to see the stone figure roadside art. They walked around and took photos. Ethan ran up to the first statue and did a goofy pose while Chance snapped a picture. This was the Ethan he liked to see. The one who wasn't overthinking why they shouldn't have a relationship or acting jealous. *Relationship.* This was the first time he'd thought about actually having one, and with Ethan, and it scared him. He thought of calling Brad, the last person he'd had one with. But they hadn't really even had one. They were more like good fuck buddies, and Brad knew Chance wasn't ready for one then. Was he now? He looked over at Ethan, who was running between the statues, patting their heads in a peculiar game of duck, duck, goose. Ethan was not like the good professor. Chance laughed, watching him. He was absolutely precious.

"Having fun, Ethan?" He snapped another picture, and Ethan held another silly pose, laughing. Yeah, he could see it. But could Ethan?

After the statues, they watched the colorful and artistic Barong dancing at the Sila Budaya Theater. Chance had more fun watching Ethan watching them. His face was glowing as he clapped to the beat of the music. Once the performance was over, they returned to the car and drove to Ubud's Museum Puri Lukisan, which had modern works of Balinese art. Chance found this the most interesting, but he could tell Ethan's attention was waning. Putu helped guide them through, explaining all the art and giving a history lesson of Balinese architecture.

The next trek was north to the sanctuary of Besakih, known as the "Mother Temple of Bali." It was the largest temple on the island, and their guide told them it dated to prehistoric times. They stood at the base and enjoyed the massive structure before walking up the many steps and reaching the top, breathless. Ethan looked breathtaking as well as he panted, his hands resting on his knees. "Wow, we're high up." He ran over to the other side. "Chance, look."

Chance met Ethan and looked out at the mountains and streams below. "It's beautiful."

They stood together with Putu behind them. "Hey, what's that?" Ethan pointed to a grassy area below that looked like a garden of some sort.

"Rice paddies," Putu answered. "Would you like to walk through them?"

"We can do that?" Ethan asked, excitedly.

"Sure. I'll drive you down after we've finished here. There's a lovely restaurant with incredible local delicacies."

"Sounds amazing," Chance said, for the both of them.

"The complete tour takes several hours, but you can at least see the fields."

"Thanks, Putu. And I hope you will join us for lunch. My treat."

The man beamed. "Thank you, Mr. Harlow."

"Please, call me Chance." He nodded toward Ethan. "And Ethan." They shook hands at the new familiarity, and Putu gave them a genuine smile.

Putu drove them down to the terraced rice paddies, and they did a mini tour through the fields, then stopped for lunch at the Balinese buffet restaurant overlooking the terrace. Chance enjoyed watching Ethan devour his smoked duck, a local specialty, while Putu gave them a lesson on the local rice industry.

After lunch, they drove south to Sanur Beach and walked along the shopping district, stopping in a few boutiques and art stores. Chance could tell Ethan wasn't much of a shopper, but even he seemed to enjoy looking at the handmade jewelry. "Look at this, Ethan." He pointed to a wide, sterling-silver band with a dragon etched through the entire circumference of the ring and an amethyst stone sitting on top. It was gorgeous.

"The dragon is the guardian of the gods," Putu pointed out.

"Guardian of the gods," Chance repeated. "I like that."

"It's totally you, Chance," Ethan told him.

He pointed to the case and had the clerk pull it out for him, and he tried it on. It looked perfect for him. "I'll take it."

The clerk took the ring and wrapped it in tissue paper. "Anything else?" he asked.

"Ethan, what about you?"

Ethan shook his head. "I'm not much of a jewelry wearer," he said, looking down into the counter. He stopped at a row of leather bracelets and peered inside, gazing longingly at them.

"What about one of those?" Chance asked, having moved closer to him.

Ethan sighed. "I don't know. "

"I'll just pay for the ring then. I'll meet you both outside."

Chance watched Ethan and Putu walk out the door and heard the little bell chime. He turned back to the clerk, paying for his merchandise. He unwrapped the ring from the tissue, placed it on his finger, and tucked a small bag in his pocket.

The tour continued south to Jimbaran Beach, known for its water sports. After a little window-shopping, they strolled down the beach and watched the surfers ride the late afternoon waves, then took off their shoes and walked along the shore. Chance took Ethan's hand. Ethan looked at him strangely at first, but then smiled and squeezed Chance's hand. Maybe they were making progress.

It was early evening before they headed back to the resort in Tabanan. They made a quick last stop at the famous rock formation, Tanah Lot. Chance got a beautiful picture of Ethan with the rock behind him, just as the sun was setting.

Putu drove them back at the hotel. Chance and Ethan were exhausted from their long and adventure-packed day. After changing into dinner clothes, Chance went into the kitchen and grabbed two beers, then met Ethan in the living room and handed him one of the bottles. "Are you ready to talk about last night?" Chance was done evading that conversation and wasn't going to let Ethan put it off any longer.

Ethan looked scared again. It was freaking Chance out, but he waited patiently for him to begin.

"I was having an okay time. Dancing was fun, but I wasn't too crazy about those guys." He wrung his hands in his lap.

Guilt racked Chase. "I shouldn't have taken their invitation to sit with them."

Ethan shook his head, as if he was trying to get the rest of the story out. "I had to pee, so I left to use the restroom. I heard footsteps behind me. At first I thought it was you, but when I turned around, it was the guy I was dancing with and he was following me, too closely. I smiled at him, but kept walking. Once I was inside the room, he grabbed me, and..." Ethan began breathing heavily, panic in his expression. Chance put his arm around him.

"Take your time, Ethan. You're safe, now." Chance was seething. Why didn't he go with Ethan to the bathroom? He'd been distracted by the attention his dance partner was giving his crotch that he'd ignored Ethan. He could just kick himself.

"He—he pushed me into the stall and then he tried to—I didn't want..." Tears fell as he recalled the incident, still fresh in his mind.

He walked through the restroom door, seeing the row of open urinals, but opted for a private stall. After he flushed and opened the door, the guy he'd been dancing with pushed him back into the stall and pinned him to the wall, kissing him roughly. His demeanor had completely changed, and Ethan was afraid. The guy's eyes were wild, and he looked wasted as he lunged for Ethan, grabbing him. Ethan tried to get out of his clutches but had the abuser's tongue down his throat, choking him, while the man pulled at the front of his jeans, tugging down all layers of clothing at once, exposing Ethan's cock and ass. He tried flipping Ethan around, one hand clutching his waist, and unzipped himself with his other hand. Ethan panicked and began clawing at the man, shoving him away. He finally used his knee, bringing it up to make contact with the man's crotch, catching him right in the nuts. The man shrieked in pain, and Ethan escaped, zipping himself up as he ran away, huffing and shaking.

Ethan was shaking as he cried in Chance's arms.

"I am so sorry, baby. I should have gone with you."

Ethan shook his head. "You couldn't know anything would happen. I'm sorry I ruined your evening."

"Ssh, it's okay, Ethan," Chance said, holding him. "I've got you, now. I'm so sorry." He petted Ethan's hair and made a pact to himself. He wouldn't push him anymore. God, he'd been such an ass. If Ethan wanted him, he'd be there for him, but no more pushing him for more. He felt Ethan relax in his arms.

"Thanks, Chance."

He looked up at Ethan. "So, you kneed the guy in the balls?"

Ethan almost smiled. "Really hard. He screamed like a little girl."

"Badass."

He snorted. "Yeah, I was, huh?"

Chance kissed him on the cheek. "Ready for dinner?"

Chapter Twenty-One

ETHAN

"I had a nice time today, Chance. Thank you—for everything," Ethan said, smiling across the table at Chance as they ate dinner and sipped on expensive wine. Ethan had tried arguing about the price, but that never did any good. Chance, if anything, was tenacious. He appreciated the way Chance took care of him and listened to him. He really *was* a great guy. It would be so easy to give in to him. But what about when they got home? Would anything change?

"I had a great time too," Chance said. "And you're welcome." He gave Ethan a tired smile. "We need to turn in early tonight, though. We have a huge day tomorrow."

"We're ready," Ethan assured him. They'd worked so hard—the entire team.

"I have all the confidence in the world, Ethan. You're going to be fantastic."

Ethan beamed. "We make a great team."

"That we do." Chance winked, causing Ethan to blush as he registered the double meaning.

After dinner, they headed back to their suite. "How about we stay in tonight and just watch a movie?" Ethan suggested as Chance pushed open the door.

"That sounds perfect. Meet you out here in five."

Ethan retrieved a bottle of wine and two glasses from the kitchen and met Chance in the living room. Chance had chosen a romantic comedy, and they cuddled together on the sofa, sipping their wine. Ethan was finished thinking about that incident at the club. Nothing had actually happened; it was just scary. And he did get away from the guy, after doing some serious damage to his balls. He'd left him huddling in pain. The movie helped distract him from that, but Chance's warm body was so close to him. He thought about kissing him, but where would that lead? Right to the bedroom, he was sure of that.

Instead, Ethan leaned his head against Chance's chest and concentrated on the movie. Before long, he was sound asleep.

Ethan woke a little while later when he felt himself being lifted. Chance was carrying Ethan to his bedroom. He allowed Chance to lay him on the bed and pull the covers over him. Ethan didn't have the energy to stop him when Chance kissed his cheek. He heard the door shut and promptly fell right back to sleep.

CHANCE

It was just the two of them swimming in the pool. The night sky cast a shadow from the lights in the pool, illuminating the water. Both men had long ago shed their swimsuits.

Chance watched Ethan do laps, that ass moving back and forth, just above the water. God, he's so fucking hot. Chance licked his lips and felt himself harden. He resisted reaching for his aching cock.

Ethan stopped swimming when he reached the side of the pool and stood up, carding his hand through his hair as the water dripped down his back, making his muscles glisten. The water was shallow enough that Chance could see just the top of Ethan's crack. Ethan slid his hand down his own body and touched his ass, caressing it, looking over at a very horny Chance.

Chance swam up behind him and wrapped his arms around him.

"Baby," Chance said, kissing the back of his neck. Ethan turned around and let Chance kiss him on the lips. They began as soft pecks, building momentum, turning rough as their desire built. Chance probed Ethan's wet mouth with his tongue, licking across his teeth and meeting Ethan's tongue as they each fought for control.

They were pressed against one another, rubbing their erections together. "Fuck, you are so hot," Chance breathed out.

"Chance, I want..."

"I know what you want." Their breathing was getting heavier. Chance pressed Ethan against the side of the pool, pushing his cock against Ethan's hip.

Chance lifted Ethan out of the pool, and set him on the edge while he climbed out of the water. He pushed Ethan down so he was lying on top of him. He grabbed the lube that miraculously lay beside them. He opened the cap and poured a generous dollop onto his fingers. He then began inserting them into Ethan, one by one, stretching his hole.

Chance kissed Ethan's body while his fingers did their work. He licked at Ethan's nipples, watching them grow hard, sucking one rosy bud before moving to the other. He slid his fingers in and out, scissoring them, and found that pleasure bump inside Ethan, who was now begging Chance to fuck him. Ethan spread his legs and curled them around Chance's waist.

"Ready, baby?"

Ethan nodded, his eyes glazed with bliss. "God, I want you, Chance. Please."

Chance smiled and kissed Ethan one more time. Then he removed his fingers and sheathed his cock into Ethan's tight ass. "Ah, you feel so good, Ethan; so tight."

Chance slid his huge, throbbing cock the rest of the way inside Ethan. "Fuck me, Chance," Ethan moaned.

Chance slid his cock nearly all the way out, then slammed back into Ethan's tight hole. Ethan screamed in pleasure as Chance did it again, and again. Soon they had a rhythm going with Ethan fucking him back.

They both uttered incoherent mumblings of affection for each other.

Chance reached for Ethan's cock and pumped him with his hand. "Chance," Ethan screamed out.

"Ethan, I'm gonna co—"

CHANCE WOKE TO his cock shooting a hot stream of come all over himself. He sat up, breathing heavily as he soaked his stomach and the sheets. *Fuck.* His cock still throbbed. *That was the hottest fucking thing ever.* Chance got his breathing under control as he remembered his dream. Ethan writhing under him, begging him to fuck him, was *only a wet dream.* Damn, he hadn't had one of those since college.

He got out of bed to clean himself off and get a damp cloth to wipe away the come that had missed his stomach and landed on the sheets. When he exited the bathroom, he heard noises coming from Ethan's room.

ETHAN

He leaned against the edge of the pool, watching the dark figure swimming back and forth in the moonlight. The man was muscular, his strong arms churning through the water, his dark hair swaying back and forth. That beautiful, naked ass and long legs glided gracefully through the waves he was making.

Ethan couldn't see his face. It didn't matter. He wanted him. God, how he wanted him.

Ethan could see the figure coming closer, the man's breathing getting heavy as his cock responded. He turned around so the stranger wouldn't know he'd been staring.

He felt his breath on the back of his neck, and those strong arms wrapped around him.

"I saw you standing there—watching me," the man whispered in his ear. "I liked it."

Ethan relaxed into the man's touch.

"You want me, don't you?"

Ethan just nodded and leaned his neck into the man's body. The man raised his arms to thread his hands through Ethan's hair, and he licked his cheek. Ethan's breath hitched as he turned around to face him.

"Chance," he breathed.

Without saying a word, Chance leaned into Ethan and kissed him, hard on the mouth, forcing his tongue inside, darting all around. Ethan kissed him back as their tongues swept one another's. Chance took control and carried Ethan up the shallow steps and out of the pool. He took him over to the grassy area and laid him down. He looked deeply into Ethan's eyes. "Let me love you."

Chance lay next to Ethan, moving his hands all over his body, caressing him. Then he placed his lips on Ethan's hips, licking his way downward until he reached Ethan's cock. All at once, he swallowed him. Chance hummed around Ethan's cock, sucking, licking, and making Ethan want more.

Chance popped his mouth off Ethan and reached for the lube waiting there for them, and he opened the cap. He turned Ethan over and put him on his knees and had him spread his legs. "That's it, baby. Open for me."

Then Chance licked across Ethan's hole. Ethan sucked in a breath. Chance continued licking across the puckered entrance. He then pressed his tongue inside his lover.

"Fuck... Chaaance, feels so good."

"Mmm, baby."

Chance darted his tongue in and out, fucking Ethan with it. Ethan went to grab his cock, but Chance slapped his hand away. "Not yet," he purred.

Chance grabbed the lube and poured a generous amount right over Ethan's wet hole and onto his fingers. Then he pressed one finger into Ethan, sliding in and out. He rubbed his finger over Ethan's prostate, which made him jump.

"Do that... again," Ethan whined.

Chance added two more fingers and began lovingly stretching Ethan while he kissed his back, licking up and down Ethan's spine, driving him insane with pleasure.

Ethan fucked into Chance's fingers. "Please..." he begged.

Chance withdrew his fingers, prompting a throaty groan from Ethan. He lubed his cock and slid into Ethan's eager hole. He pushed all the way in until he was balls-deep inside Ethan.

"Fuckkkkk..." Ethan moaned.

Chance grabbed Ethan's ass and began to move. "You feel amazing, Ethan." Chance breathed heavily as he thrust deep into Ethan's willing entrance, faster and faster as skin slapped together.

Ethan fucked him back, panting and moaning.

"Please touch me," Ethan begged.

Chance reached around and grabbed Ethan's rock-hard dick, pumping him while fucking him hard.

"Fuck, Chance, I'm gonna co—"

ETHAN JUMPED UP, startled and extremely turned on as his cock pumped white streams of come all over his stomach. His heart raced as he sat there panting, wondering when his shorts had come off.

He did, however, watch Chance walk naked into his room with a clean, wet washcloth and sit on the side of the bed.

"Chance! What are you doing in here?" Ethan was mortified.

"Ssh, it's okay, Ethan; I had the same dream." He winked at Ethan, who stayed still, stunned.

Chance gently washed Ethan. After wiping the sheets clean, he stood up and pulled the covers over Ethan, leaning over him to kiss him on the cheek. "Good night, babe. I'll see you in the morning." And he walked out of the room.

Ethan lay back very satisfied. *What the fuck just happened?*

Chapter Twenty-Two

CHANCE

Chance and Ethan stepped into the empty boardroom to set up their presentation. While they arranged the boards, Chance looked over at Ethan who appeared calm and collected. He knew picking Ethan was the best decision he'd ever made. The kid just had that something about him that was warm and inviting. He was a perfect contrast to Chance. The clients were going to love him.

A caterer brought in trays of meats, cheeses, and several kinds of salads as the room began filling with men and women in business suits and stern expressions. This was the group who'd be deciding the fate of Chance, Ethan, and the entire organization of Ashton Lake. Okay, that was a little dramatic, even for him, but this was a huge opportunity for their firm. He needed it to go well, for all of them. Ethan and Chance took seats at the head of the table. The vice president, sitting at the other end, stood up and gave a small speech, explaining why they were all there. Then he invited everyone to dig into the delightful spread. Chance was too nervous to eat, but Ethan didn't seem to have that problem as he piled some meat and cheese over a bed of lettuce. As he was about to put the first bite into his mouth, Ethan looked over at Chance and smiled. They had this. Chance decided to relax and enjoy the meal.

THEIR PRESENTATION WENT well, although the display of Balinese delicacies for lunch may have helped. But it was hard to read reactions as the group showed hardly any expression, just intense stares. Maybe they were just being polite. Chance spoke first, giving the group an overview of their plan for their account, including advertising campaigns. This is what he excelled at. He grabbed their attention, making them want more. Ethan was amazing as he gave greater details of the timeline of events and showed them some of his designs and the direction they were heading. Chance was mesmerized by the younger man. He wasn't just a hot body; he had an incredible mind. Ethan really did remind Chance of himself before he was jaded by love. He nearly snorted. That was never love. He looked back at Ethan who'd absolutely charmed the audience with his easygoing personality. He could fall in love with Ethan. Hell, he might already have.

When Ethan finished his part, Chance stood again and wrapped up, bringing their presentation to a close. They were met with polite applause and a few nods, but nothing showing on their faces gave anything away. He'd hate to play poker with these guys, although the thought of this bunch playing a game of cards seemed comical.

Now they waited. The VP dismissed his team, leaving Chance and Ethan alone to pack up and carry everything back to their temporary office. Chance paced the small room, while going over everything again in his mind.

"Chance, it'll be okay," Ethan tried reassuring him. He had more pent-up energy than he knew what to do with. Ethan looked so good too. Chance thought of kissing him, but then someone knocked, startling him.

Taking a deep breath, Chance opened the door and Mr. Salomayer walked through it, looking stern. "Gentlemen," he began. "I'd like to thank you for the obvious hard work and dedication you've put into our account this week."

Chance felt a bead of sweat form on his brow. He resisted brushing it away. He glanced over to Ethan, who looked calm, but he was rubbing the back of his neck. Chance knew he was nervous, too. *This sounds like a—*

The vice president continued, "We knew from our initial contact with your company that we wanted to work with you. You took every one of our concerns and addressed them. Your presentation was well received by everyone in that room today. You were both professional and sincere." Man, could he talk. Chance stared straight ahead, expecting the worst.

The older gentleman stood right in front of them both for a few seconds. Then, after a more than brief pause, he reached out to shake Chance's hand. "Congratulations, Mr. Harlow."

What?

"Mr. Moore," he said, shaking Ethan's hand. "We would be delighted to have your company handle our account for a long-term contract. We will give you all the paperwork tomorrow to sign, and then it will be official. Thank you, both of you."

Chance let out the breath he'd been holding.

"Celebrate, gentlemen. Tomorrow, the real work begins." He nodded to both of them and exited the office, closing the door behind him.

"Holy shit, Ethan. I thought we were getting bad news." Chance sat down, relieved.

Ethan laughed. "What? I totally knew we had this."

"Yeah, right." They both erupted in a fit of nervous laughter.

The mood in the limo on the ride to the hotel was exuberant as they reveled in their moment of glory. A bottle of champagne sat in a silver bowl filled with ice in the back of the limo. Chance popped the cork, poured two glasses, and handed one to Ethan. They toasted each other and their victory.

"We kicked ass today," Chance said, taking a long sip.

"Congratulations," Putu yelled from the front seat so they could hear him.

"Thank you so much. If you weren't driving, we'd offer you some champagne," Chance answered back.

He chuckled. "I'm on the clock."

The limo arrived at their hotel a few minutes later. They thanked Putu again and watched him drive away. Chance walked over, put his arm around Ethan, and kissed his cheek. "I knew I made the right decision."

"About what?" Ethan looked over at Chance.

"Choosing you for this project. You were amazing, today."

"Thank you, Chance." Ethan blushed.

"I mean it. No one is going to think you got this opportunity because you..."

Ethan looked at the ground. Chance dropped the subject. "Let's have some fun tonight. We totally deserve it."

"No clubs," Ethan blurted.

Chance's mind immediately went to Ethan's incident the other night in the restroom. He still felt guilty that he hadn't protected Ethan from that predator. "Let's start with a nice dinner in the hotel and then hang out at the swim-up bar. Maybe dancing in the lobby bar afterward?"

"That sounds nice. Thank you."

Chance put his arm around Ethan. "Come on."

Walking up to the suite, they were still talking nonstop. "You know, Chance, you're the one that kicked ass today. You are amazing. They couldn't keep their eyes off you," Ethan said, gazing into Chance's eyes. He seemed to look right through him.

"I love what I do." Chance winked back at Ethan, lightening the mood.

"Well, you are, Chance, and I'm honored—" Ethan paused as if considering. "Yes, honored to be here with you." Ethan broke his gaze.

Chance blushed, something he never did, but Ethan's praise felt good. They went into the living room, and both fell onto the couch.

"I'm almost too tired to move," Ethan groaned.

"Oh, wait. Let's call Brad and let everyone know the good news."

"Yeah, he'd kill us if we didn't. Wait, what time is it there?"

Chance thought about that for a minute. "Shit, it's like three a.m."

"He'd really kill us if we woke him up.

"We can call him later tonight. Or will that be tomorrow?" He tried to figure out the time difference and gave up.

They cleaned up and headed down to the lobby and into the hotel restaurant, where the host greeted them as usual. "This way, gentlemen."

Chance and Ethan followed him to their usual table. They sat down and looked over the menu. "Spare no expense tonight, Ethan; this is our celebration dinner."

The waiter came over and just had to give Chance the flirty eyes. "What can I get you to drink, gentlemen?" he asked both of them, but looked directly at Chance.

Ethan glared at the guy as Chance shifted his gaze from Ethan to the waiter and nearly burst out laughing. He leaned to the side and spoke softly to the waiter so Ethan couldn't hear him. "We don't want to be disturbed this evening. This cutie and I are celebrating tonight." Then he put his arm around Ethan and winked at the waiter, who apologized for shamelessly flirting with Chance all week. Then, flustered, he walked away.

Chance gave Ethan a wink, knowing the waiter flirting with him had really bothered Ethan.

Ethan raised his eyebrow but didn't say anything. Chance now knew how Ethan felt about him by just how jealous he got of other men giving him attention. But he also knew Ethan wouldn't do anything about it, not on this trip, anyway.

He ordered a bottle of champagne and then dinner for both of them.

The next time the waiter came over, he was more subdued. Chance watched Ethan's reaction and smiled. He liked seeing Ethan happy and relaxed.

They took their time eating and enjoying each other's company. They discussed the rest of their trip and the future of the company. Chance loved to talk business with Ethan. Ethan's brown eyes lit up, sparkling as if the company's success excited him as much as it did Chance. It thrilled Chance, as he loved his work, and it was a big part of him.

"Ethan, you're going to do great things at Ashton Lake, I can feel it."

"I'm learning from the best."

They clinked their glasses together in a toast. "To us." He noticed Ethan blush at his double meaning.

After dinner, they went back to their rooms and changed into bathing suits. "Um, Chance, instead of the pool, how do you feel about going straight to the hot tub?" Ethan yelled from his room.

"Now you're talking." Chance threw on his swim trunks and met Ethan in the main living area in record time. Ethan looked so yummy, Chance just stared with lust-filled eyes.

"Chance," Ethan reprimanded. Chance remembered he wasn't pushing Ethan, but he'd come on this trip to have some fun, and he was going to do just that.

"We better call Brad."

Brad put them on speakerphone so everyone could hear the news as Chance briefed them on their presentation and outcome. They could hear their team whistling and cheering in the background.

"Bradley, take the whole group out to dinner after work to celebrate. Use the company account."

"Thanks, Chance. We have an amazing boss," Brad yelled out to everyone. Then he must have held the phone out so Chance could hear everyone could thank them.

When Brad took the phone off speaker, he cleared his throat and lowered his voice. "So, Chance..."

"No, Brad. And it's none of your business anyway." Chance rolled his eyes.

Ethan turned away, blushing, knowing exactly what Brad had just asked. Did they all think Ethan would cave? He was a tough nut to crack.

ETHAN

He and Chance walked to the poolside bar and got a couple of cocktails, then headed for the hot tub. Ethan was grateful it was empty. He wanted to relax after a long and stressful day. He was still holding out on Chance, but he also realized that not only was it probably futile, but it was what he wanted too. He decided maybe they could have a conversation tonight so he could address his concerns and they could move forward. He climbed over the side of the tub and slid down into the water, hesitating as the steam surrounded them to allow their bodies to adjust before sinking deeper. Chance let out a soft moan. Ethan looked over at him. He was so beautiful. He sighed. They sipped their drinks as the heat worked on their muscles. Ethan was still a little sore from all the hiking yesterday. They were relaxed and enjoying their cocktails while Ethan worked up his nerve to talk to Chance. They both had their eyes closed, but Ethan could feel someone invading their private space. Chance and Ethan opened their eyes in surprise as two very hot men approached them. Ethan's heart sank. His moment was gone.

"Do you mind if we join you?" the first man asked in a thick accent Ethan couldn't quite place as they climbed in without waiting for an answer.

"Sure," Chance spoke up. Chance moved closer to Ethan to give them room, but the first one sat close to Chance while the second one moved right next to Ethan.

The two men were partners but also swingers, and were here on vacation from Spain. Ethan felt uncomfortable as they appeared to be interested in more than just talking, but Chance seemed oblivious as usual.

Chance revealed he and Ethan worked together and were here on business, which the first guy seemed very intrigued about. He kept inching closer and closer to Chance, which made Ethan jealous, even though he knew he didn't have a right to be. He noticed the second man attempting to distract him so the other could make his move on Chance. He asked Ethan questions while maintaining constant eye contact. It was unnerving. He flashed back to the other night at the club. He tried scooting away to give the guy a hint he wasn't interested. Then he glanced over at Chance, who was in deep conversation with the other man, and before Ethan knew it, the guy kissed him hard on the mouth. Ethan stared wide-eyed as Chance kissed him back.

Ethan abruptly stood up. "What the fuck?" He was so upset he tried to run off, but the other dude stood up too and grabbed Ethan.

"Hey, I thought you two weren't together."

"We're not," Ethan spat, trying to get away.

"Then party with me." He leaned over and tried to kiss Ethan, who pulled away with a shocked look on his face.

"Sorry, but I am not into this," Ethan said. "Chance?" Chance hadn't come up for air yet, so Ethan stomped off.

He stormed back to the room, totally pissed off at himself. He'd left Chance with that—that molester. *God, I'm such an idiot.* He grabbed a beer from the refrigerator and immediately downed it, then grabbed three more and went into the living room. He turned on the television, and fumbled with the remote until he found a funny movie to watch. Then he settled in and drank. About twenty minutes had passed and Ethan was feeling a little tipsy. He was still upset Chance let them get in that situation, especially after what happened before at that nightclub. But who was he kidding? He'd told Chance he couldn't be with him because they worked together. It wasn't fair of Ethan to keep him from having a good time. But he didn't want to watch, either. He was going to tell him that he wanted to try. *Fuck.* What did he just do?

He was buzzed, working his third beer and watching the television, when a very pissed-off Chance barged in, slamming the door behind him.

"What the hell, Ethan?"

Chapter Twenty-Three

ETHAN

Ethan looked up with the bottle against his lips and gazed at Chance, who looked fucking breathtaking, even through his obvious anger. "Chance," Ethan whispered, the alcohol causing a warm burn in his stomach.

"If you don't want me, that's fine. But stop fucking cock-blocking me," Chance ranted, waving his arms as he stomped around the room. Even angry, the man was so sexy.

"Chance, I'm not," Ethan interrupted, perplexed at the man's attitude.

"Yes, you are." He planted his feet right in front of Ethan. His blue eyes blazed. Then he continued pacing.

"I just didn't want to watch you and him—g—going at it," Ethan stammered, staring right back.

"And, why not, Ethan? You're obviously not into me, so..."

"Chance...that's not true. I—"

"Yeah, well, I couldn't be with those guys 'cause all I could think about is you," Chance said a little more calmly, staring at the floor. "Are you happy now?" he spat. He folded his arms while Ethan sat contemplating his actions over the past week.

"Chance." Chance was clearly upset with him. *And what did he mean, those guys? Was he with both of them?*

"I've made my intentions with you very clear, Ethan."

Ethan stood up, anger instantly enveloping him. He was feeling looser from the alcohol. "What? That you want to fuck me in between your lunch hookups?"

Chance's eyes widened for a second. "That's not what I want, Ethan." Chance shook his head, looking guilty.

"Really?" Ethan shouted. They were now inches apart from each other, and Ethan wasn't sure if Chance was going to punch him in the face or kiss him.

"Really—God, you make me sound like an asshole." he said, calmer. "But, you clearly have issues with being with me, so stop fucking with my sex life."

"Chance, I don't want you getting together with anyone else." Now, he sounded like the asshole.

"Why not, Ethan?" he goaded.

"Because—" He turned around.

"Fuck, I knew I made a mistake."

"What?" Ethan shouted again. "You picked me just so we'd have sex." It wasn't a question.

Chance glared at him, and Ethan knew he'd blown everything.

"Chance, I didn't mean that."

"Yes, you did." Chance looked hurt. But he was too.

Ethan stood facing Chance again and leaned forward so their foreheads were almost touching. He shook his head. "No, I never thought that, but—what mistake are you talking about?"

"You."

Ethan's blood chilled. He was a mistake? What, hiring him, sleeping with him, what? He wasn't sure he wanted to know.

"Falling in love with you," Chance said instead.

Ethan blinked his eyes twice. He couldn't have heard that right. "What did you say?"

"I let myself fall in love with you." Chance turned to walk away and Ethan grabbed his shoulder, stopping him. Had he done a good job hiding his feelings for this man? Did he want to keep doing that?

"You're in love with me too?"

"Too?"

Ethan nodded, tears beginning to fall. "I thought I was doing the right thing." He lifted Chance's chin with his hand.

"I know," Chance whispered, still avoiding Ethan's eyes.

"Obviously, I was wrong." He smiled, waiting for Chance to react.

"You were." Chance gazed into Ethan's eyes, and Ethan saw him melt.

"Yeah, totally and completely wrong. Can you ever forgive me?" Ethan pressed himself against Chance and kissed him. Surprised at first, Chance kissed him back, letting their tongues get reacquainted. They made out for several minutes, standing there kissing with hands all over each other, not believing this was real.

"Do you mean it, Ethan? Because—I can't do this anymore."

Ethan nodded, and then kissed Chance. Then he kissed him again—and again.

"God, Ethan, I need you so badly." Chance stood looking at him, the tension of the trip melting away as Ethan kissed him again, and Chance resumed worshiping Ethan's mouth.

They stayed as one and made their way into Chance's room, tossing off what few clothes they had along the way, hands never leaving each other's bodies.

"Are you sure?" Chance breathed.

"Yeah, Chance. I give up—in—everything," Ethan said, giving himself fully to the man he was in love with.

"Finally." Chance pushed Ethan toward the bed, and climbed on top of him. Ethan spread his legs to accommodate Chance's body. They wrestled on the bed, Chance winning the round by pinning Ethan down, kissing him.

"I want you, Chance. Please," Ethan said, breathless and aching.

"Please what?" Chance replied through kisses.

"Fuck me, Chance. I've missed this. I've missed you."

"Me too, Ethan—me too."

Chance spread Ethan's legs, bending his knees and pushing them open, exposing his leaking cock. He kissed the inside of Ethan's thigh while he pressed his lubed fingers into Ethan's ass. "Mm, you're so beautiful.

They made up for lost time. Chance carefully opened him up, hitting that bundle of nerves, then fucking him till they were both spent. After they came down from their orgasmic high and had a few moments to calm, Chance said something Ethan never thought he would ever hear from this man. "Ethan, make love to me."

"What? Are you sure?" Ethan kissed Chance's face, neck, chest, slowly moving down his body.

"I'm very sure. Fuck me, baby."

He didn't need to be asked twice. Ethan grabbed the lube and spread it on his fingers. He pressed a single digit into Chance's tight heat, working it back and forth. He crooked his finger just as he himself always liked, found Chance's prostate, and brushed against it. Chance moaned for him, egging him on. "Fuck. God, that feels so good. Please..."

Ethan added a finger, continuously hitting that spot, driving Chance crazy. Then he added a third and began stretching Chance. "Chance, you're so tight. He looked at Chance—really looked at him—and realized he didn't do this very often, if at all. "I'm a lucky guy, aren't I?"

"Yeah, you are," Chance said, trying not to laugh at his comment. "Fuck, please, Ethan."

"Please what, Chance?" Ethan teased.

"Don't fuck with me, Ethan. Or, do, just hurry." So Chance liked to give it, but not—he knew his partner well. Chance pushed into Ethan's fingers, kissing him, willing him closer... Ethan pulled out his fingers, and Chance groaned as he grabbed a condom to put on Ethan. He slid on the rubber and guided Ethan's cock into his ass in one stroke.

"Fuck," Ethan breathed as he bottomed out. Chance was so tight, Ethan was afraid to move.

They held like that for a moment. "Chance—God, you feel amazing."

"Ba—Ethan," Chance hissed. "Fucking move." *Damn, he's a bossy bottom.* Ethan giggled and kissed him.

"Fuck, Ethan." Ethan slid his cock nearly out and then slowly pushed back in. When Ethan pulled almost out again, Chance grabbed his ass and thrust him back in, grunting in pleasure-pain. Ethan caught on and slammed into him once more, his balls slapping against Chance's ass. Ethan sped up, pumping his cock in and out of Chance, building a rhythm. Chance moaned, and Ethan knew he was close.

"Touch me," Chance ordered.

Ethan reached out and stroked Chance's cock. Within a few tugs and pulls, Chance cried out Ethan's name as he shot heavy ropes of come all over himself and Ethan, who stroked him through his orgasm while still pumping into Chance's ass. "Chance, oh, fuck." Ethan came inside him, still thrusting until he couldn't anymore. "God... I love you so much." Ethan rested on top of Chance while he stroked Chance's hair.

"I love you too, Ethan. I think I have since the moment you first walked into my office and I realized it was you."

They both knew that first night meant something more than just a one-night stand. It meant much more to Ethan.

"Can we please stop the bullshit now?" Chance was still panting, coming down from his orgasm, rolling Ethan over so he was on top and kissing him.

"No more bullshit." Ethan giggled again.

"Good," he said, kissing the top of Ethan's head.

"Chance?" Ethan laid his head on the larger man's chest. "Can we go back down to the hot tub?"

Chance chuckled. "Why?"

"I want to show those two guys you belong to me."

He kissed the top of Ethan's hair. "Of course, baby."

They put their bathing suits back on, walked through the lobby hand in hand, and out the back to the hot tub. Those two men were still there, sitting alone, necking.

They perked up when they saw Chance and Ethan. "You two all right now?" one asked. They genuinely looked happy for them. They seemed like okay guys, but Ethan still wondered what happened out there after he left. Did they both come onto Chance? *But he said he didn't do anything with them.*

"Yeah, we're good," Chance said, kissing Ethan on the cheek. They sat down and edged their way into the hot tub.

"Well then, let's finish this party, shall we?" One of the guys pulled out a bottle of wine, and somehow, four glasses appeared. "You know, we aren't at all surprised. You two look head-over-heels in love." Chance smiled, and Ethan blushed into his chest.

They stayed for a while in the hot tub and talked with their new friends. Ethan kept glancing at Chance, not quite believing this gorgeous man was his. He also watched the other two guys, and they seemed only interested in conversation. After an hour, Chance and Ethan left and headed back up to their suite. Since they hadn't cleaned up the bed after their makeup sex, they moved to Ethan's room.

CHANCE

Standing in the doorway, Chance placed his hands over Ethan's cheeks and kissed him. This felt so right. Ethan was his. When he opened his eyes, Ethan was smiling at him. He could see Ethan was as happy as he was. Chance stepped back and pulled Ethan's bathing suit down past his knees, admiring his nakedness. Then he slipped out of his own suit and kissed Ethan again, their cocks greeting each other at last. Chance wanted to go slowly this time and show Ethan how much he meant to him. It was more than sex for him. He loved Ethan, and he was ready for this.

He led Ethan over to the bed and lay over him as they scooted to the head of the bed. Chance propped himself on one elbow and raked his other hand down Ethan's gorgeous body, laid out for him. He stroked Ethan's chest, fingering each nipple, watching them harden under his touch. Ethan's breathing changed the lower Chance traveled, until his hands were on Ethan's balls, gently stroking. Ethan scooted his butt forward as Chance moved his fingers toward Ethan's hole. "Roll over, sweet baby."

Ethan flipped onto his stomach, and Chance spread his legs apart and kneeled in between them, rubbing his hands over the soft globes of Ethan's ass. He leaned forward and kissed each one. Ethan moaned as Chance spread his cheeks apart and dipped his tongue into Ethan's pucker. Ethan made sweet, encouraging noises as Chance licked and sucked his most intimate place.

Chance replaced his tongue with his fingers, stroking Ethan's hole with two and then three, rubbing that nub inside, causing him to curse like a sailor. He loved making Ethan do that. He was normally so sweet and innocent, but he let go so beautifully. Through panted breaths, Ethan pleaded for more.

Chance reached for the lube and a condom. He put on the condom and spread a large amount of lube on his hard length and poured some extra directly on Ethan, before resuming the finger-play.

Then he flipped Ethan over again and kissed him as he pressed himself into his lover. "Ethan. Fuck, you feel so good."

Ethan's eyes were wide as Chance's cock breached him. The stretch had to burn, but Ethan wrapped his hands around Chance's ass and pushed him in farther. A couple of inches at a time, Chance finally slid in the rest of the way. He kissed Ethan again, giving him a second before he slowly slid out and back in. Ethan snapped his hips to meet Chance's thrusts.

Sex was always amazing with Ethan, but this was making love and this beat amazing. Chance could feel the emotions coming off Ethan as they kept their eyes locked while Chance fucked him. He went slowly, not wanting to rush this. Ethan wrapped his legs around him, and

Chance could tell he was close as his eyes fluttered shut and the pitch of his grunts got higher. "Chance, please."

"Knees up." Chance changed position so he could stroke Ethan's penis while still pumping his ass.

"Oh God—fuck." Ethan's pants became erratic, and he was right there. Chance stroked him harder, and the first shot hit his stomach. The second landed near his chin.

"That's it, Ethan. I got you." Chance milked Ethan's cock until there was nothing left, and Ethan groaned. Chance released him and then chased his own orgasm, thrusting hard into Ethan until he felt it and clenched. "Fuck." He leaned over and kissed Ethan as he spilled into the condom. He kept pumping until he was spent, then fell on top of Ethan, kissing him. Ethan had recovered enough to kiss him back, and they became a tangled mess of limbs and come.

"I love you, Ethan."

"I love you too."

CHANCE AWOKE FIRST and carefully slid out of bed so he wouldn't wake Ethan. He ordered from room service and then he jumped in the shower and quickly dressed before breakfast arrived.

He took the tray from the waiter and placed it on the table by the bed. Then he sat on the bed, leaned over, and kissed Ethan awake. "Morning. Sleep well?"

"Hmm. Never better." Ethan sat up in bed and noticed the spread. "Wow, breakfast in bed?"

"Nothing but the best for you," Chance answered, sitting next to Ethan and feeding him.

"I don't know what I was thinking." Ethan appeared regretful he'd wasted so much time resisting Chance.

"I don't know either, honey, but that's all over, right? I meant what I said last night. I am hopelessly in love with you." Chance placed his hand over his heart as he spoke his feelings.

Ethan beamed. "I love you too, Chance. I always have." Chance kissed Ethan on the top of his head.

After breakfast, Chance pushed the dishes outside for room service to pick up. Then he crawled back into bed with his boy.

"Don't we have to get up soon?" Ethan asked.

"Yeah, but we have time for this." Chance rolled over onto Ethan and kissed him into the mattress, spreading his legs and feeling his way into Ethan's ass.

After another round of amazing sex, Chance pulled Ethan out of the bed toward the shower. He turned on the water and let it get warm, then faced Ethan and held him, kissing his face.

"Are you ready?"

"Again?" Ethan reached out for Chance's cock with a sly grin.

"To get to work," Chance said seriously.

"Oh, that."

Chapter Twenty-Four

ETHAN

Once the details were hashed over and the paperwork was signed, the company's execs sent Ethan and Chance on their way for the day. They met Putu, their driver, outside. He clearly noticed the change in demeanor between the two men and gave them a knowing look, smiling.

They climbed in the backseat, nearly sitting on top of each other in their rush. Chance took Ethan's hand and kissed him on the lips. "Ready to go?"

Ethan nodded, returning the kiss, which Chance deepened as the car pulled away. Their short journey became more interesting as Chance made love to Ethan's mouth.

"Sirs, we have arrived," Ethan heard from the front seat of the limo as Putu pulled up to the curb of the resort. It felt as if they'd just pulled away from the company building. *Time flies*. Ethan chuckled to himself.

"Thank you," they both said, fumbling out of the car. Why weren't they inside already?

The man tipped his hat. "See you tomorrow, gentlemen."

They returned the good-bye and walked hurriedly into the lobby, holding hands. Chance pulled Ethan into the elevator, pushing the button for their floor. It took too long to arrive. Then they sped down the hallway to the suite, and barely making it inside before their clothes came off. Chance carried Ethan to the bed and proceeded to kiss him all over. "God, this was a long day. I wanted to take you so bad right in the office."

"See, that's why I thought I was doing the right thing. Now you're too distracted," Ethan said, throwing his hands in the air.

"Wow, you think a lot of yourself, don't you?" Chance smirked, and Ethan smacked him on the ass.

"I think about myself under you all the time."

"You're in trouble now, Ethan." Chance chased Ethan around the room, easily catching him. Then he pushed him onto the sofa and kissed him hard. "I'm gonna fuck you so good."

He placed kisses everywhere on Ethan's face and gradually moved down his body, licking and kissing the whole way. He arranged Ethan's legs so he had perfect access to his cock. He licked the tip, which was already leaking. Ethan was too far gone already to speak coherently, so he just made little noises of pleasure while Chance licked around the sensitive area just below the head. Chance sucked the tip into his mouth and then swallowed him whole, letting Ethan's cock hit the back of his throat. He took it like a champion, bobbing up and down and caressing Ethan's balls. Somehow, Chance grabbed the lube and poured a dollop on his fingers. He slowly pressed one finger into Ethan's ass, then gently moved it in and out.

Ethan reacted to the intrusion by pushing back into Chance's finger. "Gah" was all that came out of his mouth. Then Chance crooked his finger just so, to hit Ethan's prostate, which made Ethan yelp in pleasure.

Chance added another finger, and now Ethan was panting with want, moving against his fingers. When Chance added the third finger and began stretching him, Ethan whimpered, begging Chance to enter him.

Chance quickly pulled out his fingers, leaving Ethan a mess, and whipped on the condom so fast, he didn't leave Ethan time to miss him. He aligned his cock with Ethan's hole and gently pressed in, a little at a time to let Ethan adjust to his length.

"Chance, please."

"Wanna go slow, so you feel every inch of me."

Ethan was pushing his ass back to try to get more of Chance's cock.

Chance eased in a little more and started moving in and out, each time going in a little farther, slowly increasing his speed.

One more push and Chance was fully inside. He stopped and let Ethan breathe, kissing him. "I love to see you like this, underneath me, begging me to…"

"Fuck me, Chance, please." Ethan ran his nails against Chance's back.

Chance fucked Ethan's hole, slowly building speed with every thrust, as Ethan jerked his hips in sync with Chance's movements. They had a beautiful rhythm going, moaning and grunting, Chance's cock hitting Ethan's prostate every time.

"Chance," Ethan panted, "I need to come."

"Do it," he commanded. Ethan clenched his ass cheeks and spilled all over Chance's stomach without ever being touched.

"That was so hot, baby."

Chance let Ethan's cock go. He thrust into Ethan and came inside him moments later.

"Fuck."

Chance pulled out and lay on top of Ethan, both panting.

They slowly came down and just stayed together, basking in the glow of their lovemaking.

"God, that was the most amazing experience I've ever had in my entire life, Chance."

"Better than last night?"

"It keeps getting better and better."

Chance planted kisses on Ethan's chest while Ethan recovered, a blissful expression pasted on his face. "You're so beautiful, Ethan."

Reluctantly, Chance and Ethan got out of the bed, cleaned up, and went downstairs for dinner. Their friends from the hot tub the previous night were in the lobby right outside the restaurant and spotted Chance and Ethan right away.

"Hey guys, over here," one said, and they waved.

"Hi, you two."

"Miguel," one of the men said, indicating himself, "and Rodrigo. We never properly introduced ourselves last night."

"Sorry about that. I'm Chance, and this is Ethan." They held out their hands to shake their new friends' hands.

"So, Rod and I couldn't decide whether we should treat you to dinner to apologize for the way we behaved at the beginning of last night, or if you should buy us dinner for being the reason you two finally got together."

"Well, we can decide after we've eaten, all right?" Chance said, and they all agreed, chuckling.

Their regular waiter came over and gave Chance that same lusty look he'd been giving him all week. Chance ignored him, but noticed Ethan roll his eyes, which caught Miguel's attention too. He snorted. "Wow, your man does draw attention, doesn't he?"

"What? He's just being friendly," Chance said innocently.

"That's what he always says." Ethan snickered. "It's okay 'cause I get to take him home," he said, kissing Chance on the cheek. Chance quickly turned his head, though, and slid his tongue into Ethan's mouth so he wouldn't forget that.

"Yeah, you two are definitely buying," Miguel, the chattier one, concluded.

The four men laughed together.

They had a nice dinner, and afterward they went to the bar for cocktails.

"So how long are you boys here for?" Rodrigo asked.

"Only a few more days; we just landed a huge advertising account here in town," Chance told them.

"That's exciting. We're here for a week. Then, it's back home for us too."

They chatted for a while before Chance and Ethan looked at each other, quickly making the excuse that they were tired.

"We've had a very long day. We'll see you tomorrow?" Chance winked at Ethan.

"Good night, you two. And thank you for dinner.

"Like you said, we owed you."

Ethan blushed, embarrassed at his outburst last night but forever grateful it had happened. He might have wasted the entire trip acting like a complete idiot. They walked out of the lounge with their arms around each other.

"So, Chance."

"Yeah?"

"Are we dating now?"

Chance snorted. "Yeah, I'd say we're dating now."

"Do you think we should we tell Brad? I'm positive he has a pool going on at the office whether we end up together or not. He asked me again last night."

"I think we should let him figure it out when we get back. No use spoiling their fun while we're gone."

"Are you really tired?"

He shook his head. "I just wanted to get you alone."

"Good." Ethan walked over to Chance and took off his shirt, feeling his chest. He nuzzled into Chance, breathing him in. "What was I thinking?"

"You were trying to be a good boy and not sleep with the boss."

"Yeah, well you're kind of hard to resist." Ethan pouted. "There is one thing, though."

"What's that?"

Ethan looked deep into Chance's eyes. "You can't have lunch alone anymore," he said in complete seriousness.

Chance broke into laughter.

Ethan's face dropped, making Chance feel bad at once. "Baby, I am all yours; I promise. There's no one else for me," he assured him.

Ethan beamed as Chance led him into the bedroom, kissing him all over. "God, Ethan, I can't get enough of you. I want to make up for lost time."

"I'm so sorry, Chance," Ethan said with his head back while Chance kissed and licked his neck, obviously in ecstasy.

"Mm, no more, sorry. All right, Ethan? Just let me love you." Chance undressed him carefully and laid him on the bed. "I'm going to make love to you slowly, baby."

Afterward, Chance laid his head on Ethan's chest and felt his breathing, and kissed him there. He rolled over, lay on his back, and turned his head toward Ethan, who looked blissfully fucked out.

"Ethan, I've been an idiot too, you know."

"I know." Ethan smirked.

Chance threw a pillow at him, laughing. Then he got up to get a washcloth to clean them both. They decided to sleep in Ethan's room again instead of cleaning up Chance's bed. Chance pulled down the covers, and they climbed in. Ethan curled up in Chance's warm embrace and promptly fell asleep.

ETHAN

They had only two days left in Bali. There would be multiple meetings to come up with a game plan for the account and determine how they would handle it over the next year, long distance. They decided on weekly Skype calls to work on issues and suggestions. Chance wanted the client to feel very involved, and that meant staying in regular contact and being readily available. They planned a return trip to Bali in about six months.

Those last two days went by too quickly, both at work and at the resort. The boys tried to make the most of the rest of their time together. That evening, they had a romantic dinner at the hotel. Their waiter obviously noticed a big difference in them and seemed to respect that by not flirting any more with Chance. Ethan was grateful.

After dinner, they went for a swim. While they were in the pool, they swam over to the bar. The bartender took one look at them and started laughing. "Well, I see you two finally made up your minds about each other."

Chance leaned over and kissed Ethan. Then he turned back to the bartender. "Yeah."

Ethan just blushed.

"I am honestly happy for you."

Chance turned back to Ethan and took his face in his hands. "Me too." And he kissed him again, as Ethan melted into his embrace.

ETHAN

"So, this is your last day. How did you two enjoy our country?" Putu asked once they got into the limo after the final day of work in Bali.

"We loved it," they chimed.

"Our favorite part was spending the day with you on our city tour, right, Ethan? Thank you so much for doing that." Chance wished he could do something for Putu in return.

"Anytime; you two have become my favorite guests," he said, tipping his hat.

"Please come and have dinner with us tonight. We'd like to repay you just a little," Chance added.

"No, my wife is expecting me home, but thank you, Mr. Harlow. I'll see you at four o'clock tomorrow afternoon to drive you back to the airport for your flight."

"Thank you so much," Chance said. "See you tomorrow."

They climbed out of the limo and took a long look at their hotel. "I'm going to miss this place, but I can't wait to get you home."

Ethan nuzzled himself into Chance's arms.

"What do you want to do on our last night in Bali? I've made plans for the morning, but tonight is totally up to you."

Ethan looked questioningly at Chance. "What plans?"

"You'll see." Chance winked.

"Well, I'd say let's stay in our room and make love all night, but I guess we can do that anytime, so..." Ethan said shyly.

They decided to spend the night on the town. They walked the streets and had a lovely dinner. Then they tried a club again. Ethan was okay with it as long as Chance stayed close to him. "I won't let anyone touch you. I'll take care of you, I promise."

"I know," Ethan answered, curling into Chance's embrace. That was the truth. Ethan honestly trusted him with his life and his heart.

They chose a different club than last time and danced all evening, but only with each other. Ethan was grateful for Chance's presence. It allowed him to be comfortable so he could enjoy the night with his new boyfriend. Ethan was nearly giddy when they finally went back to the hotel for a cocktail from the lobby bar. Drinks in hand, they took a stroll in the moonlight. They passed the pool and hot tub.

"Do you want to get our suits and swim?" Chance asked.

"No. I just want to walk with you tonight. We can swim one last time tomorrow." They walked arm in arm, causing quite a few heads to turn.

A little while later, they went back to their room. They were both tired and just wanted to be together.

"Whose bed are we sleeping in tonight, Chance?"

"Let's start in yours," Chance said, obviously knowing they'd end up in both at some point anyway.

After making love in Ethan's room twice, they cleaned up in the bathroom and moved to Chance's room. Chance turned down the covers, lay down, and pulled Ethan over to him so they could spoon. Ethan loved the feeling of being surrounded by Chance.

"I love you, Ethan," Chance said, kissing the back of Ethan's neck. They fell asleep sated and happy, yet Ethan wondered what was in store for them once they returned home.

Chapter Twenty-Five

CHANCE

Chance awoke first and rolled over onto his side, propping his head with his hand so he could watch Ethan sleep. *He's so beautiful. And he's mine.* He smiled as he used his other hand to pet Ethan's hair. He hoped he could be what Ethan needed and he wouldn't want to leave him. He felt that young insecure guy surface again. Ethan was nothing like the professor, but Chance had turned into him, hadn't he? No, he'd never hurt anyone like that. And he'd never hurt Ethan. He'd be the guy Ethan needed him to be.

After a bit, he leaned over and kissed his boyfriend awake. "Morning, baby," he said to a sleepy Ethan.

"Mmm...morning, Chance." Ethan kissed him back.

"Are you ready to go home today?" Chance asked, brushing Ethan's hair out of his face. Big brown, sleepy eyes peered back at him with nothing but love and trust in them.

"No. I want to stay here with you forever," Ethan replied, nuzzling in closer to Chance.

"Me too, Ethan, me too." They both got lost in their thoughts for a moment. Chance leaned over and kissed him once more. "But right now, we have things to do, so get up, sleepyhead."

"Why?" Ethan groaned as he buried his head into his pillow.

"Because our breakfast will be here in just a few minutes." He pecked Ethan on the cheek. "And then we have appointments for a massage right afterward."

"I don't want to leave this room." Ethan pouted.

"Good, because the masseuses are coming here." Chance winked at him, jumping out of the bed. He rushed into the bathroom and turned on the shower. "Join me." Chance peeked around the corner, giving that lustful look he knew weakened Ethan in the knees.

Ethan climbed into the tub and Chance took him in his arms, turning them so the jets washed over Ethan's gorgeous body as he kissed the back of Ethan's neck, smelling his unique scent. He never ceased to be amazed at how Ethan fit against his body, like they were made for each other. Chance reached around and caressed Ethan's balls as the water ran between them. Ethan's soft moans filled the shower, and Chance sucked a mark onto his neck, moving his hand up to softly stroke his cock. He didn't want him coming just yet. He had plans for him later.

Breakfast arrived while they were still in the shower. They threw on minimal clothes and sat down to eat. Chance fed Ethan bites of food and chased each with a kiss.

"Chance," Ethan whined, still hard from the shower.

"What?"

"You need to eat too."

"I am."

"I mean food," Ethan said, rolling his eyes.

"You're right. We'll need our strength for later," he suggested, steering the bite on his fork to his own mouth.

"What's that?"

"Nothing, Ethan. Keep eating." He smirked.

When they finished, Chance opened the door to put the breakfast trays outside and spotted the two masseuses walking down the hallway with their portable tables. Chance held the door open for them. "Right this way, gentlemen." Chance pointed them in the direction of his room to set up their tables while Ethan and Chance got undressed in the other bedroom.

"I don't know about this, Chance."

Chance held out a robe for Ethan to put on as he slipped on his own. "Ethan, don't worry. I promise you're going to enjoy yourself." Chance put his arms around Ethan, kissing his cheek.

"That's not what I'm worried about." Ethan lowered his head and glanced over toward the bedroom, then down at Chance's chest.

Chance started laughing. "Oh my God, Ethan, are you afraid a man massaging you will turn you on?"

"Um, no..."

"Yes, you are. It's okay. Don't you worry about a thing. I'll be right next to you."

Ethan snorted. "Yeah, that'll help."

Soon they were ready to begin, and the masseuse called Chance and Ethan back into the other bedroom. They each hopped on a table and covered themselves with the sheet that lay on top after dropping their robes.

Each masseuse went to work on his client. "Relax, you are so tight," Ethan's masseuse told him in a sexy Balinese accent. Ethan groaned.

Chance chortled from his table. Ethan was still so shy in his sexuality, something Chance would change eventually. For now, though, Chance enjoyed the blushing innocence of his man.

After a full hour of the best massage he'd ever had, Chance looked over to Ethan, who looked so relaxed he was almost falling asleep. Without Ethan noticing, Chance nodded to the two masseuses to stop, as he hopped off his table and went over to Ethan. He watched them quietly leave the room, and then he placed his own hands over Ethan's back, sliding them up and down his strong body. Ethan felt so good. Chance leaned close to breath in Ethan's scent, inhaling in the crook of his neck. The sensation startled Ethan into flipping over in a flurry of sheet and flailing arms.

"What are you doing?" Ethan spluttered before realizing it was Chance standing over him.

"Ssh, just finishing your massage." Chance went back to kissing Ethan's neck and rubbing his hands over his lover's body, stopping only to drip more scented oil on his man. "You can keep pretending I'm the masseuse, if you like."

"No, this is better," Ethan said, visibly relaxing into Chance's touch. Chance swept his hands over Ethan's chest, gliding down to Ethan's cheeks, spreading them apart, letting the sheet fall away.

"Oh, Ethan, you are so pretty down here." His mouth watered at the sight of Ethan's open hole.

Ethan giggled. "I like your hands on my ass."

"Well then, let's see how you like this." Chance bent over, ghosting his mouth over Ethan's most intimate spot, demanding entrance with his tongue. Ethan spread his legs in agreement, moaning.

"That's good, Ethan. Open up for me." Chance licked at his hole, pushing with his tongue while he massaged Ethan's ass, spreading the cheeks apart for better access. He made the tip of his tongue into a point and dove in farther, tasting his essence.

"Fuck, feels so good."

Chance soon replaced his tongue with his fingers, hitting Ethan's prostate. Ethan groaned his delight and pushed back on the probing digits.

Chance patted Ethan's butt. "Roll over for me."

Ethan rolled himself over and looked up lovingly at Chance, who leaned over and kissed his cock, swirling the precome dripping from the tip, then he swallowed him whole.

Ethan writhed on the table as Chance sucked his cock. He spread his knees apart, giving Chance a better position.

"I've got you." Chance lubed his fingers and, one by one, pressed them inside Ethan's tightness. He moved his fingers in and out, brushing against Ethan's prostate repeatedly, leaving Ethan a moaning mess.

"Oh God, Chance, please."

"Please what?

"Fuck me."

"On the bed, baby." He took Ethan's hand and gently helped him off the table. They walked into Chance's bedroom, and Chance giggled at Ethan running toward the bed, jumping on it, then splaying himself across the top with this knees spread. "Eager, are we?" he teased.

"Please, Chance. Get inside me like right the fuck now." Chance quickly sheathed himself with a condom, and then Chance was on top of Ethan, his leaking cock pressing against Ethan's entrance. Ethan grabbed Chance's ass and pulled him in all at once.

"Oh fuck," he yelled, panting.

"Ethan, did I hurt you?" Chance asked, worried. But he looked at Ethan's blissful expression and knew Ethan was okay.

"Just give me a second," Ethan breathed.

Chance held still and kissed Ethan on the mouth until he felt Ethan start to move. "Ready, baby?"

Ethan just nodded, grinning stupidly.

Soon they were both grunting and thrusting, balls slapping against each other. Ethan was so far gone, Chance knew he was going to come soon, so he wrapped his hand around Ethan's cock, pulling and pumping his length. He felt Ethan clench his sphincter muscles as he yelled Chance's name. "That's it, come for me. God, you are so fucking beautiful, Ethan."

Chance pumped Ethan's ass, harder and harder. "Oh, God." Chance released inside Ethan's ass. He continued thrusting through his orgasm.

Then he lowered himself gently on top of Ethan, their naked bodies pressed together, both still breathing heavily from their lovemaking.

"I love you so much, Chance," Ethan said as he lay pinned by Chance's larger body.

Chance had never been happier in his entire life, hearing those words from Ethan. "I told you you'd enjoy yourself."

Ethan just giggled, and Chance kissed him some more.

AFTER ONE LAST swim and a nostalgic dip in the hot tub, it was time head back to their suite to pack their bags. They took one last look around their home for the last ten days. Chance shut the door, and they followed the bellman to the elevator.

While they were checking out, the limo driver, Putu, came inside the lobby to help with their luggage. "Are you ready to leave Bali, gentlemen?"

"No," Ethan blurted.

"But we'll be back in six months," Chance added.

On the way to the airport, Ethan was quiet.

"What's the matter?" Chance asked, caressing his thigh.

"Nothing, I'm just thinking about when we get home."

"It's gonna be fine, Ethan," Chance tried reassuring him. He hoped that Ethan hadn't had a change of heart and would go back to being "professional" at the office. He wasn't sure he could do that. He wanted Ethan. He loved him. Ethan looked over at him with adoring eyes, and Chance knew he loved him too.

After they checked in at the airport, they found the members-only club as they had on the way to Bali. Chance knew Ethan liked going into the clubs. He walked taller and grinned, obviously feeling important.

Chance pecked the top of his head, knowing how nervous Ethan felt. He'd do anything to make sure Ethan didn't regret his decision.

The club was nearly empty at that time of the day, so they enjoyed privacy as they ordered drinks from their table in the back of the room. They toasted to their success and to each other and sealed it with a long, wet kiss. Soon it was time to board the plane, where they had first-class seats again.

"I want to make out with you the entire trip home," Chance said as they walked down the aisle to their section.

"Chance." Ethan blushed.

"What? Last time we were on a plane together, you were trying to be professional, remember?"

"I remember," Ethan responded, getting quiet again. They settled in their seats, and Ethan snuggled against Chance's chest.

"It's going to be okay, Ethan."

Ethan looked up at him and smiled. "I know."

Chapter Twenty-Six

ETHAN

Before the plane took off, the flight attendant came around to offer pillows and blankets for the flight. Chance took two of each and placed a pillow behind Ethan's head. He helped Ethan wrap a blanket around him, and placed the other blanket over his and Ethan's lap.

"Chance, don't you want to wrap the other blanket around you?" Ethan asked innocently.

"I don't want anyone to see us," he said, with that wicked grin Ethan had come to love.

"See us? What do you...?" He saw the mischievous look turn guilty. "Really? Here?"

Chance leaned over to Ethan and pecked his cheek as he placed his hand under the blanket and rubbed Ethan's cock over his clothes.

"What are you doing, bad boy?" Ethan raised his eyebrow at his lover.

"Mm, just giving you a taste of what's to come later, Ethan." Chance sat back in his chair and pulled up the blanket, smirking.

"Tease."

The flight attendant came back down the aisle to close all the overhead compartments. Chance sat up and asked her for another blanket. Ethan giggled. They waited until she was gone again, then Chance leaned over and pulled Ethan toward him and they kissed, melding into each other. They made out until the plane was in the air. Soon after takeoff, the flight attendant came around with the beverage cart and took their dinner orders. She smiled at the men cuddled together, holding hands.

During their meal, they talked about the trip, how much they'd miss Bali and the resort. Ethan tried not to think about how much time he'd wasted fighting Chance or what the reaction of their coworkers would be when everyone found out about them. The flight attendant came back to take their trays and brought them each another drink. They knew they'd be alone for a while. Well, almost alone. There were a few other passengers in first class, all in front of their seats so Chance and Ethan weren't visible to anyone else.

"Ethan," Chance whispered, scooting closer to his man and once again covering him with the blanket.

"Yeah, Chance?"

"I want you."

Ethan's eyes grew big. "You are not serious. Here?"

"Yeah, I'm going to blow you." Chance reached over, fumbled with Ethan's pants, and pulled out his cock. He stroked it a few times and looked up at Ethan for a reaction.

Ethan spread his legs a little and closed his eyes, and Chance took that as an invitation, bending over him, and burrowing his head under the blanket. He used his hand to caress Ethan's balls while he took Ethan's whole cock into his mouth and bobbed up and down a few times. Chance lifted his head.

"Fuck my mouth," he whispered and went back to sucking Ethan's leaking cock.

Ethan thrust into Chance's mouth, trying not to make any noise, but then Chance felt around, stuck a finger inside Ethan's ass, and hit his prostate. "Fuck, Chance," he breathed.

Chance answered him with another finger, gliding in and out of Ethan's ass, and soon Ethan came. Chance swallowed all of it, leaving no mess. He sat up and kissed Ethan so he could taste himself.

"Bathroom, now," Chance hissed.

Ethan put his softening cock back into his pants, and they both scrambled down the aisle to the bathroom. Fortunately, it was unoccupied and no one noticed them both go inside. Chance closed the door behind them and tugged Ethan's pants down. He thrust three fingers into Ethan and hurriedly stretched him. Then he pulled his own pants down, slipped on a condom, and lubed his dick.

"Hurry, Chance."

Ethan bent over the sink, anxiously waiting for Chance's cock. Chance pushed in through Ethan's tight ring of muscles and didn't stop until he was all the way in. Ethan groaned, and Chance waited for him to relax.

"That's it, Ethan. Are you ready for me?"

Ethan just nodded and pushed back. Chance fucked him hard, thrusting in and out, while Ethan held on to the sink. "Fuck, touch me."

Chance reached around, grabbed Ethan's cock, and stroked him while they fucked into each other. Ethan came first, right into the sink. With just a few more thrusts into Ethan, Chance came too.

"Fuck. That was good, and quick." Chance held Ethan while they came down. "Welcome to the club, baby." Chance kissed his neck.

Chance pulled his cock out of Ethan's ass and wrapped the used condom in a tissue, then threw it into the waste can. They pulled up their pants and splashed some cold water on their faces, and Ethan rinsed the remnants of their activity from the sink. Chance slowly opened the door to make sure the coast was clear. No one paid any attention, so he signaled Ethan to follow him. They both walked out of the bathroom and hurried back to their seats. Chance strutted confidently while Ethan slinked behind him, feeling as if everyone knew what they'd just done.

A few minutes later, the flight attendant came by with two more drinks. "Have fun, boys?" She winked, handing them their cocktails. Chance snorted and Ethan blushed.

After a long nap, Ethan woke up to the captain announcing they'd be landing shortly. He had wished they could've left the airport during the long layover in Hong Kong.

"I'll take you there one day. It's fabulous; great shopping," Chance told him.

"You've been here before?" Ethan asked in surprise.

"I've been lots of places, Ethan."

"Oh." Ethan looked down, not sure he wanted Chance to continue.

"For business," he reiterated. "I usually traveled alone, and when I did take a colleague, it was never like this, okay? Never," he promised, picking up Ethan's chin, looking him in the eyes, and kissing his lips.

Ethan smiled into the kiss.

"You know, before I met you, and when I met you, I was a real playboy."

"I know." Ethan just didn't want to think about it.

"I never knew I could fall for someone like this."

"No? Not even Brad?"

"No." He chuckled. "Definitely not Brad. I walked into the club that night, and Andre pointed you out to me."

"I remember."

"You were supposed to be a one-night stand."

Ethan just nodded.

Chance lifted his chin again. "Look at me." He smiled. "Andre told me you were having the same drink as me."

"So that's how you knew."

"Anyway, you were so cute, and then we danced, and then..."

"Then I took you home with me, but I woke up alone."

"I left you my number. I've never done that before, not ever."

"Never?" Ethan felt a little better at hearing Chance's confession.

"Never."

While the plane began its descent, the boys sat back and finished their drinks.

"So when we met again, in your office..."

"I was surprised, that's all. Then when you said you didn't know what that night meant, my feelings were hurt, which surprised me and even scared me a little. Anyway, I didn't know how I felt except confused."

Ethan grabbed Chance's hand.

"You were so adorable, and I remembered how much I had enjoyed our night together and..."

"Me too, Chance."

"Anyway, that's all over now, right?"

"Yes," Ethan agreed.

"There's no one else for me, Ethan. I want to be exclusive—with you."

Ethan looked up, surprised. "Exclusive, as in boyfriends?"

"Sounds better than just dating, don't you think?"

Ethan threw himself on Chance's lap and kissed him hard, right there in the cabin.

"I guess that's a yes?" Chance laughed and kissed his boyfriend back.

"So, I guess I tamed the great Chance Harlow, huh?"

Chance laughed. "I'm glad that you 'took a chance' on me."

Once they made their descent into San Francisco International, both men were ready to be off airplanes for a while.

"You up for seeing everyone?" Chance asked a sleepy Ethan.

"I guess." He sighed.

"It'll be fine, Ethan."

Chance had called Alex from the plane to tell him their exact arrival time, so once they were out of customs and had their bags, they went outside and into the California sunshine, the limo was waiting for them.

Alex jumped out and gave Chance a hug. "Welcome home, boys." He looked from Ethan to Chance and burst out laughing.

"What?" Chance smirked.

Alex just shook his head. "About time," he murmured.

"Take us to the office, Alex, just for a little while."

"The office? Aren't you two exhausted?"

"No, we slept a lot on the plane. I want to report in to Brad and everyone. Then we'll take the rest of the day off."

The limo arrived downtown at the agency late that morning, and the boys climbed out. They walked into the building holding hands, and when they saw Brad come around the corner, they immediately dropped them. Brad spotted them and ran over to them. He stopped, slapped his hands on his hips, and looked from one man to the other. Chance stood smirking, and Ethan knew he looked guilty as hell.

"Oh my God," Brad said before he ran down the hall yelling, "I knew it!" and leaving a befuddled Chance and Ethan.

They walked into Chance's office and dropped their things. "Let's get this over with. I want to take you home and have my way with you," Chance said, pulling Ethan into a hug. Ethan was still nervous about everyone's reaction to their new relationship, but Chance convinced him it would be okay. He trusted him.

"Ahem." They heard Brad as he walked into the office. "So when were you going to tell me, huh?" He looked annoyed. *Serves him right.*

"Oh Brad, we just wanted to keep this to ourselves for a while. Besides, we knew you had a pool going," Chance said.

Brad shrunk into the wall. "Pool?"

"Can't fool me, Bradley Parker; I know you too well. So who won?"

"Okay, you're right. And I don't know yet. I need details."

"We're not giving you details," he spat.

"Just the day, that's all," Brad said, hands up in the air.

"Um, day six, I think. Right, Ethan?"

Ethan had been standing there petrified that everyone knew about them. "Yeah, it was the night we found out we won the account," he recalled, rubbing the back of his neck.

"Right." Chance nodded.

"Hey, that's the day you called from the hotel. I asked if you two had..." Brad accused.

"We hadn't yet, Bradley."

"So what happened?"

Ethan spoke up first. "I realized I'd been acting stupidly all this time," he said, walking over to Chance and pulling him in close.

"Aw, you're not stupid, baby," Chance said as he kissed Ethan on the mouth.

"Well, as fun as this is to watch, I have a pool winner to announce. Me!" He cackled as he left Chance's office to spread the news. Ethan groaned.

When Brad returned, they gave him a rundown of the business part of the trip. Afterward, they left the office and climbed into the waiting limo together.

"Well, that wasn't so bad, was it?"

"What? Brad gloating or everyone else smirking at me?" Ethan groaned. But no one seemed surprised or cared, so he guessed it would be all right.

"At least it's over now. Let's go home."

Chapter Twenty-Seven

ETHAN

Chance lived in a quiet neighborhood in the suburbs. It wasn't what Ethan expected from the extravagant man as they pulled up to the three-story, modern home and drove up the driveway. He'd imagined a penthouse suite with a hot tub in the living room. Well, he hadn't seen the inside yet.

Alex helped them bring in their luggage, and he and Chance said a few words while Ethan looked around the foyer. There was a long hallway on one side, the entrance to the living room on the other. He peeked in and gasped. The large picture window had a gorgeous view of the city below. Underneath was a smart, black leather sofa with matching love seat and recliner facing a huge television screen hanging on the wall. No hot tub. He chuckled to himself. The other side housed shelves with leather-bound books and closed cabinets beneath. This room was gorgeous, just like Chance: strong and confident. It definitely suited him. Ethan heard Chance call him, and he walked back into the foyer to say good-bye to Alex. Alex gave them a knowing smirk as he shut the door behind him.

"Mm, that took too long," Chance said as he wrapped his arms around Ethan and pressed him against the front door. "I'm so glad to get you home."

"It's beautiful—what I saw of it."

"How about I give you the grand tour?" Then he smirked. "Later."

Ethan nodded as Chance kissed the breath out of him. "Let's get cleaned up first, then I want to take you to bed," Chance said wickedly.

Ethan blushed, his approval apparent as he followed Chance upstairs. "Wait, I don't have any clothes up there. Should I bring my suitcase?"

"You won't need clothes, Ethan—not for a while, anyway." Chance smirked.

"Bad boy, Chance."

"Isn't that what you fell in love with?"

"No, it was your eyes." Ethan stared into Chance's eyes longingly. "And those leather pants." They both burst out laughing before they made their way upstairs and into the huge bathroom. "Wow, this is incredible." Chance had a huge counter full of products. Ethan looked around in awe. "Can I brush my teeth?"

"I have a brand-new toothbrush just for you," Chance replied, handing him the unopened package from the cabinet.

Ethan raised his eyebrow. *We weren't together before the trip. Why did Chance have an extra toothbrush?* He brushed that thought from his mind and took the package.

They brushed their teeth in silence, watching each other lustfully. After they rinsed, Chance turned on the water to the shower. He walked over to Ethan and slowly undressed him. Ethan felt himself getting hard with just Chance's touch.

Then Chance undressed himself while Ethan watched, licking his lips.

"Like what you see?" Chance posed for him.

"Mm," Ethan said.

"Shower?"

They climbed into the large Jacuzzi bathtub. "Wow, this is a huge," Ethan exclaimed as he scooted close to Chance.

Chance smirked, taking Ethan's hand and rubbing it on his erect cock.

"I meant the tub, Chance." Ethan rolled his eyes.

"Well, maybe later we'll take a bath together," Chance suggested as he rubbed soap all over Ethan. They kissed and washed each other. When they were finished, they were both painfully hard. Chance didn't want to waste his erection in the shower, even though Ethan pouted and tried everything to persuade him.

Chance's erection was not wasted once they got to his bed. Coming down from the high of an orgasm, Ethan felt perfectly sated as Chance lay on top of him. Once their breathing came back to normal, Chance pulled himself out of Ethan and tossed the condom in the wastebasket.

"I can't wait until we don't need those anymore."

Wow. Ethan wanted that someday too. He had never thought about it before, but yeah. "Um, Chance?"

"Yeah?"

"Were you always careful with—you know?" He didn't want to think of anyone else with Chance.

"Always. And I get tested regularly. Besides, believe it or not, I never fucked that guy."

"Really?" He'd just assumed. Not wanting any details though, he added, "I've been tested too." He made his decision. "I want to feel just you inside me. I love you."

"I love you, too." Chance placed gentle kisses on his face. "I love you, Ethan Moore."

They must've fallen asleep, because Ethan woke up feeling rested and needing Chance. They made love again, Ethan positioning himself on top this time. He loved to be inside Chance, but he usually wanted Chance to be the one taking control. It made him feel safe and loved. Still, he'd never turn down the invitation to take Chance. Ethan was fairly certain he belonged to a unique club.

"Hey, Chance, has anyone ever done this to you, before me?" Ethan hesitantly asked.

"Yes." Ethan's heart dropped, but the look on Chance's face told him there was a story there. He swallowed down his questions and waited for Chance to tell him more.

"But not in a very long time. I was young and stupid and—someday I'll tell you all about it, okay? Just not now."

"Okay." He wanted to know about Chance's past. It was part of him.

Chance leaned over and kissed him, pulling Ethan on top again.

As they lay cuddled that evening, Ethan asked, "We have a big day tomorrow. Should I go home now?"

"No, stay with me?" Chance nuzzled him closer.

"But I don't have any clothes," he argued.

Soon they were taking out clothes from their suitcases and doing a load of laundry together. "I could totally get used to this," Ethan thought he heard Chance say under his breath.

"What, Chance?"

"Nothing, I just like doing this with you."

Ethan smiled. "You like doing laundry?"

"I do—with you," he said, pulling Ethan to him and wrapping his arms around him.

They went back upstairs and into Chance's spacious kitchen to make some dinner. Chance's housekeeper had stocked the refrigerator so he wouldn't have to go shopping immediately. Once their laundry was finished and they'd cleaned up the kitchen, Chance poured two glasses of wine, and they sat in the living room on his leather sofa.

"So I've seen this room, the kitchen, and your bedroom." Ethan chuckled. "Oh, and the laundry room. When do I get to see the rest?"

Chance beamed and jumped up from the couch, grabbing Ethan's free hand. "I'd love to show you my home," he said, smiling.

Chance gave Ethan the grand tour, all three levels, from the kitchen to the dining room and living room. He took him downstairs to the basement, where he had a theater room with another monster television and a large, comfy couch. He even had a weight room. Ethan had already seen Chance's bedroom, but he had two others, both made into guest rooms. He wondered who would stay in those. They eventually made their way outside to the large yard with a swimming pool and hot tub. Ethan's face lit up as he noticed the yard was completely fenced in, giving it total privacy.

"Is it heated?" he asked, looking at the illuminated pool.

"Yeah."

"And no one can see us?" Ethan grinned like a goof.

Chance must have caught on. "Why, Ethan, do you want to skinny-dip in my pool?"

"Hell, yeah," he answered, slipping off the robe and boxers Chance had lent him. He dove into the pool, before standing up completely naked, crooking a finger and inviting Chance to join him. Ethan felt bold, more sure of himself with Chance.

Chance took the invitation Ethan offered, tore off his clothes, and jumped in after him. Swimming to him underwater, he reached Ethan quickly and pressed him into the side of the pool.

"You are so hot," Chance said into Ethan's mouth. "I may just take you right here."

"Please do," Ethan said lustfully, grinding his erection into Chance's and rubbing his ass with both hands.

"As tempting as that is, Ethan," he said, chuckling, "I don't want to have to sanitize the pool tomorrow."

"Oh. Oh, right." Ethan giggled.

"So instead..." Chance reached to grab Ethan but missed him.

"Come and get me, Chance," Ethan said, sliding down and swimming away from him, laughing.

"What? Come back here," Chance said, faking anger.

"Catch me first," Ethan teased.

They played around until Chance was out of breath, then Ethan climbed out of the pool and jumped into the hot tub. Chance swam up to him, the barrier still between them. He put his arms on the side, breathing heavily. "You're caught now, Moore," he said wickedly.

"Yeah?" Ethan raised his brows in a flirtatious manner. "And what are you going to do with me?"

Chance jumped from the pool into the hot tub, grabbed Ethan's waist, and kissed the breath right out of him. Chance ground his crotch into Ethan while forcing his tongue inside Ethan's open mouth. "I have to punish you now for running away from me and teasing me and getting me all hot and bothered."

"Okay," Ethan agreed a bit too eagerly. He was done playing and ready to be caught.

"Fuck." Chance pressed Ethan into the side of the hot tub, both men still grinding into each other. Chance cupped Ethan's cheeks with his hands, licked around his lips, and worked his tongue into Ethan's gaping mouth. Chance continued pressing into Ethan as they grew harder and harder. Both were panting. "Ethan."

"Mmm—Chance, want you now."

Chance kissed Ethan hard and lifted him up so Ethan was sitting on the high seat in the hot tub. It was shallow enough his cock peeked out of the water, fully hard and resting on his stomach.

Chance sat down in front of Ethan, cupping his ass cheeks, as he bent down and licked across the tip of Ethan's cock, sucking on the sensitive rim just underneath. With his other hand, he caressed Ethan's balls, tugging them gently.

"Baby, you taste so good," Chance insisted.

Ethan lay back with his head leaning on the side.

Still teasing just the edge of Ethan's cock, Chance began pressing fingers into his ass, slowly at first and one at a time.

"Um, Chance, what about the water?" Ethan panted.

"This isn't the pool, Ethan—easier to clean," Chance explained, then got back to Ethan's throbbing, leaking cock.

"Oh." Ethan couldn't keep the smile from creeping on his face as Chance prepped him with the lube he'd thankfully brought with them. Then Chance sheathed a condom on himself.

Keeping fingers in his ass, Chance lay on top of Ethan. In one smooth move, he replaced the digits with his cock, easing in slowly.

Ethan groaned and grabbed Chance's ass to pull him in while he put his legs up on Chance's shoulders for perfect access.

Chance went back to kissing Ethan and sunk his cock deeper inside Ethan.

"God, Chance. Fuck, you feel so good, Chance. So good..." Ethan was gone, mumbling.

Chance thrust deeply inside Ethan. They came together without Chance even touching Ethan's cock.

"That was incredible," they both said together. Chance pulled out, and they held each other for a moment.

"Let's get back inside. We do have a big day tomorrow. Are you ready for bed?"

"Uh-huh." Ethan caressed Chance's bare ass as they walked back into the house.

Exhausted, they crawled into Chance's king-sized bed and cuddled together, their bodies intertwined.

"Ethan?"

"Hmm?"

"Stay with me," Chance whispered. There was a pleading tone to his voice.

"I am, Chance. Tired..." Ethan shut his eyes and curled into Chance.

Chance sat up and stroked Ethan's hair. "I mean, stay here," he repeated.

A sleepy Ethan melted into Chance's touch. He rolled over and pressed his smaller body into Chance's larger frame. A few minutes passed and Ethan sat up. "What do you mean?" he asked, looking up at Chance, who was now looming over him.

"I want you to be with me, Ethan. Not just tonight, but every night." Chance looked deep into Ethan's eyes. Ethan felt as if he saw into his soul.

"Are you sure? This is all new to you, Chance." *And very sudden.*

"What's new to me?" Chance asked, shrugging.

"Me, a relationship, all of it."

"I know what I want, Ethan. I've been alone a very long time. It's not as if I'm on the rebound and don't know how to be alone. I want this; I want you."

"I still have four months on my lease," Ethan said, thinking aloud.

"I know."

Ethan relaxed into Chance. "Yes," he said after a few moments.

"Yes?" Chance answered in a surprised but excited tone.

Ethan giggled. "Yes, Chance. I love you!" he said, kissing Chance gently on the lips. "I love you," he whispered.

Chance rolled on top of Ethan and showed him how much he loved him back.

Chapter Twenty-Eight

ETHAN

The next full day at work was nothing short of drama-filled. Chance had a list of demands for the team as he went back to his professional self. Instead of intimidated, Ethan was intrigued. He wasn't expecting special treatment, and Chance didn't give it to him. He barked orders into the workroom, and everybody jumped at the commanding sound of his voice. Even Ethan, who chuckled to himself. *He's all mine.*

He heard grumbling from a few of the team, and a couple looked over at him glaring. What, like they thought he could do something about him?

"Well, you heard the man," Bradley bellowed. "We have work to do." He gave everyone a friendly, reassuring smile, and Ethan realized that Brad was the buffer for Chance. He seemed to intimidate everyone, but Brad softened the blow. They just didn't know him like Ethan did.

But then Chance peeked his head around the corner. "Great job, everyone. I mean that." He flashed him that winning smile Ethan loved. He ducked back out and Ethan smiled outwardly.

He noticed a few eyes rolling, but nothing more was said. They had eight weeks to come up with an entire campaign for the group in Bali. This was what he'd been hired for, and Brad ran a great team. They worked diligently for the rest of the day. He did notice a few glances thrown his way and some off-topic whispering. He'd been afraid of this. People looking at him differently, snickering behind his back, thinking he slept his way to the top. Well, he wasn't anywhere near the top, but still.

Ethan looked over at one of the guys who was shaking his head. "Do you have a problem with me?" Ethan asked him.

He snorted. "Not at all."

"What's that supposed to mean?"

One of the girls spoke up, smiling apologetically. "He's never come back to say sorry before. I guess you're good for him, Ethan."

"He was kind of a dick before you got here, man."

"That's the senior exec you're talking about, Cliff," Brad spat, saving Ethan from speaking.

Instead, Cliff threw Ethan a glare before looking away and mumbling, "Sorry, boss."

"All right, everyone. Back to work," Brad snarled. He gave Ethan a sympathetic glance and looked away.

They worked through lunch, and Ethan didn't see Chance until the end of the day when he peeked into his office. "Ready to go home?"

Ethan looked up at him, tears threatening to spill. "What's wrong, baby?" Chance's tone sounded more like panic than concern as he came into Ethan's office and sat down in front of his desk.

Ethan shook his head, and his hand shot to the back of his neck. "Nothing, it's just the guys..."

"Giving you a hard time?"

"Not really, but now that everyone knows, they keep staring and whispering. It's just like I thought it would be."

"Oh." Chance sounded defeated, like he expected Ethan to end it right there.

Ethan looked up abruptly to see Chance stand and begin pacing. "What do you want me to do, Ethan? This is what you were worried about, wasn't it?"

Ethan stood up and joined Chance, taking his hands. "Yes, but it's all right. We'll get through it." He didn't feel as convinced as he sounded, though. This *was* what he'd worried about. But he'd proven himself somewhat. That Bali trip had brought everyone job security. Who the hell were they to judge him anyway?

Chance had stepped back and was now staring at Ethan with a huge smile.

"What?" Ethan asked.

"You've got that determined look on your face. It's sexy."

"You know, I was worried that I'd be treated differently if everyone knew, but now that they do, I don't care."

"You don't?"

"No." He really didn't.

Chance leaned over and kissed Ethan on the lips just as Bradley walked in, clearing his throat. Chance turned around, covering Ethan in a protective move and making him giggle.

"Well, at least you two waited till the end of the day for that. You all right, Ethan? I know today was a little rough."

They both looked over at Ethan, waiting for an answer.

Ethan went back over to his desk and sat down with his hand folded on top. "I don't want any special treatment, at all."

Chance smiled.

"I'll actually be harder on you, Ethan," Brad told them both. "I expect a lot from you. The big guy over here can't protect you from me."

Chance snickered and Ethan shivered. "Fair enough."

"Great, let's go out and celebrate."

The three men walked to the elevator together, and Cliff, Ethan's teammate, got in just behind them. Ethan felt his stares, though, and he heard the guy snort. Ethan stood close to Chance, but they weren't holding hands or anything, thank God. He waited until the elevator stopped, and as Cliff walked out, Ethan tapped him on the shoulder. "Do you have a problem with Chance and me?"

Both Chance and Brad followed them out, but stood off to the side, apparently waiting to see what Ethan was going to do.

Cliff shifted, looking like a canary who found himself just outside his cage with a tabby cat prowling toward him. Ethan grabbed his shirt by his shoulder and pulled him to the side. Then he stepped back and put his hands down to his side. "Tell me what's going on, Cliff." Ethan wasn't sure he wanted the answer, but knew it was necessary.

"Chance is a player, a real tool."

"What?"

"You didn't know?" Cliff looked surprised, but a little triumphant.

"I know exactly what Chance is, or was, but why would you call him *that*?" Cliff didn't seem to know how to answer that, by his excessive squirming. "Are you gay, Cliff?"

"What? No!"

"Sorry, I thought that maybe you were interested—never mind."

Cliff snorted. "That's hilarious." He bent over, laughing.

Ethan laughed too, making light of his comment. Both Chance and Brad were staring at them now, looking thoroughly confused.

"I just don't want to see you hurt. It's happened before."

Ethan wasn't sure what he meant by that, but he wanted to know. "Did he date someone in the office before?"

Cliff seemed nervous again, like he was giving secret information. Then he looked over at Brad and Chance and looked right back at Ethan. It took him a second to figure it out. "You mean Brad?"

He gave a slow nod, up and down.

"I know about them. It's way in the past.

"He always seems to get in the way."

"What do you mean?"

"There was a guy who worked here a couple of years ago, before Chance was the senior exec. He worked really hard and we all thought he'd go far, but then Brad showed up. Chance got promoted and took Brad with him instead and..."

Ethan didn't want to know. "So, this doesn't have anything to do with *me* dating him?"

"You're a good guy, Ethan. No one else wanted to go on that trip with Chance, anyway."

Ethan shot him a confused look. "Why not?"

"No offense, but the idea of spending ten days with the guy?" Cliff shivered, and Ethan laughed.

"He's really great."

"He's a tough nut."

"So, you're okay with me?"

"Yeah, buddy. Just be careful, all right?" Ethan nodded, and they patted each other on the shoulder. "See you tomorrow, Ethan."

"Bye, Cliff."

Ethan walked over to Chance and Brad. "Ready?"

"Everything all right, baby?"

"Yeah, everything's fine." It was and it would be.

A NIGHT AT Cruze was just what they needed. Brad found someone right away, and Chance and Ethan spent the entire evening together, dancing, kissing, and just being together. Ethan felt safer here than he did at that club in Bali. There were guys looking out for him here: Chance, Brad, even Andre. They sat at the bar, and Chance properly introduced Ethan to the bartender as his boyfriend. Andre's eyes widened as did his grin. He reached out and shook Chance's hand, and then Ethan's. "It's about time, my friend," he told Chance, and genuinely seemed happy for him. "You look different, Ethan, from that first night you came in here."

"You mean when I was terrified? You know, it was my first time in a gay bar."

"Really?" He chuckled. "It didn't show," he said with a smirk, then walked away to serve a customer at the other end of the bar.

"He warned me against pursuing you that night," Chance confessed.

"He did? Why?"

Chance shrugged. "He said you looked too innocent."

Ethan laughed.

"I saw something else though."

"Easy target?" Ethan knew it was a mistake as soon as he said it, but Chance looked tremendously offended. "Oh, come on, you came in that bar intending to pick someone up that night, didn't you?"

"But I never expected you, baby."

Andre had walked back over and put two new glasses on the table, then filled them with Chance's top shelf Chopin and a spray of tonic. "He hasn't been the same since, Ethan. You look good on my old friend."

Ethan felt his face flush, and tucked his head into Chance's chest and arms. Chance leaned forward and planted a kiss on his forehead. "He's right, you know. You make me better, Ethan."

He lifted his head and mouthed, "I love you."

"Ah, and my work here is done," Andre said, sliding their drinks to them and bowing, then walked away again.

They took their drinks and found Brad at a table with the same guy he'd met before. "Hi, Stephen, right?"

"Nice to see you both again. You always look so in love," he told them. They turned their heads to face each other and leaned in for a kiss.

"He's like a lovesick puppy now," Brad said, pouting.

"No," Chance spat, startling Ethan. "But I am happier than I've ever been."

Brad and Stephen left to dance, and Ethan couldn't get Chance's reaction off his mind. "You didn't like Brad calling you that."

Chance took a sip of his drink and shook his head. "Let me tell you about the first time I was in love, Ethan."

He wasn't sure he wanted to hear this, but Chance's demeanor changed. He looked almost angry, and Ethan knew this was the story he'd promised to tell the other day. Ethan took a deep breath, waiting to hear about the love of Chance's life.

"I went away to a big school where I didn't have many friends."

Ethan wasn't expecting that. *Where is this going?*

"I walked into Sociology 101, and there he was."

"Who? Someone you knew?"

Chance shook his head. "Dr. Wesley Montague. He was a couple inches shorter than me, had light-brown hair and the biggest brown eyes you've ever seen." Ethan flinched at the similarities. "He wore gray slacks and a bright blue shirt with the top two buttons down." Chance looked dreamy as he described him. Ethan already didn't like the guy.

"He was your college professor?" Ethan didn't mean to sound judgmental, but it came out a little harsh.

"He was gorgeous, but he noticed me right away," Chance continued, ignoring Ethan's comment.

"That's a little inappropriate, don't you think?" Ethan snapped, not liking where this was going.

"I was nineteen at the time. What did I know? Anyway..." He shot an annoyed look at Ethan.

"I'm sorry. Keep going."

"He courted me for the first three weeks of class. Just giving me extra attention, and batting those pretty eyes at me every chance he had."

"He sounds like a dick." Ethan really did hate the guy. Chance was his—now.

Chance laughed. "Let me finish, baby. I promise you, it gets worse."

Ethan sat back and let Chance tell him the story of how the classy Dr. Montague abused his status as a professor to hook up with students. He didn't blame Chance at all. He could have easily fallen for a couple of his professors in college, but they were never dumb enough to pursue him, or any other student—as far as he knew anyway.

"One day, he asked me out for coffee. He said he liked to get to know his favorite students better. I was flattered because he was so attractive." Chance had that dreamy look again, and Ethan wondered if he still had feelings for the guy. "He invited me for coffee after class every day after that. At first, we just talked, and then he'd reach out and hold my hand. When we walked out of the coffee shop one afternoon, heading back to campus, he took me over to his car and kissed me." Then Chance blinked, as if coming out of a trance.

"Are you okay?"

"Yeah, I just want to get this out." Ethan realized that Chance had never talked about this before, probably not even to Brad. He felt privileged.

"He was so sweet and I was smitten. I let him take me to his apartment and we slept together."

"Oh."

"He was older and it just seemed natural that he take charge, but he never let me top him, not once. I was falling so deep, though, I didn't notice."

"Notice what?"

"That he was never emotionally involved with me. All the feelings were mine. He was just in it for the sex."

"I'm sorry."

"I thought I was in love with him—I guess I was, for that age. What I didn't realize was that I was just the flavor of the semester."

"Oh shit."

"He dumped me a week before the term ended. Abruptly. I was devastated. He made excuses, but I knew it was bullshit."

"What an asshole."

"Yeah. Anyway, about a week into the next term, I saw him at the coffee shop with another student. Someone nudged me, after noticing me staring."

"Who?"

"Just some girl I kind of knew. She made a comment about the professor's next conquest, and my heart fell into my stomach. I felt nauseous, realizing I'd been so played." Chance looked sick.

"You should have reported him." Ethan was angry now.

"I should have, but I just moved on. He took something from me, though, that I hadn't realized until I met you." Ethan reached over and grabbed Chance's hand. "Brad called me a lovesick puppy. I was with him. But it was one-sided."

"Not with me."

"You make me want things, Ethan, and it scares me."

"I love you, Chance."

"I love you too, baby." He took Ethan's hand and kissed it.

"Can I ask you one question? Well, two."

"Anything."

"Did you ever tell him you loved him?"

Chance shook his head. "I thought it—felt it, even, but never said it. It was never romantic between us, so there was never a place for that. Just sex. It's exactly what I've been doing to other guys."

"But they're adults, not impressionable youths."

"I always picked predators who wouldn't want anything more." Chance was nothing like that guy.

"That's all over now, right?"

Chance nodded. "What's the other question?"

"The toothbrush."

"What?"

"You had an extra toothbrush for me."

"I bought that just before the trip, hoping that I'd be taking you home."

"You bought it for me?"

"Ethan, I've never taken anyone home before. Not ever." Ethan believed him.

"Dance with me?"

Chapter Twenty-Nine

CHANCE

They danced all night long. Just the two of them. Chance had never revealed that much of himself before, to anyone. Not even Bradley. He felt raw, but really good. Like something had been lifted from him. He could see the light and it was right in front of him. Somewhere along the way, Ethan had become more than just a conquest. He was Chance's air. He squeezed him tighter as they moved together to the music. "Baby, I want to take you home and make love to you all night long."

Ethan nodded and took Chance's hand, leading him out of the club this time. They passed the bar, both glancing over at Andre who gave them a finger wave and a wink. This time, Ethan walked proudly. He seemed more confident. Chance looked back at his friend who nodded, smiling. Things were good.

Chance drove to his house, thinking that one day it would be their house. He pulled into his driveway and stopped the car. "Wait here."

"What?" Ethan looked at him suspiciously.

Chance walked around the car and opened the passenger door, catching Ethan grinning.

"Remember what I said to you last time you opened the door for me?"

"Something about me being a gentleman?"

"Now I know better," Ethan teased.

"You definitely do." Chance unbuckled Ethan's seatbelt and planted a kiss on his lips as he lifted Ethan's smaller body into his arms. He kicked the door closed and carried Ethan to his front steps. Then he stopped and fidgeted, but had no hands free without dropping his precious cargo.

Ethan, who'd been hanging on for dear life, started laughing. "You need your keys." He wasn't asking.

"I put them in my pocket when I got out of the car." Chance shook his head at his predicament, laughing along with Ethan.

Ethan reached his hand down to Chance's front pocket, brushing his hand against his boyfriend's crotch and giving it a nice squeeze. "Baby," Chance croaked.

He let his hand linger, teasing Chance. "I'm gonna drop you, baby, if you don't stop."

"I could walk, you know." Ethan ignored the warning.

"Nope." He shifted his feet. Ethan was smaller than him, but he wasn't light by any means.

Ethan moved his hand to his pocket, and Chance felt him reach inside and grab the keys. He pulled them out triumphantly. Chance walked him up to the door, and Ethan put the key into the lock and opened the door as Chance carried him over the threshold. "Welcome home."

"Chance," he cautioned. "I don't live here yet."

"I know, I know." Semantics. Now that Ethan was his, he wasn't about to let him go. "Someday."

ETHAN

Chance carried him inside and took Ethan directly up to his bedroom, planting kisses on his face the entire way. Ethan never felt so safe or loved. Chance had opened up to him tonight, and he was honored and swore he'd be the best boyfriend right back. He'd never gone through anything like Chance did, but he'd never been in love before either. He'd had crushes, of course, but his heart had never been broken. That was a scary thought, but he knew Chance was worth it.

He laid Ethan on the bed and kissed him. Ethan could see himself living here with Chance, but everything was going too fast. Chance might know exactly what he wanted, but this was still new to Ethan. He'd never really had a boyfriend before. He'd never dated anyone long-term for that matter. He wanted to date Chance. "Um, Chance?"

"Mm, baby?" Chance said while peppering kisses over Ethan's body. He was losing all focus on what he wanted to say, thanks to the attention Chance was giving him. "Do you need something?" Chance asked, before swallowing his cock.

"Oh God." He had something he wanted to say, but holy fuck, that felt good. "Chance."

"Do you want me to stop?" Chance asked, playfully teasing the slit, slurping the precome with his lips firmly around the head of Ethan's cock.

"No," he croaked. Ethan did forget about talking for the next hour as Chance showed him how much he loved him. Making love to Chance was probably his favorite thing to do in the entire world. As they curled up together, Ethan finally got his chance. "I do want to move in here, someday."

Ethan had gotten his attention, but Chance looked concerned. "Someday soon," he corrected, "but..."

Chance seemed to relax, but urged Ethan to continue. "We've never really dated."

"We've gone on dates, baby. Remember the black tux party, and...the wharf."

"But we weren't dating at the time so it doesn't count." Ethan stood his ground.

"Okay, you want to date?" He looked curiously at Ethan, with a small smirk forming on his lips.

Ethan sat up, leaned over, and kissed Chance. "Yes, I want us to date—properly," he said, poking him in the chest.

Chance positioned himself upright as well. "So, you want me to wine and dine you."

"Yes, and I want to take you out too."

Chance got a huge smile on his face. "Let's date, then. Come on, get up."

"What, now?" Chance was full of surprises.

"Yes, Ethan, now. Put on your bathing suit," he said, seriously.

"Is our first date in the pool?" That didn't sound like a date.

"Of course not, baby." But he had a mischievous grin on his face, and Ethan knew he was up to something.

He never expected this. Chance led him out to the patio by the pool where dinner had been spread on the round table. The umbrella was open, and lit candles illuminated the deck and pool area. "What the heck? When did you have time to do this, while we were, you know..."

"That was just a distraction so you wouldn't notice this being set up." Chance pointed to the table, looking pleased with himself.

"You planned this?" He ignored the part where Chance said he'd distracted him with sex. It worked.

"I want to date you too, baby."

"This is perfect." Ethan fell just a little bit more tonight. Chance pulled out a lawn chair for Ethan. Then he poured two glasses of wine from the bottle chilling on the table and sat next to him, clinking their glasses together. "You're like the best boyfriend ever."

"I want to prove to you that I'm worth it."

Ethan leaned over and kissed him. "You are worth it."

ETHAN

Things began to slowly settle down at work. Chance and Ethan kept it professional during the day, and the team either forgot about them or just got used to seeing them together. Brad was still a slave driver, but he was great at his job. It made Ethan wonder about what Cliff had said. There was no way that Brad got the job for any other reason than he was the best man for it. However, it niggled at him, and Ethan decided to bring it up at lunch that afternoon.

"Ready, baby?" Chance peeked around the corner looking delicious as usual.

"Yeah," Ethan said, shutting his laptop. "I'm ready."

"Where do you want to go?" They'd been eating lunch in the office the first couple of days back and this would be the first time they ate outside the office since their trip.

"Your place," Ethan said.

"My house?"

"No, silly."

"Oh, you mean..."

"Yeah, I'm in the mood for crab cakes, and you said it yourself. They're the best."

Chance looked like he didn't quite believe him, and that was all right with Ethan. He'd been wanting to go there since they returned. He had some business to settle.

CHANCE

Chance and Ethan walked into Chance's usual lunch establishment. Much to Chance's irritation, his old hookup Kevin was sitting at the bar, seemingly waiting for him. Kevin turned around when he noticed Chance come in and glared at Ethan.

Chance wasn't sure what to do. He and Ethan were doing great, and he didn't need Kevin upsetting that applecart right now. To Chance's surprise, Ethan pulled on Chance's arm and walked him right over to a nervous-looking Kevin.

"Chance," Kevin said, looking everywhere but at the two of them.

Chance stood there, wondering what his adorable boyfriend was about to do.

"Kevin, right?" Ethan said, looking him over. "Look, I know you had, um, something with my boyfriend here, but no hard feelings, okay?" He reached his hand out to shake the confused Kevin's hand.

"Boyfriend?" He looked extremely uncomfortable, and Ethan grinned like the cat who just ate a big fat canary. Chance pictured him wiping his mouth clean of the feathers hanging out of it.

"I'm aware of your history with Chance, but it's just that, got it?" Wow, Ethan had some spunk to him. Chance was very turned on.

"Yes," Chance piped up. "Kevin, I'd like to introduce you to my boyfriend, Ethan."

"Oh." Kevin glared at Chance first, then at Ethan but eventually shook his hand. "Nice to meet you," he grumbled.

Ethan shook Kevin's hand and broke away. "Bye, Kevin," he said smugly, taking Chance's hand. He walked them away from the bar, leaving a befuddled Kevin nursing a cocktail, as the host led them to a table.

Ethan had a wide smile plastered on his face, and Chance felt nothing but pride. "Wow" was all he could think of saying, as he admired the new confidence in Ethan.

"I hope I didn't overstep there." He looked a little less confident now that the moment was over.

"Baby, that was brilliant. I couldn't have done that better myself. And he probably wouldn't have believed me anyway." Kevin was a persistent fucker.

"I've wanted to do that since we got back. I just needed..." He looked thoughtful.

"Closure," Chance finished for him. "It was perfect, baby." He picked up Ethan's hand from across the table and kissed it. "Now, how about those crab cakes?"

"Sounds great."

"I thought tonight I'd take you back to the wharf for dinner."

Ethan smiled the big gorgeous smile that Chance had grown to love. "I'd like that."

They ate their lunch, talking about everything but the office. Chance had a thing about work talk at lunch. But Ethan's demeanor had changed, and he wondered why. "What's going on?"

"Tell me about Brad."

Chance wasn't expecting that. "What about him? You know we briefly dated."

"Is that why he got the manager position?"

"What?" He about choked, and had to take a big sip of water. "Why would you ask something like that?" Ethan looked guilty, and Chance remembered the other night by the elevator. "Cliff."

Ethan nodded. "He said something, and it's just been bothering me ever since. I didn't believe it, but he's convinced that his friend didn't get the job because you were dating Brad.

"What friend?" Brad was a dynamo. Everyone knew it, and he had managerial skills that you just couldn't teach someone. He couldn't even think of anyone else being considered at that time. Besides, Chance didn't make those decisions; upper management did.

Ethan shrugged. "I don't know."

"A couple of years back? Honestly, baby, I have no idea who you're talking about. But I'll tell you that Brad came in through the management trainee program three years ago. I met him when they put him on our floor. He was being groomed for his job long before I met him, and then we dated—briefly. It was never like this, though. I never loved Bradley. I mean, I do—but not like that."

"Thanks for telling me." Ethan smiled at him, looking relieved.

"Do I need to have a talk with Cliff?" Chance didn't know him very well, but Brad always had good things to say about him. He hoped the guy wasn't trying to start trouble. He didn't need that on his team.

Ethan shook his head. "No, we're cool right now and I want to keep it that way."

"You can't keep people from talking."

ETHAN

Chance gave Ethan just enough time to get home, shower, and dress before he arrived for their date. Ethan wasn't sure how he'd top last night by the pool which was perfect. They'd ended up making love in the hot tub again. But Ethan didn't want their relationship to only be about sex. He wasn't cutting him off again or anything, but he wanted to make sure they had more than just sexual attraction. He already knew they did, but he needed to do this. They needed to do this.

The doorbell rang, and Ethan flew over to open the door. Chance wore a pair of black trousers and deep-blue collared shirt. "Wow." Chance looked incredible in his business suit, and sexy as fuck in his leather pants at the club, but Ethan thought he truly outdid himself with this look. The dark hue brought out the color of his eyes and the contrast against his raven hair was stunning.

"Wow, yourself," Chance replied, giving him a chaste kiss.

Ethan still didn't know where they were going, but it didn't matter. The fact that Chance was making an effort meant the world to him. Chance could take him bowling and he'd think it was the perfect date, because he was with the perfect man.

"Ready, baby?"

Chapter Thirty

CHANCE

Chance found a parking place just a couple of blocks away from the wharf, and they walked along the water to the Bayside Bistro. It was one of Chance's favorite restaurants down here; not too fancy, but it was on the waterfront and had a lovely view of the bay if you had the right table. He'd called ahead to make a reservation.

Ethan's mouth was wide open as they were seated at a table by the window, and he looked out to see a perfect view of the Golden Gate Bridge. "Chance, this is amazing." The look on his boyfriend's face was one of awe and appreciation.

"I thought you'd like it," he said, taking Ethan's hand across the table.

"I love it," he said, staring into Chance's eyes, and Chance saw the love gazing right back at him, making him realize something in that moment. Yes, he'd been in love before and had his heart broken, but no one had ever loved *him* before—not like this. Ethan was the first person to truly love him, and his heart soared.

"I love you," he answered, kissing the back of Ethan's hand.

The waiter came over and poured two glasses of wine from a bottle that Chance had ordered ahead of time when he made their reservation. "Can I get you sirs something to start with?"

Chance ordered a tray of baked artisan goat cheese, which Ethan balked at, but Chance promised he'd love it. And to appease his boyfriend, the Dungeness crab cake appetizer.

"Isn't that what we're having for dinner?"

"Nope, you need to try their pan-seared scallops," Chance told him. He leaned over and whispered, "You'll think you've died and gone to heaven."

Ethan laughed at the drama spewing from Chance's lips but nodded his agreement.

"Very good, gentlemen," the waiter said, collecting their menus.

Chance made sure they went easy on the wine, and switched to water during their meal. The waiter corked the bottle and placed it in a bag for them to take home. Chance hoped they'd have an opportunity to finish it later tonight. While Ethan devoured his scallops with a look of sheer ecstasy on his face, Chance began a conversation. "Tell me something about you that I don't already know." Although they knew each other intimately, the purpose of dating was getting to know each other better, and Chance relished the opportunity.

They'd learned a lot about each other on their trip and over the last couple of months, and Ethan looked deep in thought, as if he couldn't think of anything. Then Chance saw the lightbulb go off as Ethan smiled. "The first boy I ever kissed was named Dudley," he blurted.

Chance guffawed. "Really, Dudley? Like Dudley Do-Right?"

"Rocky and Bullwinkle? I loved that cartoon," he said with such excitement, Chance decided they should spend tomorrow watching old episodes.

"Me too. So, was Dudley a good kisser?"

"Not really." Ethan sighed. "And he wasn't gay."

Chance laughed again at that. "Okay, the first boy I kissed was when I was six. Harold Copenheimer."

"Harold, huh?"

"At least his name wasn't Dudley, and he was gay."

"You win," Ethan conceded, moaning into another bite of his scallop. "This is, literally, the best thing I've ever eaten."

"Told you," Chance said, putting a scallop in his mouth. He absolutely agreed.

"Chance, do you ever think about—you know?" Ethan looked guilty for asking.

"The professor?" He shook his head. "There are no good memories for me. It was all a ruse just to get me in his bed. But, no, I'm not pining for him or anything. I hardened myself after that, until..." He dropped off, looking right at Ethan.

"I'm glad I met you that night."

"You ended up working here anyway, so you would have met me regardless."

"I know, but you would have been off-limits and circumstances would have been completely different..."

"Me too, baby. It was fate." No sense dredging up something that never happened.

Chance lowered his hand to his pants pocket, feeling around for something. "Since we're officially dating now, I have something for you." He reached his hand into his pocket and pulled out the velveteen drawstring bag he'd been holding on to since their trip.

"You bought me something? You didn't have to do that." There was that blush again.

"I actually bought it in Bali." Chance placed the bag in front of Ethan. "Go on, open it."

Ethan opened the string and pulled out the braided leather bracelet he'd been looking at that day they went on the tour with Putu. "When did you do this?" he asked, looking awestruck.

"Here, let me help you." Chance unlatched the silver clasp, placed the bracelet around Ethan's wrist.

"It's perfect. I don't know what to say."

"I wanted you to have it while we were still in Bali, but I didn't want you to think I expected anything from you."

"Thank you."

When they'd finished their meal, the waiter returned. "May I suggest the crème brûlée for dessert?"

"We'll take the check, thank you," Chance replied, not letting Ethan answer.

"Oh." Ethan looked disappointed. It was cute.

When the waiter left again, Chance explained. "We'll get to dessert, but we have another stop first, and I don't want us too full."

ETHAN

"Where are we going?" Ethan asked, as they exited the restaurant. Chance was just full of surprises tonight.

"You'll see." Chance put his arm around Ethan, and they walked along the waterfront in the cool night air to Pier 39. "There are a lot of great restaurants there," Chance explained. "We could spend fifty dates at the pier alone."

"Sounds wonderful. My turn next, though, okay?"

"It's a date," Chance replied, sealing it with a kiss. He led Ethan to the pier where their boat was waiting. The captain greeted them and took their name. "Reservation for two under Harlow."

The man looked at his list and nodded. "Welcome aboard, Mr. Harlow. Right this way." He pointed to the plank leading up to a larger boat than the ferry.

"Are we going on a cruise?" Ethan asked as they boarded the vessel.

"Wine-tasting cruise. Come on, baby." They walked inside to find a cabin lined with bench-style seating, with the center open for mingling. Chance introduced himself and Ethan to a few other couples on board, and just as the boat was ready to set sail, everyone took a padded seat along the edge of the boat as the steward explained what wines they would be tasting throughout the ninety-minute cruise.

All the selections were from local Northern California wineries. Ethan and Chance started with a grenache blanc from Napa Valley and a chardonnay from Central Coast. They were given instructions on proper wine tasting and offered various snacks for in between each taste. Ethan giggled while swirling and sniffing the glass. He watched Chance and the other passengers and felt rather ridiculous, but Chance seemed totally in his element.

"Baby, like this," he instructed, slowly swirling the wine using his wrist.

Ethan mimicked his sexy boyfriend as they tasted several whites, then moved to the reds. Ethan's favorite was the dolce served last, a fruity dessert wine that went well with the pastries that accompanied it.

"You still want dessert, baby?" Chance asked when they were leaving the boat. Full and happy, Ethan declined. "No, I want to go home and ravage you."

"Are you inviting me to sleep over?" Chance looked at him, surprised. *Dating doesn't mean we can't sleep together.*

Ethan grinned. "And I have a toothbrush for you too."

"I want to get a couple of bottles. What was your favorite, Ethan?" They were given a list of wines at the beginning, so they could rate each selection and make comments. Ethan didn't even need to look. "The last one."

"The dolce. I liked that one too." They stepped up to the bar and Chance ordered a bottle of the dessert wine and then a full-bodied Bordeaux and a chardonnay.

"You plan on getting me drunk and having your way with me?" Ethan teased.

"Yes," Chance replied, kissing him on the lips. "But not too drunk. I want you to know exactly what I'm doing to you, baby."

Ethan gulped, feeling his pants tighten at the thought of Chance exploring his body.

"Let's go home."

CHANCE

The most perfect date ever was succeeded by several others over the next few weeks. They covered nearly every inch of San Francisco and ate their way through the wharf and Pier 39. They enjoyed outdoor concerts, and Ethan finally got Chance to laser tag and the aquarium. On a Saturday afternoon, Ethan took Chance to Golden Gate Park where they spent the day roller-skating and eating ice cream. That evening, Chance reciprocated with a nighttime tour of Alcatraz which started with a boat ride to the island. They stood on the edge, watching the city pass until they were in open waters and the island came into view.

"This is beautiful," Ethan said, as Chance stood behind him, his arms wrapped around Ethan, nuzzling the back of his neck as the boat churned through the deep water, illuminated by the distant city lights.

"So are you, baby."

The entire trip was two and a half hours and included a tour of the inside of the prison. "It's kind of creepy," Ethan said, walking past the cells. He imagined them occupied with notorious criminals, cat-calling and whistling at him, and he shuddered. Chance seemed to notice and put his arm around Ethan, making him feel safe. The tour guide told them stories of failed prison breaks and inmate uprising and corruption. "No wonder they closed it," he whispered to Chance, leaning into him. Chance felt his warmth as suppressed the desire to kiss him right there.

"That was the coolest thing ever," Ethan said as the boat brought them back to shore.

"You feel like getting dessert or something?"

Ethan shook his head as he wrapped his arms around his boyfriend.

THE NEXT NIGHT, Chance made reservations for a dinner cruise since Ethan enjoyed the water. "Chance, this is getting expensive," Ethan half-heartedly complained.

In response, Chance kissed him and told him he was worth it, then licked his way into Ethan's mouth, rendering him speechless. "We could stay in and make love all night instead."

"Nope," Ethan said, wiggling from Chance's embrace. "You already made reservations."

Grinning, Chance agreed. "Come on, baby. You're gonna love this." Then he squeezed Ethan's butt, making him squeal.

Chance parked his car and they walked to the pier to wait to be boarded. There was a healthy crowd in line already, and Chance knew it would be packed tonight. He'd reserved a table for two, so they wouldn't be sharing. He wanted to be as alone as possible with his delicious boyfriend.

"I can't believe it," Chance mumbled, as his eyes stopped at the man three feet away from him holding hands with a much younger man.

"What?" Ethan followed Chance's gaze and then looked back at him. "Do you know them?"

"Yeah." Chance felt sweat form on his brow, and a lump in his throat. What were the odds of this ever happening? Dr. Montague was smiling as he released his hand and put his arm around the college student.

"Is that a business client?" Ethan asked, looking confused.

"God, I wish," he spat. "Nope, Ethan, that is Professor Wesley Montague."

"No way," Ethan blurted, looking back at the odd couple. "He looks—old."

He guffawed. Chance noticed his hair had thinned quite a bit and his hairline receded, but it appeared he dyed it now. All that did was make him look desperate. When Chance was in college, Professor Montague was very good-looking, sexy even. He wondered what the younger man Wesley was with saw in him.

"That guy he's with looks half his age," Ethan said as the line started to move.

They were seated a few tables away from the professor and his date, but still in their view.

The waiter brought over a bottle of wine and poured it into the two glasses sitting on the table. Chance picked his up and took a healthy swig and set it down again and glanced over at Montague's table again.

"Do you want to go over there?" Ethan asked.

Chance shook his head rapidly, taking another sip. "No, I don't know what I'd say to the guy. He really messed me up, you know?" Chance wanted to throw up, not confront his past lover. He felt all his youthful insecurities resurface. The anger, the hurt, the betrayal... He had been so young and in love and this asshole...

"Can you really get through the evening with him over there and not say anything? This is your opportunity." Chance thought about that. He was letting the professor control his evening when he should be enjoying himself with Ethan.

"What would I say?"

"Start with hello."

"And then, what? Ask him why he's still sleeping with students? Should I warn that guy?" No, he wouldn't do that.

"Do you still have feelings for him, Chance?"

"I told you that I don't." He'd gotten over him a long time ago.

"But that was before you saw him again." Ethan was wise beyond his years. Chance looked back at the couple again. No, he decided. But he'd never got any closure, either. Maybe he should do this. "Come with me?"

Ethan stood up and walked behind Chance. "Let's do this." Chance fed off Ethan's encouragement. They held hands and walked over to Wesley Montague's table. Chance was so grateful for Ethan tonight. There's no way he could have done this by himself He swallowed. "Dr. Montague?" Chance spoke softly.

The older man looked up at him with recognition and surprise. "Mr. Harlow. How lovely to see you."

For some reason, that pissed him off. *Lovely to see me?* Didn't he have a clue as to how he devastated Chance all those years ago? Who the fuck was this guy?

Then Wesley stood up and shook both Chance and Ethan's hand. "Ethan," his strong boyfriend said, looking ready to throw a punch if Chance needed him to. God, he loved him.

"My boyfriend," Chance added, wanting the professor to know that. *See, I moved on and you're still fucking students.*

"You look well," the professor said, looking directly at him, ignoring Ethan. "It's been a long time, Chance."

Chance seethed as he looked from Wesley to the twink sitting across from him smiling, unknowing. He should really tell the poor guy who he was dating. Although this wasn't the young gorgeous professor anymore.

The student had to have his own agenda in this. Chance decided he was on his own.

"Charles, this is one of my favorite students of all time. Chance Harlow." *What the hell is he playing at? Does he even remember what we did outside of class?* Of course, he did. Chance had a brief flash of he and the professor fucking on his couch. He'd always made Chance bottom, and he hadn't been gentle or slow in his prepping. He'd used him. Anger enveloped him, but Ethan squeezed his hand, bringing him back to now.

"Charles," Chance said, reaching his hand out to shake the younger man's hand. "It's nice to meet you." It wasn't, but Chance was trying to be polite. Why, he had no idea.

Ethan squeezed his hand again and gave him a reassuring look. *What did I ever do without him?* "I just wanted to say hello, Professor. Have a nice evening."

"Wait," Professor Montague called urgently.

Chance turned around. "Yes?"

The professor looked uncomfortable and unsure of his words. Then he said, "It's good to see you, Chance. You look happy."

Wesley Montague, however, didn't. He was balding, had gained about fifty pounds, and honestly looked ridiculous with the younger man, who seemed bored.

"I am, sir. Good night." He took Ethan's hand again, leading him back to their table. Once seated again, Chance downed his glass of wine and reached for the bottle. He felt like a college boy all over again, with the same insecurities, but he wasn't.

Ethan grabbed it and poured Chance another glass. "I'm sorry. That must have been hard."

"You think that kid has any idea how many students the good professor has fucked before him?"

"What do you really want to say to him?"

That was it. Chance wanted to tell the guy off. Make sure he knew how much he hurt him, but would it do any good? Would he suddenly stop? Probably not, but Chance might feel better.

Ethan looked over at them. "Now's your chance."

"Huh?"

"The professor's alone." Charles must have gone to the restroom. "This is your chance."

Chance nodded and stood up. "Thanks, baby."

"Do you want me to go with you?"

Chance shook his head. "I've got to do this by myself." He marched over to the professor's table.

"Chance." Wesley looked around, apparently to make sure Charles was out of their sight. "What can I do for you, son?"

"Son? That's rich, considering the things you used to do to me."

"I enjoyed our time together, Chance." He kept his voice even and calm, and it was infuriating Chance.

"Why did you dump me before finals?"

"It was just over." The professor looked down. He had to know what he did was fucked up, but instead he just said, "You enjoyed it as much as I did."

Chance felt his face flush and took a deep breath as he sat down next to the man. No sense drawing attention by having this discussion standing up. "I thought I was in love with you."

"I'm sorry if I hurt you." He actually looked remorseful. Was this guy honestly that clueless? Chance wasn't getting through to him at all.

"You're an asshole," Chance said through clenched teeth. Wesley flinched, and Chance retreated. Then, in a softer voice he continued. "You took advantage of me, and countless students before and after me. Don't you feel bad at all?"

"I gave you an opportunity."

"To sleep with you?" He raised his voice louder than he intended. Chance needed to get out of there. "Do you how much time I wasted acting just like you?" Of course he didn't know that. Chance was better than this guy. He had to be.

"Is everything all right?" Charles had returned and was looking back and forth between Dr. Montague and Chance. "What did I interrupt?" He looked annoyed that Chance was back at their table bothering his date.

"Nothing, Charles. Mr. Harlow was just leaving." He sounded like a teacher.

Chance stood up. "Is he your professor, Charles?"

Charles blinked his eyes. "No, I'm an assistant professor at the same college." So, he wasn't a student after all. It wasn't any of his business. He'd said what he came over to say and now he was done. He was so done.

"You two have a pleasant evening." He walked back over to Ethan still reeling. Ethan handed him a full glass of wine.

"How did it go?" Ethan wasn't really asking. It was quite obvious that it hadn't gone well.

"The guy is a jerk, but at least he's upgraded from students to staff. And, I got to tell him what I thought of him."

"Any regrets?" Ethan reached across the table and took Chance's hand.

"I got it off my chest. Not that it did any good, but at least it's over." He picked up his glass. "Let's make a toast, baby." Ethan picked his up as well and clinked it against Chance's.

"To closure," Ethan said, reading Chance's thoughts.

Chance looked over at the man he loved. "And to you and me."

The spent the rest of the evening enjoying their meal and each other's company. Chance didn't think about the professor any more, although on the way out, he noticed the two not walking as close together as they were earlier, and wondered if something happened between them after he left.

The two of them were walking ahead of Chance and Ethan in the parking lot, and although he couldn't hear them, their body language spoke volumes. Chance held out his arm to stop Ethan from advancing further. "Wait."

"What's going on?"

"I don't want them seeing us." Chance watched Dr. Montague walk Charles to his side of the car. The younger man pulled away and slammed the door shut. The professor flinched as he slinked over to the driver side and closed his own door.

"Charles doesn't look happy."

"No, he doesn't." Charles must have pressed Wesley for information as to why Chance kept coming over to their table. Did he confess that he'd slept with at least one of his students? Maybe Chance did something good here by confronting him. If he and Charles had something real, then Charles would probably forgive him, but at least it was out. Maybe it was something that needed to be done, for everyone. He put his arm around Ethan's waist and led him over to his car, turning his back to Dr. Montague's car.

"I don't know what I'd do without you, Ethan. I love you so much. I had no idea what I was missing before I met you."

"Hey." Ethan stopped him, brushing the hair out of his eyes. He leaned forward and kissed Chance. "I love you too."

Chapter Thirty-One

ETHAN

Chance looked drained by the time they came home from their dinner cruise. Ethan was ready to just put him to bed and go to sleep, but it appeared that Chance had other ideas. He told Ethan that he needed to replace those memories from long ago with new ones. "I need you, baby. I want you to fuck me."

Ethan prepped him slowly and lovingly, enjoying the expressions of bliss on his amazing boyfriend's face. When he finally entered him, they made love passionately, yet tenderly. They loved each other with their mouths and their bodies. Ethan couldn't for the life of him remember why he hadn't wanted this for them—why he'd resisted so much. But he was grateful for everything that had happened between them because it brought them here. He was ready for the next step, and waited for the perfect time to tell Chance.

The next morning, they showered together and Ethan made them breakfast before they headed to work in Chance's car. Brad met them outside the elevator door, frowning. "Trouble, Chance. Follow me."

Chance released Ethan's hand and kissed him on the cheek. "See you later, baby," he whispered.

Ethan watched them walk away, wondering what was going on. "Hey, Ethan," Cliff said, walking up to him, looking as confused as Ethan felt.

"What's going on?"

Cliff shook his head. "I don't know, man, but it's bad, I think."

Ethan ambled to his office, dread filling him, wondering what could have gone wrong. What if it was the Bali account? No, it couldn't be that. God, what if it had to do with Chance?

Brad entered his office at that moment. "Come on, let's get to work," he said, his tone matter-of-fact, not looking directly at Ethan.

"What's going on, Brad?"

Brad sat down. "Wait until Chance comes back," he said with hushed tones.

"You're scaring me."

Brad nodded once, terrifying him further.

A few minutes later, Chance stopped at the door to Ethan's office. "Conference room in fifteen minutes. Please gather the team." He looked somber, yet determined, and Ethan's heart was in his chest. Were they all about to get fired or something?

Ethan followed Brad and the rest of the team into the large conference room. To his surprise, there was a spread of cheese, fruit, and tiny sandwiches on the table, with carafes of coffee and bottles of water off to the side. They wouldn't cater a mass firing, would they? Ethan took a seat next to Cliff, who looked just as nervous as he felt. "What do you think's going on?" he asked Ethan.

Suddenly, Chance came in and stood at the head of the table. He cleared his throat and waited till everyone settled down.

"There will be a press conference this afternoon to explain everything in detail," he began, "but I wanted to give all of you a heads-up. Apparently, the CFO, Matthew Carpenter, has been skimming the books, and he and the COO, Grant Masterson, have suddenly departed for South America with half of the earnings from this quarter." The room broke into wild chatter. Ethan sat still, waiting for Chance to continue.

"The press has gotten wind of this, and some of our accounts are expectantly nervous and threatening to pull out."

"What can *we* do, boss?"

Ignoring the chatter, Chance told the room, "We're going to need everyone to stay focused and work diligently to assure our clients that they will be taken care of. We'll have to go above and beyond for a while. I expect all of you to step up."

He waited for the chatter to subside again. "I will be taking over Bill Larkin's place as vice president of operations as he will assume the position of chief operating officer. Bradley is now promoted to senior executive of our division." Between the wows and the congratulations for Brad, he continued. "I want each of you to contact your clients and reassure them that operations will continue as always. We will move someone into Bradley's former position, so I will be speaking with each of you individually."

Cliff made a noise that sounded like a snort, and Ethan caught him rolling his eyes. He glared at him, willing the guy to stop right now. Chance was also looking at him intently. "Cliff, do you have something to say?" Chance asked, with a note of irritation to his voice.

"No, sir."

"Good, I'll see you first. Please meet me in my office in five minutes. That's all, everyone. Please enjoy the spread."

Then Chance stood up and walked out, with Brad following behind him.

"What's with you?" Ethan asked his friend, softly enough not to draw attention to them.

"Isn't it obvious?" he spat. "You are the newest guy here, and now you're about to be promoted to manager." He left off the intended, *just like Brad*, sitting back with his hands folded.

What? "That's ridiculous. I'm a designer, not a manager. And, I just got here," he added. Chance and Brad wouldn't do that to him, would they?

After grabbing some food, Ethan took it back to his office and shut the door. Instead of eating, he paced the tiny office, stewing. This wasn't good. He liked his job. He liked working with Brad and Chance, and everything was changing.

Someone knocked on the door and it opened, slowly. "Ethan?"

It was Brad. "Hey, come in."

"Chance wants to see you now." He sounded formal—too formal. Ethan was nervous as he walked through his office door and followed Brad to Chance's office. They walked slowly, with Ethan just slightly behind Brad. He didn't dare speak, for fear he'd puke. Brad stopped at Chance's door and knocked once, then opened it and walked through. Ethan followed, shutting the door behind him.

Chance sat behind his desk and motioned for him to sit. Then he took a deep breath.

"Hi, baby." Ethan melted. "I'm meeting with everyone, but I wanted you to know who is being promoted to manager."

Ethan sat, eyes closed, mumbling, "Please don't let it be me."

Chance came around his desk and leaned forward. "I'm promoting Cliff to creative manager. He has the most experience, and besides a little animosity toward me for some reason, he's honestly the most qualified."

Ethan looked up at him, not quite believing the words. "That's great."

Chance grinned. "Well, I'm glad you approve."

"I mean, I think he'll make a great manager."

"Good. Now, I expect all of you to support him the way you do Brad."

"Brad's taking over for you?"

"Yes."

"What about the Bali account?" Would Chance hand that over to Brad? What about their return trip? The concern on his face must have shown, because Chance moved closer and took Ethan's hand.

"The account is yours."

"What?"

Brad stood up and moved next to Chance as they both faced him. "You were a big reason we closed that account, Ethan. And they are used to working with both you and Chance. That isn't going to change. We expect you to take the lead role now that Chance will be running the entire company, but he'll still be involved."

"Wow." He wasn't expecting that at all. What if he couldn't do it? *I can do this.*

"I'll be transferring everything to you by the end of the day. I want you to go over it and let me know if you have any questions."

"And I'll expect a report on my desk by next Monday," Brad said, looking more confident than Ethan felt.

"Yes, sir. Thank you." He stood up ready to leave.

"You got this, baby," Chance said, giving him a wink. "Oh, you might want to call them today before they get wind of our troubles."

"Will we be all right?"

"We're going to be just fine. They didn't take everything. I'll be talking to the press shortly to give them our side of the story and to reassure all our clients. I want the entire team there in support."

Ethan left and wandered back to his office and found Cliff right outside.

"Did you hear?" Cliff asked, grinning like the Cheshire cat.

"Congratulations, Cliff." He really meant that. "You're gonna make a great manager."

"Thank you. I hope so. I didn't think Chance liked me that much."

"Brad respects you. And I've seen how you interact with everyone. Chance sees that too."

"What about you?"

Ethan shrugged. "Nothing's changed. Oh, except I'm the lead in the Bali account now."

Cliff nodded, looking relieved. It wasn't like Ethan deserved to be promoted after only being there for a few months. He was still very green. "You need to trust them. I don't believe for a second that Chance got Brad promoted for any other reason than he deserved it."

Cliff looked sheepish, but he nodded. "I know. I acted badly."

Ethan wasn't one to hold a grudge. Certainly not with his new manager. "Well, boss. When is it official?"

"Immediately, but Brad will be with me, transferring responsibilities and training me at the same time for the next few weeks."

"He's a great teacher. I owe him a lot."

"I know. Thanks, Ethan. I appreciate your support. I wasn't very nice to you at first."

"I understand. It's why I resisted Chance for so long. But..."

"You love him." Cliff wasn't snorting or smirking.

"I really do."

"He needs that, I think."

"I need him too."

"Let me know if you need any help, Ethan, with the account. It's a big job."

"Thanks, Cliff."

He left, and Ethan pulled out the file with their contact information and made the call. They hadn't heard the news about Ashton Lake's COO yet, but appreciated Ethan being up front with them and assured him that they were still onboard. Ethan then went over the plan and confirmed their next video conference call to go over the progress. When he hung up, he felt good.

ETHAN DIDN'T SEE Chance until the end of the day when Chance went to his office to pick him up. "Ready for our date?"

"I have a better idea," Ethan said, noticing how exhausted his boyfriend looked.

"What did you have in mind?" Chance asked. Ethan loved dating Chance. They had so much fun together, but Ethan just wanted the man alone tonight.

"Dinner at your place?" Ethan hoped he wasn't overstepping. "I'll bring everything."

Chance gave him a huge smile. "Sounds perfect."

CHANCE

Chance went home to straighten up his house for Ethan's arrival. He wondered what his amazing boyfriend had in mind for this date. He knew what he wanted to do. In his bedroom, he checked the drawers to make sure they had plenty of lube and condoms. He hoped he'd proven to Ethan that they had more than just sex between them, but tonight, he wanted to remind him how great sex was between them.

He made the bed and picked up his clothes from the floor. Ethan wasn't a neatnik or anything. He laughed when he thought of Ethan's apartment and the clothes strewn everywhere. But Chance wanted tonight to be perfect, and for him, that meant an immaculate home.

He ran a vacuum over the carpet throughout the house, lightly dusted, and cleaned up the kitchen. Fortunately, his cleaning lady had been there a few days ago. Ethan had promised to bring everything, and Chance wasn't sure if that meant he was cooking or bringing takeout. He'd just finished cleaning the bathroom when he heard the bell. Why didn't Ethan have a key? He should give him a key. Why hadn't he ever thought of that before? That would mean more to Ethan than just an extra toothbrush.

He opened the door to find his boyfriend looking spectacular in white jeans and a very tight-fitting T-shirt. Ethan looked so much more confident that he used to, and hot—really hot. He was also carrying two grocery bags and looked ready to drop them. Chance grabbed one and kissed him on the cheek. "You look amazing."

Ethan just smiled and walked through to his kitchen as though he belonged here. *He does belong here.* Chance would convince him tonight. "What can I do to help?" This was the first time either had cooked for the other. Chance wasn't much of a cook, other than scrambled eggs and the occasional pasta toss.

"You can sit and talk to me while I make you my mom's beef stroganoff with garlic mashed potatoes and green beans."

"Wow, it sounds—um—suburban family?"

Ethan turned around and laughed at Chance's expression. "It reminds me of home." Then he set the ingredients on the counter and began peeling potatoes. "My mom always said the only way to make mashed potatoes was from scratch."

"Do you miss home?"

He looked like he was giving his answer some thought. "All I ever wanted was to get out of there and find an adventure."

Chance stepped behind Ethan and wrapped his arms around him, nuzzling his neck. "And now?"

"I'm having it, and I couldn't be happier." He turned around to face Chance and kissed him. "But, I do miss Mom's cooking. I know it's not crab cakes and fancy wine, but..."

"It'll be perfect, baby," Chance assured him, smacking him on the butt. Ethan yelped and shook a spatula at him.

Chance sat back with a vodka tonic and watched Ethan peel the potatoes, then dunk them in a boiling pot on the stove. Ethan kept glancing over at a piece of paper which Chance assumed was the recipe. Probably in his mom's handwriting. Then he took out a package of meat and dumped it into a pan of oil. Chance watched him intently as Ethan rubbed the back of his neck, a sure sign he was nervous or worried. "You're doing great, baby."

"Can you tell this is my first time doing this?"

"Making this meal?"

"Cooking. I eat a lot of peanut butter and jelly sandwiches." He laughed. "I called my mom and she sent me one of her easier recipes."

Just the thought that Ethan had gone to this trouble for him made his heart soar. By this time, Ethan had whipped up a wine-and-cream sauce that was cooking along with the meat and the kitchen was filled with the most incredible aroma. "Baby, if this tastes half as good as it smells, it'll be amazing." While the meat cooked in the sauce, Ethan steamed green beans in a large pot and mashed the potatoes, adding chicken broth. "What can I do to help?"

"Set the table?"

He kissed Ethan on the back of his neck and brought the silverware and dishes to the dining room table. He didn't use this room very often, but it felt right for tonight.

He chose the bottle of red from their wine-tasting cruise, and poured two glasses. Then he brought out never-used silver candlesticks with white, long-stemmed candles and placed them in the middle of the table. He grabbed a pack of matches from the kitchen cabinet and lit each one.

Ethan entered the living room, carrying a platter, and gasped, then smiled at Chance. "Dinner is served."

Chapter Thirty-Two

ETHAN

The table was beautiful. Chance had put the place settings right next to each other, even though the table and chairs accommodated eight, and it gave Ethan an idea. "Sit down and let me serve you," he told Chance.

Chance placed a kiss on his lips. "Okay, baby."

Ethan left the room and returned with the mashed potatoes and green beans almandine. He hadn't cooked on his own at all, but he was proud of his accomplishment tonight. He hoped Chance liked it.

After serving their plates, Ethan sat next to Chance and scooted his seat closer to him. He picked up Chance's fork and swirled it through the potatoes, then dipped them into the meat and sauce. Giving Chance a very seductive smile, he brought the fork to his lips, as Chance opened his mouth to accept the bite.

Ethan looked sternly into Chance's eyes, watching for his reaction. Chance closed his eyes as his mouth closed over the fork, and Ethan slid it away. He actually moaned, as he chewed and swallowed.

"Oh, baby. Wow. Comfort food, huh?"

Ethan giggled. "My favorite."

Chance opened his eyes. "Mine, too."

They fed each other while their legs rubbed together under the table. It was the most erotic thing Ethan had ever experienced while eating.

"Baby, this was *so* good. You're a natural," he said, playing footsie with Ethan under the table.

Ethan snorted. "I just followed my mom's recipe. She's the most amazing cook."

"Well, you can cook for me anytime," Chance said, taking another bite.

"Why don't we do it together?" Ethan asked, innocently."

"Together, as in you'll be here?" Chance looked hopeful.

Ethan felt as though he was about to bust at the seams. "My lease is up at the end of next month, but I gave my notice," he blurted, hoping Chance would be happy about the news.

Chance put down his fork and stared at Ethan, as if he didn't quite believe it. He blinked twice. Then with a stoic look on his face, he asked, "Oh? And where will you live?"

Was he serious? Ethan first felt shock, then embarrassment, until he noticed the tiny smile form at the corners of Chance's mouth. He jumped up and landed on Chance's lap and kissed him hard. "I'm moving in with you." It wasn't a question, and Chance showed his happiness through his kiss.

"I love you."

Ethan beamed. "Dessert?"

"You're my dessert, baby."

CHANCE

Chance and Ethan walked into the office the next morning as though nothing had happened the day before. Except, instead of dropping Ethan off and walking down the hallway to his office, Chance kissed him at the elevator and rode ten floors up to the executive floor. He looked around and greeted Ms. Barrington, the executive secretary for the vice president of operations. Him, now.

"Good morning, Mr. Harlow. Welcome."

"Thank you, Judy."

"Let me show you to your office." Chance had been up here many times for meetings in this very office, but it was strange to realize this was his now.

She opened his door, then handed Chance the keys to his office. He walked over to the large mahogany desk, set down his briefcase, and went over to the window overlooking the city. The view was breathtaking. "Mr. Harlow, you have a busy agenda today," she told him, handing him a typed sheet of paper. He read the first line and looked up at his new secretary.

"The police?"

She nodded. "They're waiting outside. Just buzz me when you're ready."

He went back to his desk and sat down. "Send them in, Judy." He knew the investigation was coming. There wasn't much he could tell them, but he'd give them his full cooperation.

"Right away, Mr. Harlow."

"Please, call me Chance." He didn't like being formal.

"Oh, Chance, sir." She blushed, then left. Chance gathered that Mr. Larkin never let his secretary call him by his first name.

Two police detectives entered moments later. "Sorry to bother you, Mr. Harlow, but we need some information…"

They stayed only briefly. Chance explained his new role and that the former vice president had taken over the role of COO, and he could probably give them more details. He did offer to let them look at the files from his office, which they took him up on.

After a long day of meetings and damage control, Chance was exhausted. He longed for his old position where he could at least go out for lunch.

He heard a knock on his door. "Come in," he said, expecting Judy, but the sight before him was much more welcome. Ethan stood at the door with two bags from Chance's favorite dive lunch place, where he hadn't gone since their last encounter with Kevin. "Crab cakes," Ethan said, walking in. He let out a low whistle. "Wow, Chance," he said, placing the bags on his desk, then walking to the window. That's exactly what he'd done. He joined Ethan, putting his arm around him. "Thank you."

Ethan turned from the window to face Chance. "I thought you'd be hungry," he said and then added, "Mr. Vice President," in a bad Marilyn Monroe impersonation.

Chance kissed the top of his head. He was such a breath of fresh air.

"I am. Let's eat." Chance told Ethan all about the police visit and them looking through the files in his office. "I felt guilty even though I had nothing to do with any of this."

"I'm sure they knew that."

"I know, but it's all so weird being up here. Everyone is too formal. I think I freaked out my new admin by asking her to call me Chance."

"Well, you're a hotshot now. It's sexy."

"*You're* sexy. So, how's Brad and Cliff?"

"Brad's taking your position very seriously," he deadpanned.

Chance laughed. "Good. I always knew he'd take my job one day."

"Cliff—is a work in progress."

"Yeah, I figured that too. I think I'll have a chat with him this week."

"I think he's just a little insecure. He'll be fine."

"How's my favorite account?"

Ethan lit up like a Christmas tree. "Great. I called them, and they said they were happy for me. We have a Skype call next week. Will you be there?"

"I wouldn't miss it. I knew it was the right thing, putting you in charge. You're a charmer, baby."

"Thank you."

ETHAN

Ethan's favorite thing about living with Chance was *not* waking up every morning next to the man he loved, although that was pretty fantastic next to making love and falling asleep in his arms. No, it was the private swimming pool and hot tub in the backyard. Ethan loved swimming laps after work with Chance, and the two of them spent many evenings cooking on the patio grill and sipping on wine in the hot tub, reliving the first night they came home after their business trip. However, Chance made a rule of only blowjobs in there because it was a bitch to clean, which was fine with Ethan as he dragged Chance over to the comfy, padded lawn chairs that reclined. He leaned his legs against the back, giving Chance easy access to his ass, which Chance promptly licked, probing Ethan with his tongue. Ethan was glad for his own flexibility. They kept a small supply of lube out here as well, so when Ethan felt wet fingers enter him, he knew what was next. They'd each gotten tested after their trip and then again three months later just to be certain. They celebrated that night by finally ditching the condoms, for good. Sex with Chance was always amazing, but bareback was incredible. Ethan was grateful for the padding under the chair as Chance thrust inside him. They tried being quiet, because although no one could see them, they didn't want to give anyone an audio show of their outdoor activities.

The day Ethan's lease was officially up, they drove over to his apartment, where he hadn't slept in over a month, to clean it up and turn in his keys. Ethan wanted them to make sure this was right before he gave up his place completely. He knew Chance had been afraid Ethan wouldn't want to give it up. He never let on, but Ethan could feel Chance's tension slip away the day they packed up the rest of his things and he turned in his key.

"I'm so happy," Ethan reassured Chance as they drove away from his apartment building for the last time.

Chance gave him a kiss and whispered a relieved, "Thank you, baby."

When they returned to Chance's house, Chance picked Ethan up and carried him over the threshold, kissing him as if they were newlyweds. "Welcome home," he said, very seriously.

Ethan cracked up. "It's been my home, silly," he said, nuzzling into Chance's neck.

"I know, but I want to make it official." Chance kissed Ethan again, carried him upstairs to their bedroom, and made sweet, passionate love to him all night long.

They celebrated that night with a home-cooked meal that ended up with sex on the sofa, because Ethan refused to let Chance take him on the dining room table and Chance didn't want to wait till they got upstairs. "The cleaning lady is going to get a quite an eyeful, if we don't clean this up first."

"You have a cleaning lady?" Ethan looked up at Chance in wonderment, as if he was confessing that he could walk on water.

"I'm the vice president of an international advertising firm," he said, with a hint of charm and playfulness.

"That you are," Ethan purred, stroking Chance's cock, bringing it back to life

THE FIRM RECOVERED from their financial misfortune. The former chief operating officer and chief financial officer were caught trying to move funds from their US accounts and were now facing embezzlement charges. Everyone gave their full cooperation to the feds while they investigated. Fortunately, those two had worked alone; not even their admins had known what was going on. Everyone else was cleared, so after a couple of weeks, things settled down and got back to normal. Chance was incredible as vice president. It was like he was born into it. Ethan was so proud of him.

After some growing pains, Cliff turned out to be a pretty good manager. He left Ethan alone for the most part since Brad and Chance were still involved with the Bali account. Ethan was the lead, though, and ran the weekly Skype meetings. He'd gained so much more confidence in the months he'd worked at Ashton Lake. Both Chance and Brad commented after their last meeting.

"Girl, you rocked it," Brad said. "I trained you well," he added, proudly.

"Bradley, we'll have to have you over for dinner."

"You two are cooking?" He looked at them suspiciously.

"Ethan makes great comfort food," Chance explained proudly.

Brad gave them a look that suggested he'd just smelled something terribly bad. "Like meatloaf?" he said with such distaste that both Ethan and Chance laughed.

"Even better. Bring Stephen. We'll see you at seven."

Brad just tsked at them, but agreed.

"Our first dinner party," Ethan said after Brad had left.

"I can't wait. Let's blow them away, baby." They sealed it with a kiss.

Epilogue

Chance

ASHTON LAKE WAS back on solid ground, thanks to Chance and the new COO. Everyone else had settled into their new positions. Ethan was such a wiz, and kept the Bali client very happy with their progress. The client hinted they had more work for the firm. Six months passed quickly, and it was time for Ethan and Chance's return visit. The company arranged for them to stay at the same resort.

Chance surprised Ethan with his own membership to the airline club. He presented it to him just as Alex dropped them off at the airport. "Really?" Ethan beamed when he gave it to him. They checked their bags and received their boarding passes before heading over to the club. Ethan proudly showed his card to the maître d' before sauntering confidently through the entrance of the club, passing the bar, and heading straight for the comfy chairs, still holding his card as if it was precious. Ethan was precious.

They sat down and a waiter promptly came over to take their order. "Two Chopin tonics with a twist."

"How does it feel, baby?"

"Fantastic. The first time you brought me here, I felt like an imposter. I was intimidated by everything."

"And now?" Chance smiled at his amazing boyfriend.

"Now, I have my own membership to an exclusive club." His smile was contagious, as he patted the soft leather armchair.

"And you fit right in, baby."

ETHAN

The limo was waiting for them as they exited the airport. Putu jumped out of the car and hugged Chance and Ethan. "Welcome back. I see you two look—happy," he said, smiling.

"We are," Chance said, nudging Ethan into the backseat of the limo.

"It looks good on you," Putu told them as he placed their luggage into the trunk.

When they walked into the lobby of the resort, it brought back so many memories for Chance. "Ready for the spa?" Chance asked Ethan.

"Hell, yeah. Then a swim, and I want to enjoy the hot tub this time and..."

"You are too cute." Chance kissed the top of Ethan's head.

They had reserved the same suite, and when Chance and Ethan walked into to the room, they stood there in awe. "Do you remember—"

"The first time we made love in here?" Chance answered before Ethan finished. They did that a lot now.

"Yeah, I was a little buzzed and you walked in, so hot—so fucking hot," Ethan said dreamily.

"I was pissed off because I turned down those two guys for a threesome."

"What?" Ethan yelled.

"I said I turned them down." Chance wrapped his arms around his beautiful boyfriend and kissed the top of his head. "I knew then you were the only one for me."

"I knew it too, Chance."

They went downstairs to the hotel restaurant for dinner and saw their old waiter, who recognized Chance right away with a lustful stare. Chance snorted as Ethan gave the poor guy a wicked stare. *Some things never change.* One thing had changed, though. Ethan was more confident, a lot more confident. Chance loved that about him. He was sweet but knew when to take charge too. It made Chance feel cared for.

"Great to see you two gentlemen again," the maître d' told them as he walked them to their table. They sat down, and the waiter glanced over at the two of them. Ethan scooted his chair closer to Chance and petted his hair, smiling. The waiter looked down in defeat but just shrugged it off.

Chance kissed Ethan. "I'm all yours, baby."

After their meal, they changed into their bathing suits and visited the pool. They swam up to the bar and saw their favorite bartender, who recognized them right away. "Hey, you two. Chance and Ethan, right?" he addressed them as they sat down. "Welcome back, boys."

"Nice to be back," they said in unison.

They had a successful trip. The company was pleased with their efforts and complimented Ethan on taking over their account. They added two more years to their contract and a couple more projects which meant a lot more money for the firm.

"He's talented, this one."

"Don't I know it," Chance replied.

They stayed just five days this time, and soon it was time to head back home.

On the last night of their trip, they were eating in the hotel restaurant. "Ethan," Chance said as they were sipping after-dinner drinks.

"Hmm?" Ethan answered, gazing at his gorgeous boyfriend.

"I love you," Chance said, scooting his chair right next to Ethan.

"Mm, I know that, Chance; I love you too." Ethan placed his hand in Chance's and nuzzled in his neck.

"I mean, I really love you, Ethan." Beads of sweat were forming on Chance's brow as he stumbled with his words. He took his free hand and placed it in his jacket pocket, fishing for something.

"What's the matter, Chance?" Ethan had no idea what was going on, but Chance was pale and not his normal chatty and confident self. At first, he wondered if Chance was coming down with something, but then Chance pulled out a little black box and held it out to Ethan.

Now Ethan felt as nervous as Chance looked. "Chance?"

Taking his other hand, Chance opened the box and pulled out a beautiful diamond-encrusted gold ring with an inscription on the inside.

"What is that?" Ethan whispered, knowing exactly what that was but needing to hear it out loud.

"Ethan. I love you, and I want to spend the rest of my life with you," Chance began.

Ethan was shaking and tearing up.

"Ethan, I want to marry you. This ring is my promise..." He held up the ring as he spoke the inscription. "My promise to you—I'm forever yours," Chance said, placing the ring on Ethan's left ring finger.

Ethan leaned into Chance's chest, soaking him with happy tears, holding out his hand with the ring on it.

"Say yes?" Chance picked up Ethan's chin and kissed his cheek. Ethan turned and placed his mouth on Chance's, hungrily pushing his tongue inside.

"I love you, Chance. I want to be with you forever too."

Chance looked lovingly into Ethan's eyes, still waiting for an answer. "Yes."

About the Author

Emjay Haze is a pen name for a wife, mother, and writer of gay romance. She resides in Northern Virginia with her husband, two teenagers, a new puppy, cat, gecko, and several fish. She always loved writing and fell in love with the genre seven years ago after discovering the world of fanfiction. She went back to school to pursue a Bachelor's Degree in Creative Writing from SNHU where she graduated in April 2015, with a renewed desire to make her dreams of becoming a published author come true.

She has a wide and diverse work history in the fields of travel, hotel management, high-tech communications, web development, real estate, and the nonprofit health care industry where she has held positions such as travel agent, hotel concierge, web programmer, Realtor, account manager, and many, many others, giving her a varied and unique set of experiences that she draws upon in her stories and characters. Her interests include music and pop culture, and she is an advocate for the LGBT community.

Her stories delve into all types of romantic relationships, regardless of sexuality, with a focus on first times and new encounters in a lighthearted style with a goal to gain a diverse readership and broaden the minds of those who might not normally pick up an LGBTQ romance because it's more about the person than the sexuality. She'll take you on a roller-coaster journey, but you'll always get a happy ending.

Facebook: www.facebook.com/emjayhaze
Twitter: www.twitter.com/cmjayhaze
Website: www.mjhauthor.com/emjayhaze
Blog: www.mjhauthor.com/news-and-events/
Goodreads: www.goodreads.com/author/show/14254769.Emjay_Haze

Also Available from NineStar Press

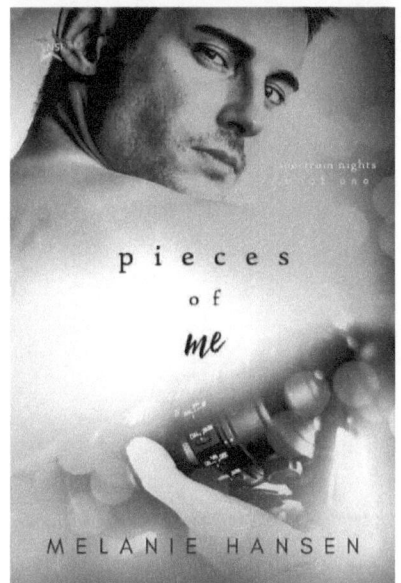

www.ninestarpress.com

www.ingramcontent.com/pod-product-compliance
Lightning Source LLC
Chambersburg PA
CBHW050038180626
46810CB00002B/784